EVA CHASE

VILE
SORCERY

ROYALS OF VILLAIN ACADEMY

Vile Sorcery

Book 2 in the Royals of Villain Academy series

First Digital Edition, 2019

Copyright © 2019 Eva Chase

Cover design: Christian Bentulan, Covers by Christian

Ebook ISBN: 978-1-989096-42-0

Paperback ISBN: 978-1-989096-43-7

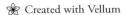 Created with Vellum

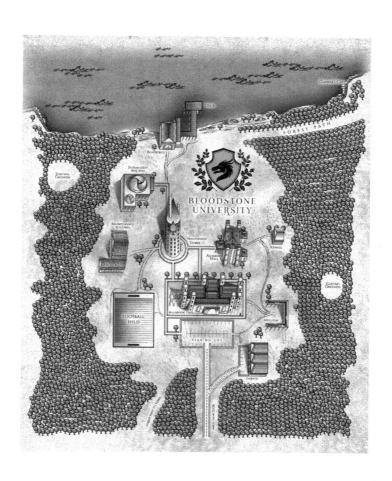

CHAPTER ONE

Rory

The morning after I was declared the most powerful mage to attend Villain Academy in decades, I dreamed about my parents' murders again.

The moment didn't play out exactly as it had in real life. This time, my legs refused to move as one of the blacksuits slashed his hand through the air with a snapped spell. Mom's throat tore open with a gush of blood, and I stayed locked in place, straining to run to her.

A scream ripped up through my chest but caught in the back of my mouth. I couldn't even force out that sound. Couldn't throw any spell of my own at the attackers. Couldn't take a single step to defend Dad when the man spun on him and gouged an X in his chest.

The smell of blood, thick and metallic, flooded my nose and washed over my tongue. My stomach lurched.

I woke up shaking and watery-eyed with the

wrenching sense that I had no power at all—none that mattered, anyway.

Early morning sunlight streamed through my dorm bedroom window, thinner here in upstate New York's early May than it'd be back in California, where I should have been. Where I would have been if I could have saved my parents.

I pulled the duvet up over my head to hide from the day. No part of me felt ready to face it. I'd just spent the last month fighting to make sure I could stay here at the school more properly known as Bloodstone University. The school named after a birth family I'd never known and didn't particularly want a part in. The school that was full of the cruelest people I'd ever met.

I'd won. I'd proven myself more capable than I could have hoped. After yesterday's assessment, I should have been full of confidence. But the truth was, I was exhausted.

The fight was far from over. I'd worked my ass off to stay here so that I could figure out a way to take down the university and the vicious mages who'd destroyed my *real* family, the parents who'd raised me. No one here was going to make that easy for me, least of all my four fellow scions, the sons of the other ruling families. Malcolm, Jude, Connar, and Declan—all of them as brutal as they were gorgeous.

Maybe Headmistress Grimsworth wouldn't mind if I took a whole week off to recover instead of just one day? Ha.

The sheet twitched, and a small furry body nestled against my arm. *How are you doing, sweetheart?*

The voice of a sixty-something woman that traveled into my head came from the pet mouse tucked in the crook of my elbow. Before I'd even known I was a mage myself, my parents' people had arranged for Deborah's soul to be relocated into the animal, and for the mouse to be bound to me as my familiar so that she could protect me... and keep an eye on me. Just in case some of the magic my parents were suppressing in me leaked out.

They and the mages they worked with were joymancers, getting the energy for their spells from the happiness they stirred in others. Like everyone else here at Villain Academy, I was a fearmancer, with powers that came from provoking terror. Having now met a whole bunch of fearmancers, I couldn't exactly blame Mom and Dad for worrying about how I might turn out.

"I'd like to go back to sleep for about a year," I murmured to Deborah. The walls in the dorm room weren't super thick, and while the secret that I *had* a familiar was out now, no one except me knew my mouse had a joymancer's soul along for the ride. Deborah's life depended on my keeping that secret.

"Are *you* okay?" I added. Yesterday she'd been kidnapped by the other scions in an attempt to force me into bowing down to them. I'd managed to outsmart them and get her back, but being in their hands even for a little while couldn't have been fun.

Don't you worry about me, Lorelei, Deborah said with a tickle of her whiskers against my skin. *I'm already on my second life—I'm grateful to have it at all. What matters to me is making sure you make it through these trials all right.*

My chest tightened up. I ran my thumb over the soft fur on her back. At least one person here had my best interests at heart... even if she wasn't exactly a person anymore.

"I'll be fine," I said. "I'm just feeling a little overwhelmed. No one knew what to expect from me before. After that assessment, they're going to be watching for incredible things. I still can't cast much if I'm not stirring up fear in people, and I still don't like doing that." I let out a little groan. "And now I'm going to have a full schedule. Even more classes with these assholes."

Don't you think the other scions will back off now that they know how strong you are? Your classmates seemed to respond quite positively to the news yesterday.

"Those ones were just hedging their bets, I guess. Figuring they should fawn over me a bit while I'm in the spotlight. If I can't keep up, they'll go right back to taking jabs at me. And the scions... I don't think I can count on any mercy or respect from them. Malcolm Nightwood made it *very* clear that he's not finished with his campaign against me."

His exact words had been, *We're just getting started.* Definitely not extending a hand in friendship. Not that I'd have accepted his hand any more than I had the first time he'd come sauntering in here, figuring he could simply introduce himself and I'd be honored to enjoy his company.

I couldn't let him or the others get to me. I'd focus on learning everything I could until I was ready to destroy this school and the cold-blooded psychopaths it taught all its students to be, and then I could prove to the joymancers back home that I wasn't like the other fearmancers. That they didn't need to be afraid of my powers. I'd go back to them and back into the life I really wanted.

If it took me a while to get there, so be it.

I pushed back the covers and sat up, careful of Deborah. "We'd better find you a new hiding spot in case they decide to use you to mess with me again," I said under my breath. The sock drawer wasn't going to cut it anymore. "Any ideas?"

I've found some comfortable nooks right in the walls. It'd be difficult for them to catch me in there. And I can keep more of an ear out for anyone coming into your room who doesn't belong.

"Okay, that sounds good."

I should have been able to keep intruders out with all the magical strengths I supposedly had. Unfortunately practice counted for a lot too, and my most enthusiastic enemies had plenty of talent of their own along with their years of experience.

A couple of my dormmates were sitting on the sofas in the common room when I walked through, but not any of the girls I'd really interacted with. They watched me pass by with a curious if wary look and went back to their conversation. When I'd finished my shower and headed into the kitchen to grab breakfast for me and my mouse, those two had disappeared, and Shelby was pouring herself a bowl of cereal.

A smile leapt to my face at the sight of the dorm's one Nary student. Bloodstone University brought in a limited number of Naries—short for *ordinary*, or *Nary a bit of magic*, as Mom used to say—on scholarships more for our benefit than theirs. As mages living in secret among human society, we needed to learn how to act and cast around them without raising suspicions. That was *all* they were supposed to be: a tool. Fearmancers didn't make friends with Naries.

But I wasn't your typical fearmancer, and I'd rather have Shelby's company over that of the mages here any day, even if there were a whole lot of things I could never talk to her about.

"Hey," I said as I opened the fridge to retrieve my eggs and Deborah's cheese. "You're looking better. Totally recovered?"

Shelby glanced over at me with a swish of her mousy brown ponytail and smiled back. A faint but healthy-looking flush colored her cheeks. She'd been suffering from a flu for most of the last week, pushing on with her schoolwork despite a serious fever, because she was scared the teachers would send her home if she didn't seem committed enough to her classes. Despite the chilly treatment she got from most of the student body, the music program here apparently offered her opportunities she'd endure just about anything to hold onto.

"Back in ship-shop shape," she said, and paused.

"Other than hearing that stupid tree. The maintenance staff obviously didn't listen to me about it."

"Tree?" I repeated as I cracked my eggs over a frying pan, and then remembered. "The one you think might be rotten?"

"Yeah. It's still making that weird sound when the breeze is moving in the right direction. It's pretty faint—maybe they think I'm making it up. But I swear it sounds just like the one that collapsed on my street way back when, and I'm not feverish anymore, so…" She grimaced.

The fearmancer staff just assumed they knew better than any Nary. I doubted they'd even checked it out. When I'd told my assigned mentor, Professor Banefield, about Shelby's complaint, he'd brushed the sound off as a prank one of the magical students must have been playing on her.

I'd just have to raise the issue again. I couldn't imagine anyone getting enough fear out of some faint weird tree sound for it to be worth keeping up the illusion for days on end.

"I have to talk to the staff about something today anyway," I said, which was only sort of a lie. Banefield was staff, if not maintenance staff. "Maybe if they hear about it from more than one person, they'll take the problem more seriously."

"Thanks. I'd really just like them to take a look. People could get hurt. Anyway… I was wondering… Do you want to go grab drinks in town again sometime? I'm busy with rehearsals for the end-of-year concert the next couple evenings, but maybe after that?"

She eyed me hesitantly. I was the first dormmate she'd had who'd been anything close to friendly. I gave her my warmest smile in reassurance. "That'd be great. I'm still getting to know what the best places are."

We chatted about the town's somewhat meager offerings for food and entertainment as I finished frying my eggs. Just as my toast popped up, a door at the far end of the room opened, and Victory Blighthaven stepped out.

Victory's auburn hair curved in perfect waves around her angelic face, and her blouse and skirt clung to her hourglass figure so smoothly it was obvious they'd been tailored for her. She'd have been lovely to look at if it hadn't been for the pointed glower she aimed my way.

She was one of Malcolm Nightwood's biggest fans, which meant she wasn't a fan of me at all. It didn't help that I'd inadvertently stolen the best bedroom in the dorm from her when I'd arrived. Obviously the announcement about my exemplary assessment hadn't warmed her up to me.

I decided not to find out what Victory might contribute to the conversation and hustled my breakfast into my bedroom. Deborah gave a happy sigh when I set down her plate of cheese, crackers, and blueberries. I sat at the little desk crammed between the bed and the window and dug into my eggs and toast.

As I gulped down the last few buttery bites, my gaze meandered over the green outside toward the domed shape of the Stormhurst Building and then on to the glittering waters of the lake. If it hadn't been for the people, this place really would have been beautiful. I could just imagine...

A haze crept over my mind. I couldn't have said I was thinking about anything, really, only that all at once I blinked and the scattering of clouds had scudded farther across the sky—and my hand was jerking a pen across a paper I didn't remember getting out.

I yanked my arm back with a hitch of my pulse. The scrawled words stared back at me. The same sentence was dug into the paper over and over all the way down its white surface.

I killed them. I killed them. I killed them.

A chill shot through me from gut to throat, just about propelling my breakfast with it. The pen slipped from my fingers, and my hand came up to grip the glass dragon charm hanging from a silver chain around my neck. The last piece of my old life I'd been able to hang onto.

How—What had even just happened there? I'd never blanked out like that before. Even when I'd acted without meaning to in the grip of one of Malcolm's persuasion spells, I'd been conscious the whole time. And there was no one in here with me to have cast any spell on me anyway.

Why had I written *that*? I'd thought it more than once remembering my parents' deaths. The blacksuits who'd come to "rescue" me from the joymancers would never have killed them if they hadn't taken me in and raised me in the first place. But I didn't think I'd ever admitted that guilt to anyone. It'd been in my head during my first desensitization session, but I could have sworn I hadn't said anything out loud. I'd been sobbing too hard to say much of anything.

Had that daze been caused by magic or simply the emotions I'd tried to bury?

Lorelei? Deborah's voice reached me from a greater distance than it normally sounded. She scurried across the floor to touch my socked foot. *Thank goodness! You came out of it.*

"What happened?" I whispered.

You tensed up all of a sudden, grabbed that paper, and started writing. I tried to talk to you, but you didn't seem to hear me. It looked like some kind of spell. I peeked out into the common room, but I couldn't see anyone who looked as if they were casting on you. Of course, who knows what awful magic these fearmancers might be able to work?

That wasn't terribly reassuring. I crumpled the paper into a ball and tossed it into the little garbage bin under the desk.

What were you writing?

"Just…" My throat constricted. "Nothing important. Just gibberish." I glanced at my phone and winced. "I should get going. I'm supposed to meet my mentor in ten minutes."

The chill in my nerves lingered as I hurried out of the dorm. None of my usual tormenters were around. If I'd been in the grip of a spell, *someone* had to have cast it.

I loped down the five flights of stairs to the ground floor with my thoughts in a jumble. I'd just reached the hall by the library when four striking and all-too-familiar figures came ambling my way.

Malcolm Nightwood's voice rang out with its usual smooth cockiness. "Well, if it isn't Glinda the good witch. You look a little frazzled. Is the pressure of all that talent we're expecting to see getting to you already?"

I swiveled on my heel to face the four scions. They must have been coming up from the basement room where they had their private lounge area—which meant, I was pretty sure, that they'd all been much too far away to cast any targeted spell at me.

Malcolm smiled at me with a cool glint in his dark brown eyes. The restrained hostility in his expression eliminated any heat his breathtaking looks might have sparked in me otherwise. His golden hair and his face with its perfect mix of hard and soft lines had made me think of him as a divine devil when I'd first met him. These days I had no doubt that he leaned much more toward the devil side in personality.

At his left, Jude flicked back his floppy dark copper hair and offered me a smirk. The Killbrook scion was just as good-looking as Malcolm in his lean, angular way—and could be just as vicious when he decided to be. But it was the muscular guy at Malcolm's other side who made my stomach clench up. Connar Stormhurst met my eyes, his chiseled face set in a stern expression that didn't waver for a second. I couldn't see any hint that he remembered, let alone cared, about the conversations we'd had away from the others… or the intimacy we'd shared.

I should have known better. Just like I should have known not to have any hopes for Declan Ashgrave the second I'd found out where he and the blackshirts had brought me. The oldest scion, bringing up the rear of the bunch, had shown more than once that he'd protect me only when it didn't interfere with his obligations to the other guys or his job as teacher's aide. Now, he ducked his head, his black hair falling forward to shadow his bright hazel eyes.

"I'm just fine," I said as evenly as I could manage. "Thank you so much for your concern, though."

I spun back around and strode toward the main doors. Malcolm's chuckle rolled after me. "We'll see you around, Glinda!"

He turned that friendly comment into a threat so easily. A shiver ran through me as I headed along the path toward the teachers' offices in Killbrook Hall. Whether someone had magically induced my little episode this morning or not, clearly my first priority needed to be working on my mental shields. If I could be sure of protecting myself from outside influence, I'd be safe from any more unnerving episodes—or I'd know that whatever was wrong was coming from inside me.

CHAPTER TWO

Rory

"Congratulations again on yesterday's exemplary assessment," Professor Banefield said with a grin as he ushered me into his office. "I knew your talent would shine through once you had a little more time."

His warm confidence put me a little more at ease. "You've got my new schedule for me?"

"I do. Lots more learning to be done, but you're clearly up to the challenge. Why don't you look it over before I say my piece."

He handed me a paper showing two weeks' worth of class times, mostly the same across both weeks. A lot more of them than had been on my initial "easing the Bloodstone scion into her magical education" schedule for the last month.

When I'd had a few minutes to read it over, Banefield leaned forward, rubbing the side of his round head. His light red hair stuck up in tufts as if he'd slept on it funny, but I'd seen him often enough to know that was just how it always looked.

"You'll see that you only have one official session with me each week now that you're getting settled in," he said. "You can drop in during my office hours any time you feel you need additional guidance, of course. I'll always be available to you, but my primary role now will be to help you continue to adjust to school life in general rather than magical lessons. From here on, you can see you'll have two seminars a week in each specialty to help catch you up."

"And now a Desensitization session every week… but at a different time?" I glanced at him quizzically.

Banefield's upbeat expression faltered for a second. "Professor Razeden and I felt—and Ms. Grimsworth agreed—that in light of your circumstances, it would be ideal for you to get frequent one-on-one instruction in that area until your control has improved."

A flush rushed to my cheeks. Yeah, my control had been pretty crappy the first two sessions I'd done. The whole point of Desensitization was to master your reactions when faced with your greatest fears—the weaknesses other fearmancers could get the most mileage out of targeting. Both times, I'd needed Professor Razeden to end the illusion for me because I hadn't been able to stand up to it even with his advice.

At least private sessions meant I wouldn't have any scions watching my weaknesses laid out on display.

"We're avoiding placing you in any of the general interest courses with the Naries for similar reasons,"

Banefield went on, avoiding lingering on my failure. "Not that your use of magic has lacked control, but you haven't been practicing it enough for us to be certain there won't be problems. Better not to risk exposure. I expect you'll move into those in the fall term with the new school year."

"That makes sense," I said. I wasn't in any hurry to add even more to my workload. But the mention of the Nary students reminded me of my conversation with Shelby.

"If you have any other questions…"

I folded the schedule. "I do, but not about this. I was talking with the Nary student in my dorm this morning—she's still worried about that tree I told you about before. Do you know if anyone in maintenance has checked it out—and if they haven't, can we get them to?"

In general, I found Professor Banefield to be one of the most pleasant people at the university. Something shifted in his demeanor whenever the nonmagical people living alongside us came up, though. His jaw tensed beneath his scruffy beard, and his mild eyes took on a harder sheen.

"As we discussed earlier, Rory, I think it's best not to get caught up in the concerns of the Naries. This is an… unusual environment for them, but they accept it because of the benefits we offer in return. We don't want to encourage them to question the unusual occurrences that may come up around them."

They accepted this environment partly because they had no idea we were using them to generate fear and test our magical stealth.

I made a face. "That doesn't mean she's wrong about this. How long would it take for someone to check it out?

A falling tree is going to hurt a mage just as much as any Nary who ends up in its path."

"I'm sure the maintenance staff is already monitoring the grounds as per their job."

His voice had gone firm. This was around the point I'd given up last time. Today, resistance prickled through me. Maybe the day I could take down the university felt way too far in the future, but I could make sure at least *one* person was treated properly.

"If one of the magical students had reported it, someone would make sure to look into it, wouldn't they?"

"That's different," Banefield said. "We trust that you would be able to tell the difference between a real problem and a prank."

"Yeah," I said, "and this sounds like a real problem to me. Shelby is a musician—she obviously has a good ear. And she's experienced this before. It makes sense that she might pick up on a sign that most of us would miss, magic or not. I get that fearmancers generally don't want to lower themselves to listening to Naries or whatever, but don't you think there's a certain point where that crosses the line from sticking to your own to being stubbornly stupid?"

A little more irritation than I'd meant to reveal leaked into my tone. Banefield stiffened in his chair. For the first time in the month I'd known him, he looked *angry*. I braced myself with a hiccup of my pulse, but whatever way I'd provoked him, he mastered his reaction. The first thing he let out was a sigh, and his shoulders came back down.

"*I* have plenty of experience dealing with Naries," he

said. "The one thread that has carried through all those interactions is carelessness. They only care about their own individual discomforts and desires without a thought to any larger purpose. We cannot have our staff distracted from their regular jobs to track down a 'weird-sounding' tree on one likely misguided report."

There were a whole lot of things I could have said about fearmancers and their selfishness, but I didn't think most of those paths would take us anywhere productive. I did have to point out, "It's not as if *we're* all that careful with the Naries. At least when they screw up, in my experience, it's usually a mistake rather than purposeful malice."

"And yet mistakes can have such wider reaching consequences compared to malice thoughtfully planned." Banefield gave me a tight smile. "I know you're still adjusting to the expectations and practices of our community, Rory, but I can assure you one thing—we expect every student here to choose their actions with full consideration of the impact."

Was that supposed to be reassuring? I shifted in my seat and opened my mouth again, but Banefield cut me off before I could say anything else.

"Your first new seminar will be starting shortly. I think this discussion has run its course."

We'd see about that the next time I got his ear. I stood up, clutching the schedule. "There was one other thing. I'd like to get in some concentrated practice on shielding my mind. To, ah, reduce the 'impact' of any spells that get thrown at me."

Banefield relaxed a little more with the change in subject. "The timing works out well then," he said. "I believe it's Insight you're off to now. Professor Sinleigh should be able to give you even better advice for advanced tactics—she has a couple of decades' experience on me. And it's best if you're working on your magical techniques with your seminar professors rather than me so they can accurately judge your progress."

I tugged open my schedule again. Yep, I was off to Insight. This seminar was a new addition to my schedule, so I could hope Jude and Victory wouldn't be there, eager to pry open my head.

I set off through the building toward the green at a brisk pace. The sooner I got to Nightwood Tower and my classroom there, the more choice I'd have in seating. Professor Sinleigh liked to pair us up with our nearest neighbors.

Killbrook Hall held the junior residences as well as the staff quarters. I passed several younger students on my way out, and a mix of juniors and seniors heading to their own classes outside. Many of them glanced at me with a glimmer of recognition, their eyes widening a bit or their heads turning to watch after I passed. A cool shudder of sensation rippled up through my chest.

It was fear, I realized as another waft of it hit me. Not one of the kinds I'd felt before: the sharp quivers of animal nerves when I ventured into the forest, the jolts of panic the few times I'd been able to land a jab against one of my tormenters. This flowed through me with a sensation more subtle and yet more sweeping.

Apprehension. Beneath all the awed fawning I'd gotten yesterday, just seeing me made quite a lot of the student body awfully wary. And why not, after the way the established scions with their multiple strengths lorded it over this school?

That thought settled uncomfortably in my gut as I reached the tower and trudged up the stairs. I couldn't say I minded getting this top-up of magical energy, now tingling behind my collarbone, but I didn't exactly like the idea of becoming some frightening figure either.

It was a good thing I'd made it to class a bit early, because I was able to choose a spot between a few students who'd never been overtly nasty to me, just a couple minutes before Cressida walked in. Victory's partner-in-crime lifted her chin haughtily at the sight of me and flicked her white-blond braid back over her shoulder as she took a seat at the opposite corner of the room—a reasonably safe distance.

Of course, sitting at the front didn't give me much distance at all from the other person in the classroom I'd have wanted to avoid. When the professor came in, peering at us with her owlish eyes, Declan Ashgrave arrived right behind her. Insight was his main specialty—the league he'd chosen from his strengths—and in those seminars he was working as Professor Sinleigh's aide.

His gaze settled on me for a second, and I tensed in my seat. He stopped by the far side of her desk.

Declan hadn't been as much of an asshole as the other scions, but he hadn't done anything to stop their torment either, even when I'd challenged him to his face. And then there was the whole library incident when he'd dragged me out of sight of Victory and her crew for my apparent safety, but ended up kissing me and then yelling at me about it.

The kiss had been pretty enjoyable, I had to admit. The yelling, not so much. Better to avoid any possibility of either happening again.

"All right, class," Professor Sinleigh said, clapping her delicate hands. "Today we'll be focusing on narrowing the scope of an insight spell through the use of questions. As some of you will be aware, asking a specific question with your spell can help you home in on more useful impressions, but they are also more hindered by mental defenses. Those of you who are relatively new to the concept, begin with more basic and unthreatening inquiries. Those of you who are more practiced may attempt to dig deeper if you're confident enough. But first let's run through a warm-up exercise..."

———

By the end of class, I knew that the girl sitting next to me had a fox for a familiar, favored mint tea, and loved the color green. I wasn't sure whether I'd broken through barriers she had up or she just hadn't tried that hard to stop me, but at this point, I'd take the success as a win.

As the other students filed out of the room, I approached Professor Sinleigh. She was so petite I found I was looking down at her from about half a foot—and I was hardly an Amazon.

"Miss Bloodstone," she said in her soft, precise voice. "It's an honor to have you joining us in the League of Insight. What can I help you with?"

"I'd like to work on my mental shielding skills," I said. "Professor Banefield, my mentor, said I should talk with you about that."

Sinleigh nodded. "That's a very valuable skill to develop. We will cover several techniques in class."

"I was hoping to get caught up a little faster, since I've missed so much time here."

"Yes, of course." She tapped her lips. "I think what would work best is for you to begin with some additional tutoring from Mr. Ashgrave. It wouldn't be a bad thing for the two of you to become better acquainted as scions at the same time. Once he's sure you have all the core skills solid, I can arrange some time to coach you on the more advanced strategies." She looked to Declan. "You should be able to fit that into your schedule, shouldn't you?"

Er, that hadn't been the scenario I'd been going for at all. I crossed my arms over my chest instinctively.

Declan trained his bright hazel eyes on me for a moment before turning to the professor. I couldn't read his expression. "I can definitely find the time if that arrangement works for Miss Bloodstone."

Okay, so we were sticking to professional courtesy now, were we? My body balked, but if I refused to work with him, Professor Sinleigh would think *I* was the problem.

I couldn't start my time here as an official student

running away scared from the guys I'd spent the last month standing up to.

"All right," I said. "That sounds fine."

Sinleigh considered me as if she'd picked up on my lack of enthusiasm, but she didn't remark on it. "I'll leave you two to work out the best timing. Let me know when you're ready for your advanced coaching."

She slung her bag over her shoulder and slipped out of the room.

I stayed where I was by the corner of the desk, and thankfully Declan didn't come any closer. He looked at the floor and then at me, swiping back his smooth dark hair.

"This wasn't my idea."

"Obviously. I was here for the entire conversation."

One corner of his lips quirked up slightly at my tone. "If you're sure—"

I shrugged. "If you can manage not to be an asshole and just do your job, it'll be fine. Unless you're worried that someone will see the extra tutoring as favoritism."

The hint of a smile disappeared at that little jab. "Sinleigh assigned me to do it. I don't see how anyone can criticize me for that. I only have about ten minutes before I need to head out now, but we can arrange times during my office hours. There's a joint aide office in the staff wing of Killbrook Hall."

"Okay." Despite my claim that all this was fine, my thoughts had scattered too much for me to think through the least awkward way of handling this. "I just got my new schedule. Let me—let me see when I seem to have the best openings, and then I'll let you know."

"Of course." He paused and then backed up a step as if to give me more room to pass him without coming near him. The gesture set off a twinge in my chest. He just couldn't help sort of protecting me in between all the times he didn't, could he?

As I headed for the door, he sucked in a breath. "Is your familiar okay?"

I stopped on the threshold, my head snapping around. "What?"

"Your familiar. It seemed all right, after—they only had it in a cage in another room—but you can't always tell when you don't really know the animal."

Something clicked in my head with his gaze on me and the guilt slanting his mouth. "You're the one who brought her back to me." In the commotion after my assessment announcement yesterday, someone had slipped Deborah into my hand so swiftly I hadn't seen who it was. Declan *had* looked awfully uncomfortable during the charade Malcolm and Jude had orchestrated yesterday, when they'd made me think they were feeding my mouse to Jude's ferret familiar.

"They didn't have the right to hold on to her," he said.

"But they had the right to take her in the first place? What if they'd decided to *really* let the ferret at her?"

"They wouldn't have," Declan said firmly. "You don't have to worry about that. No one here would risk it. To purposefully kill someone's familiar—even a scion wouldn't get away with breaking that rule. Jude might think a lot of himself, but he knows he doesn't have perfect control over his animal."

"But no one knew I even had her." If the four of them and the four girls who'd been spectators hadn't told anyone, then hardly anyone knew even now.

"It wouldn't have mattered. When someone's familiar dies, especially if it's traumatic—it affects you. If you reported it, the staff would be able to confirm, whether they knew you had a familiar beforehand or not." Declan ducked his head. "I know it's not a lot of comfort, after everything, but there are lines we don't cross."

We meaning fearmancers in general or my fellow scions in particular? I wasn't sure it mattered. The twinge in my chest had expanded, filling the space inside my ribs with a faint ache.

"Maybe you should look into finding a few more of those," I said, and left before the growing mix of gratitude and disappointment could wrench at me any harder.

CHAPTER THREE

Jude

My mother tried. I knew she did, and I could summon some gratitude for that. The thing was, most of the time I couldn't help thinking she was trying a hell of a lot more for Dad than for me when by any available metric it should have been the other way around.

Her voice carried tinnily through the phone into my ear. "He's mentioned the comments Baron Nightwood made a few times since the last meeting of the pentacle, and he always looks so grim. I can tell it's bothering him."

I shifted my weight against the worn stone wall I was leaning against and rolled my eyes in the general direction of the green. Of course she could. Dad wore displeasure like a parka, heavy and hooded on his skinny frame. You could practically hear it rustling when he moved around a room.

"Maybe he should take it up with Baron Nightwood

then," I said, even though I could tell where this line of conversation was going.

Sure enough: "I just thought, since you see Malcolm so often at school, you could feel things out through him. I'm sure your father would appreciate any insight you're able to offer."

"I don't think the baron would appreciate me poking around in his son's head."

"That's not what I meant. You're friends. You must talk about things."

Yeah, and I knew better than to bring up Baron Nightwood around Malcolm. His dad was a prick on a completely different level compared to mine. When Malcolm got back from visits home, it was a good policy not to talk to him at all until he'd had at least a few hours to let off steam on whoever happened to be in his vicinity.

I tipped my face back to the sun, inhaling the sharp grassy scent from the recent mowing. "If Dad wanted me to look into this for him, *he* should be the one asking me. He's got my number too." Not that I could remember the last time he'd used it.

Mom probably couldn't either. "He doesn't like asking for help," she said in a placating tone.

That was an all-out lie. He'd known perfectly well he was "asking for help" by fussing about the subject in Mom's hearing. He just didn't have the balls to do it directly.

"I'll see what I can do," I said, by which I meant, no way in hell was I hassling Malcolm over this. It was the fastest way to end the conversation.

When I shoved the phone back in my pocket, students were just starting to trickle out of the tower across the way. A smile crept across my lips. I straightened up, scanning the various figures for a good target. A cluster would make for maximum impact. I had to time it right to make sure they were still reacting when the teachers departed after them so someone would be around to award the credit to my league.

There. A clump of five young Naries came straggling along behind most of the others, their gold leaf pins glinting in the sun. They veered across the grass to head toward the football field, and I rolled a few slithery syllables off my tongue, aiming the picture in my mind with a serpentine flick of my hand.

The trick was making the illusion potent enough to be frightening but not so over-the-top I'd be docked for potential magical exposure. I spoke my casting word again, feeling the scales and seeing the pattern along the sinewy body with the slide of the sounds off my tongue.

Bigger than the garter snakes you'd expect to find naturally around here, but not quite as big as Connar's ball python familiar. Just large enough to freak the feebs out without them thinking it was impossible for a creature like that to be weaving through the grass. All I needed was a little more concentration and another quick gesture to draw it fully solid, etching in every impression it needed to offer their senses with a prickling at the back of my skull...

One of the boys yelped and scrambled to the side, nearly tripping over his feet. A girl shrieked as she yanked the guy next to her backward. I couldn't see my creation perfectly from this distance, but their reactions and the rippling of motion through the grass between them gave me a good enough view.

Fear flowed sharp and potent through my lungs with my next breath. Fainter flutters carried from all around me as the other students turned to see what the commotion was.

I closed my eyes for a second, savoring the most delicious sensation in the world. I was never going to get tired of drinking that cocktail of alarm and panic.

All I needed was for one of the teachers to pass by on their way to the offices, and the gambit would have scored in every possible way.

I looked back toward my targets in time to see a familiar slim figure marching up to them. Shit. The breeze tossed the Bloodstone scion's dark brown waves back from her pale face, which was set with a frown. She held out a hand as if to reassure the Naries and bent down.

What the fuck was she— Seriously?

I'd cast the illusion with enough strength for it to stay solid to touch as well as sight for several minutes, and I couldn't dispel it now while the Naries were staring, even though Rory Bloodstone was lifting the snake up from the grass with her fingers clamped just behind its jaws. To avoid getting bitten, I supposed. If she'd taken it for real, at least I'd won that much even if I'd lost my chance at earning a league credit.

The snake's body twisted and squirmed beneath Rory's hand as she scanned the crowd. Several of the spectators hurried on to escape her notice, more afraid of her than of the damned creature I'd drawn for them. Cowards.

Annoying as her intervention was, I had to admit she also looked pretty spectacular standing there, fierce as an avenging angel. Too bad Blood U wasn't any place for angels.

Her gaze settled on me and stopped there. If she thought I was going to run off as if *I* were scared of her, she could forget that. I relaxed against the wall of Ashgrave Hall as she strode across the green to confront me. It was a nice enough view with her hair still swaying across her shoulders and her dress pants swishing against her slender legs below where the fabric clung to her perfectly curved hips.

"I assume this is yours," she said, shoving the snake at me.

There was no one standing close enough to see it except the two of us now. I gave a careless wave, and the snake disappeared from her hold so quickly her fingers clenched into a fist grasping after it. She blinked at her empty hand and then wiped it on her pants as if my magic might have left behind an unpleasant residue.

I offered her a grin. "If you like playing with snakes, you only had to ask. There are plenty to go around."

It was so fucking easy to get that fire to flare even brighter in her deep blue eyes. "I'd just prefer they weren't terrorizing anyone," she said. "Mission accomplished."

She swiveled as if to go. Hardly satisfying. I could get more of a rise out of her than that.

"Hold on a minute," I said. "I was going to get at least

one credit out of that. You owe me something in return, Ice Pop."

Rory's gaze jerked back toward me. In that instant, I saw the same searing cold anger that she'd glared at me with in the moment when she'd realized the mouse I was letting Mischief toy with was only an illusion, not her familiar. Apparently it was going to take more than a couple days for her to get over that little transgression.

She took a quick glance around. "I'll give you ice," she said, and muttered a word under her breath with a jab of her hand. Before I had a chance to react, a glittering substance sprang up from the earth beneath my feet to encase them in a chilly coating. Like she'd done to Malcolm the first time we'd met her—the whole reason I'd gone with those icy nicknames to tease her.

I laughed and moved to stomp myself free, except where Malcolm had been able to crack through the sheen of frost she'd conjured with one jerk, she'd tossed a whole lot more ice at me. Neither of my feet would budge beneath the thick layer.

Rory was already stalking away. She vanished into the hall before I could shout after her. Although maybe I wouldn't have wanted to shout anyway. I didn't need the newbie's help, did I?

A few of the other students were looking my way, having noticed the exchange. With a quick murmur, I drew an illusion over my feet to make it look as if the ice had melted away. Then I leaned against the wall again. With a few more surreptitious murmurs and shifts of my fingers, I tested the magic in the ice.

She sure as hell hadn't held back on me. Damn, that conjuring was tight. Physicality was *supposed* to be one of my areas of strength, but the truth was, I mostly got by using particularly careful illusions. And no illusion could actually dislodge a well-cast conjuring.

A strong talent in all four domains of magic, Ms. Grimsworth had announced yesterday after Rory's assessment. She hadn't been kidding, had she?

Rory's spell hadn't been the most artful ever, and it lacked endurance too. The edges of the ice were already melting in the spring warmth. I'd just have to wait here a few more minutes until it softened enough, and then I'd be able to crack it. Still, if she kept picking up her skills at this speed, as full of righteous spirit as ever and with more capacity for power than even Malcolm had, we might have real trouble on our hands.

The declaration of her strengths clearly hadn't left her complacent. She was going to keep following her own joymancer-tainted moral directive no matter who she pissed off along the way. We hadn't broken one bit of her.

I should have been peeved, standing there waiting for that fucking ice to melt. Instead, remembering Rory as she'd marched across the green toward me clutching the illusion of the snake, an unexpected sense of possibility unfurled in my chest.

She had more power than any of us and all that determination to prove she was better. Different. Not like all the other fearmancers. Why the hell had I ever *wanted* that broken?

I'd let myself get caught up in Malcolm's crusade

without thinking through everything her presence here could mean for me.

From the moment I'd arrived on this campus, my life had felt more and more like a trap slowly closing in on me. That girl—that girl could be my doorway out.

I just had to make her want to be.

CHAPTER FOUR

Rory

I was paging through a book on Theories of Deception that my Illusion professor had recommended, propped against the pillows I'd set against my headboard, when someone tapped on my bedroom door.

"Rory, can we talk?"

It was Imogen's voice, low and hesitant. Imogen, who'd been my only friend among the fearmancers during my first month here.

Imogen, who'd sold me out to the scions and Victory's crew. She'd also been the only person who'd known about Deborah and her hiding place. She'd led them right to my familiar so they could enact their game of emotional torture. I hadn't talked to her since then, hadn't wanted to even look at her. My gut twisted into a knot right now at the thought of answering.

But we were sharing a dorm for who knew how long.

Maybe it'd be better if we cleared the air.

I left the book on the bed and eased the door open a crack—just far enough to see half of Imogen's lightly freckled face framed by her tawny blond hair. As always, a silver clip held back some of the shoulder-length strands. Today she'd picked one shaped like a crescent moon.

"What do you want to talk about?" I asked.

She clasped her hands together in front of her, her mouth tight with discomfort. "I know I really screwed up, and maybe you're never going to accept an apology, but— but I'd like to at least try to make one. And to explain what happened, even if I can't justify it. If you're willing to hear me out?"

I would actually really like to know what had made her turn on me like that, but at the same time I suspected hearing it wasn't going to be much fun.

Imogen eased back a step. "There's no one else around right now if you don't want me in your space. We could talk out here."

That suggestion loosened a little of the tension inside me. I stepped out, glancing around to make sure Victory and her cronies weren't lurking after all, and followed Imogen over to one of the couches. The lingering scent of someone's rosey perfume rose off the fabric as I sat down. I curled my fingers around the edge of the firm cushion.

Imogen looked down at her hands and dragged in a breath before raising her head. Her light brown eyes met mine pleadingly.

"I never wanted to tell them anything," she said. "I hope you can at least believe that it wasn't my idea at all.

I'm *so* sorry about everything that happened—what they made you think they were doing to your familiar—it was awful."

I didn't need her to tell me that. She couldn't imagine how awful it'd been for me, not least because she had no idea I'd have lost not just my animal familiar but the human guardian residing inside the mouse.

"Why did you tell them, then?" I said.

Her gaze dropped again. "Victory had seen us hanging out together. It wasn't really a secret that we were friends. She guessed that I might know something about you that they could use. She must have cast an insight spell on me and seen enough to realize there was something secret in your room. And then she threatened that she'd make up a false complaint against my dad, something bad enough to get him immediately fired, if I didn't tell her the rest."

"So you did."

"I tried not to," Imogen said, her voice strained. "I pretended I had no idea what they were talking about, but they didn't believe me. Victory called up Ms. Grimsworth and was about to say something—I knew whatever she'd tell them about my dad, they'd believe her over him and me. Her family is friends with the barons. We're not really anybody. If Dad lost his job over some scandal, I don't even know if he could find another one in the community."

I leaned back on the couch, rubbing my forehead. She'd thrown me under the bus to protect her dad. I wasn't sure I wouldn't have done the same if our positions had been reversed. I would've given in to Malcolm's demands, gotten down on my knees and offered my unwilling allegiance to him and the other scions, if I hadn't realized that Deborah wasn't really under threat.

Imogen had only known me for a few weeks. How could I expect her to have felt more loyal to me than to her family?

The betrayal still stung, though. Victory knew how to manipulate her now. What was to stop her from doing it again? Regardless of whether I understood why Imogen had done what she had, I could never completely trust her again, could I?

"I really am sorry," Imogen said with a miserable expression. "I was so relieved when you figured out the trick."

I'd seen that too—it was a bit of insight into her frantic mind that had tipped me off about the trick in the first place. She'd been in agony, not gloating like Victory and the others.

"I get it," I said. "I mean, I'm never going to be happy that it happened, but I'm not going to stay mad at you when it was Victory pulling the strings. I believe you that you didn't want to tell her."

Imogen studied me. "But you don't really want anything to do with me now either."

"It's not that. I—" I pulled my hands into my lap where they clenched. "Apology accepted, okay? The rest, we'll see how it goes."

"Okay. That's fair." She sighed and stood up. "Thank you for listening. Most people here would have sooner set my hair on fire than find out what really happened."

"Well, I think we've thoroughly established that I'm not like most people here," I muttered, and her mouth twitched with the start of a smile.

"I need to go into town to grab some groceries," she said. "Do you—do you want me to pick up anything for you?"

A peace offering? A few days ago, she'd have asked if I wanted to go with her, but she could obviously tell I wasn't in the mood to jump right back into our previous friendship. I might have taken her up on the current offer if I *had* needed anything.

"No, I'm good," I said. "But thanks."

She bobbed her head and headed out. I flopped back on the couch. My thoughts were still churning in my head, but it was kind of nice getting to stretch my legs out here in the common room rather than hiding away in my little bedroom all the time like I normally did to avoid dealing with the rest of my dormmates.

How long would it take Victory to come around? She couldn't hate me *forever*, right? As far as she knew, eventually I was going to be one of those barons her parents liked chumming up to.

Well, I was getting the hang of this magic thing, and my mere presence supplied me with a decent supply of fear now. Let her try a few more tricks on me and see how she liked being embarrassed when I turned the tables. I wasn't going to stoop to her level, but she'd better believe I'd be defending myself with every strength I had.

The relative peace lasted about five minutes. Then a knock sounded on the outer door to the dorm.

A measured voice filtered through, clear enough for me to recognize it instantly. "Rory?"

I sat up with a hitch of my pulse. Why the hell had Declan Ashgrave come calling at my dorm?

I walked cautiously over to the door. I'd seen the scions walk right past it when I'd first arrived, but I guessed it'd been Malcolm or maybe Jude who'd magically unlocked it. Declan respected the deadbolt. A minor kindness.

"What do you want?" I asked, hugging myself like I had in class a few days ago, as if the folding of my arms could protect me.

"Can I come in? It'll just take a moment."

What was the worst he could do? I didn't actually think he was out to hurt me, even if he wasn't willing to stop his friends from doing that.

I gritted my teeth and opened the door. He walked a few steps inside and stopped there, his handsome face as striking as ever, his hair neatly swept back above his bright eyes.

Apprehension prickled through me. The last time he'd been in a rush to talk to me, he'd dragged me into that closet in the library where things had taken an unpleasant turn.

"How did you know I was here?" I said abruptly. If I'd been in my bedroom, I might not even have heard the knock. "Aren't you worried about my dormmates hearing you coming calling and wondering what's up with that?"

Declan gave me a crooked smile. "Insight specialist, remember? I guess that might not have come up in any of the seminars you've been to yet. Once you've got enough practice, you can get a sense of how many people are nearby and who they are, if you know them. My dorm is right under yours."

The prickling shot deeper. "You've been *spying* on me from down there?" He was a scion, which meant they'd have given him the corner room—his bedroom would be right under mine. It wasn't as if he could watch me through the floor, but suddenly it felt as if he might as well have.

"No, nothing like that." Declan held up his hands. "I only checked because I wanted to talk. And I can't tell anything other than that you're in the room. I don't know any mage who can look inside someone's head without actually seeing that head to focus on it."

My hackles came down a smidge. I did remember Professor Sinleigh mentioning something about that. And I was glad Declan had waited until my conversation with Imogen was over before coming up. All the same...

"All right, you're here and I'm here. Again, what do you want?"

He gave me a slightly exasperated look that I didn't think was completely fair. "You asked for those extra shielding lessons, but you haven't gotten back to me to set up some times. I thought, considering... everything that's gone on, it'd be a good idea to get started sooner rather than later. I've got time right now, if you want to come back to my office, or you can tell me—"

He broke off at a sharp laugh on the other side of the door. Victory's laugh.

My heartbeat stuttered. Maybe I'd give as good as I got from Victory, but I didn't exactly want to hand her ammunition. That's exactly what she'd make of the idea that I was getting extra help. No doubt she'd use it as an excuse to test my mental shields in every possible way at every possible opportunity.

I already knew Declan wasn't going to be on board with pretending he'd come to visit for non-professional reasons. I grabbed his arm. "Come on." I hustled him across the common room and yanked him into my bedroom just as the lock clicked over.

Declan moved away from me as soon as the bedroom door had closed. I released his arm automatically, and he backed up to stand near the window, leaving plenty of space between him and me. Not really enough, though. The room felt abruptly twice as small, especially with my bed right there less than a foot from both of us. I very studiously did not look at it.

Victory's voice carried in from the common room. "If she tries to make us go over the project *again*, we'll just have to... convince her otherwise."

"You'd think they'd know better by now," Cressida replied, alongside a giggle I thought was Sinclair's.

They kept chatting away, sounding as if they'd gone into the kitchen. I caught Declan's eye where he was standing tensed with one hand gripping the back of my desk chair. Now that he was in here, there was definitely no way he could leave while they were there without raising a whole lot of questions he wouldn't be happy about.

"Sorry," I whispered. "I heard them coming and sort of panicked. They probably won't stay out there too long."

He nodded and inhaled slowly. With his exhale, he raised his hand and spoke a few words made of the nonsense syllables all the more experienced mages used to cast their spells. Once you could create a strong enough association between whatever sounds you picked and the magic you wanted to evoke, fearmancers preferred to ensure no one around could guess what they were casting and prepare.

My back went rigid, but all that happened was the voices from the common room snapped out. The room fell into silence.

"I conjured a sound barrier," Declan said. "Physicality isn't one of my strengths, but as long as they don't go prodding it, it should hold just fine. It's easier if we don't have to worry about them hearing us."

It was. I swallowed hard. "We won't know when they leave."

"I can pay attention to my impression of them out there. Don't worry, as soon as the coast is clear, I'll get out of your room."

Right. "Just like you knew when Imogen left."

He grimaced. "I promise you, I haven't generally been monitoring your comings and goings. It's just a skill that comes in handy from time to time."

He did have a point there. "Maybe you'll need to teach me that too," I said, leaning against the wall to increase the distance between us.

"Shielding seems like the more important skill to

begin with." He paused. "Do you have time to come with me now—after they leave—or do you want to decide on another time to meet? We might as well get that sorted out while we're stuck here."

I had a pretty good sense of my schedule now. I probably should have sought him out to make arrangements earlier, but part of me had still been balking at the thought of spending more time in his presence. He clearly intended to hold up his side of the deal, though, and having someone I didn't trust as my tutor would at least give me extra motivation to develop my mental defenses fast.

"I have a seminar in about half an hour," I said. "But if you'll have time later this afternoon...?"

He nodded. "I've got my own classes too, but I'll be free from five onward. Meet me at the aide office then? It's right at the start of the hall by the professors' quarters."

"Okay." There, we had a plan. For everything except how to get him out of my dorm room unnoticed. I tipped my head toward the door. "They're still out there?"

"Yeah. If they don't get going soon, there are a few tricks I can try. We just have to be careful with Victory, since she's pretty sharp... as I guess you've noticed."

"Kind of hard not to."

He motioned toward the book on the bed. "If you want to get back to your reading or whatever, don't let me stop you. You didn't ask to play host. Feel free to pretend I'm not here."

I definitely didn't want to be *on* my bed with Declan Ashgrave just a few feet away. "I'm fine right here," I said.

"We don't exactly have the best track record with tight spaces."

A shadow crossed his face, and his gaze twitched away from me for a second. His jaw worked. "I'm sorry," he said. "For what happened in the library—I handled it badly."

Understatement of the century. But the fact that he'd apologized—and looked legitimately pained about it— softened me a little.

"Is that a big problem of yours?" I said, more wryly than I might have otherwise. "Preventing yourself from kissing your students?"

Declan gave me a narrow look, but a faint flush crept over his cheeks at the same time. He hesitated for long enough that I started to think the glower was the only answer I was going to get.

"No," he said quietly. "Only with the ones I'm strongly attracted to. Or rather, the one."

Heat flared beneath my skin at that remark. I fumbled for my tongue. "Well, um, I'm sorry for existing in your general vicinity, then?"

"No apologies necessary." He exhaled in a rush. "Just to be clear, I'm not saying that as a come-on. It's not going to happen again. I just don't want you to think I go around leching on every girl I see."

"Just me."

"Rory. I can control myself. I'm generally very good at it. That was… a particularly unfortunate combination of circumstances. I promise you, it was the first and last time."

Remembering the kiss, the demanding passion he'd somehow hidden behind that strict and often cold exterior, part of me couldn't help thinking that was kind of a shame. Which was maybe why my mouth kept talking without bothering to consult my brain.

"So... if you weren't a teacher's aide, then this wouldn't be a problem at all? You'd—I don't know—ask me out or something?"

He laughed, but there wasn't any humor in the sound. "No, the circumstances are never going to be *good*, with the positions we're in." He paused at my quizzical look. "Has no one explained about the pentacle inheritances yet?"

"I know there's a pentacle of barons and of scions," I said. "The five ruling families—I think that's how Ms. Grimsworth put it. And the authority is passed on from parents to kids. I don't think anyone's mentioned more than that. Why? Are the families not supposed to mix?" Connar hadn't seemed worried about that, but then, as far as I could tell, he'd simply been stringing me along until he got what he wanted.

"There aren't any rules along those lines. But you can't be part of two families at once, and you're the only living Bloodstone. Whoever you end up marrying, they'll have to be a Bloodstone too. If you partner with another scion, they'd be giving up their barony."

"Oh." That possibility definitely hadn't occurred to me. "Then what happens to that barony?"

"It'd go to the next blood relative, assuming there is one," Declan said. "But I don't have any plans to throw away my position. I've spent my whole life working to make sure I can take it in the first place."

Well, that made sense. I wasn't sure what to say to that, though.

Before I could decide on an appropriate response, Declan's head twitched toward the door. "They're heading out," he said. "I'll give them a minute to go down the stairs, and then I'll get out of your hair."

Now that he'd actually been talking to me like a human being, I didn't completely want him to go, regardless of the circumstances. I'd see him in a few hours for our tutoring session, of course. But the thought of Connar had stirred up too many little knives of emotion for me to ignore.

"I get that the favoritism, and rules, and circumstances, and all that are important to you," I said with a vague gesture. "But—can you pick how you're going to act with me and just stick with that, no matter who's around? Because I would really prefer not to deal with being jerked around between friendly and asshole any more than I already have been, if that's all right with you."

My voice might have gotten a little raw. Declan considered me. "You're not just talking about me."

"I—"

His expression tightened. "Did Malcolm—"

"No," I said quickly. "No, Malcolm has been an asshole the whole way through."

Declan hadn't stopped studying me. With a jolt of panic, I concentrated on the steel shell around my mind I'd pictured before, however useful that amateur shield would be against a guy who'd specialized in Insight for years. "I'd also appreciate it if you didn't go magically poking around inside my head."

He blinked. "I'm not. I was just thinking back. When Connar tore into you the other day... you looked shocked."

Fuck. "I'd really rather not talk about it."

"Okay," Declan said, even though his expression was still puzzled. Given the alternately stern and ferocious demeanor his friend had shown any time I'd seen them together, it probably would surprise him to think Connar and I had somehow found common ground, even if it hadn't lasted. "I'll do my best to be predictable. We're still on for five?"

"I'll be there."

He dipped his head to me and waved his hand, I assumed to bring down the sound barrier he'd conjured. "I'll see you then."

It was only after he'd ducked out that the other implications of his confusion sank in.

He hadn't known that anything had happened between Connar and me. Which meant Connar hadn't told the other scions. Why not, if he'd only buttered me up so he could get his rocks off and then taunt me afterward? Shouldn't he have been celebrating how he'd landed that blow?

And if his betrayal hadn't been part of their whole scheme to knock me down, why the hell *had* he done it?

CHAPTER FIVE

Rory

We were all getting up to head out of my second Illusion seminar of the week when the door shifted. In the space of a second, the wooden surface twisted into a gigantic demonic face, gnashing its teeth at the nearest students, who stumbled backward.

The demon let out a harsh cackle that set my nerves jangling and then was absorbed back into the door. A guy at the back of the class—Alex? Alan? I had a lot of names to pick up—chuckled and gave a bow.

"Very nice detail and combination of visual and auditory components, Mr. Rutland," Professor Burnbuck said in a dry voice. "Credit to Illusion."

And a nice jolt of fear for the caster too.

I hurried on out with the rest of the class, but somehow Alex-or-Alan Rutland caught up with me, sauntering down the tower stairs with a smile that could only be described as self-satisfied.

"I think that was my best work yet," he said.

I glanced around. As far as I could tell, he was talking to me, even though we'd never spoken before. "Ah," I said, with as clear a lack of enthusiasm as I could pack into one syllable. What did *he* want from me?

"I'm strong in Physicality too—it makes for a pretty potent combination. While you're getting the hang of things around here, I'd be happy to give you a few pointers."

If this had been my regular college back in California, populated by regular people who didn't make a living out of terrorizing everyone around them, I wouldn't have blinked at the offer. But I was at Bloodstone University, accurately nicknamed Villain Academy by the mages who didn't attend it, and this was the first time in a month anyone had volunteered a helping hand, unless you counted Malcolm's initial posturing offer of friendship.

There was not looking a gift horse in the mouth, and then there was not being a total idiot.

"Thanks," I said mildly. "I think I'm picking things up okay, though."

"Maybe I could treat you to a night on the town then," the guy said as we stepped out into the cool morning air. The day had started out damp and dreary and was continuing in the same direction. "And not that dinky town down the road. Much better nightlife if we take an hour's drive in my Jag." He slung his hands in his pockets, putting on a casual stance even as he purposefully flexed his arms.

Oh. *Oh.* Was he *flirting* with me?

I had to catch myself before a laugh sputtered out of me. This guy clearly hadn't paid much attention to me if he thought the promise of nightlife and a fancy car was the way to my heart. Why the hell was he even—

Declan's explanation about the fearmancer laws of inheritance came back to me. *Whoever you end up marrying, they'll have to be a Bloodstone too.* Although the way these people jockeyed for power, to anyone not already a scion, that "have to" was probably more like "gleefully get to."

My affections were a ticket straight to the ranks of the barons.

"I don't think that's a good idea," I said.

"You won't know until you give it a shot, will you? I promise I'll show you a good time."

I stopped and spun on the guy. "What do you know about me other than my name and the fact that I was assessed with all four strengths?"

He just stared at me for a second with his mouth half-open. Yeah, obviously nothing, because those two facts were all that mattered to him.

"You don't get along well with Malcolm Nightwood," he ventured after way too long a pause.

I restrained a snort. That fact was almost as obvious as the other two. "I don't think I'm going to get along very well with you either, all right?" I said. An instinct took over to step a little closer, to draw myself up straighter, as I let steel lace my voice. "I'm not here to be your stepping stone, and I don't think you want to find out what'll happen if you try."

A wave of fear raced from him into my chest. He backed up, his eyes narrowing. "Message received," he snapped, but he hightailed it out of there so fast you'd have thought I'd sent a demon charging after *him*.

The rush of power I'd felt in that moment faded with a queasy twist in my stomach. I hadn't needed to be that harsh with him.

Making him scared shouldn't have felt that good.

I was built to enjoy it. Built to seek out every opportunity to absorb people's fear. That didn't mean I had to give in to those impulses, though. I'd just keep a closer rein on myself the next time I got frustrated.

And maybe I'd be less inclined toward those impulses if I made sure I had plenty of magical energy already stockpiled.

Instead of heading to the library like I'd planned, I set off across the field toward the forest that surrounded most of the campus. Making the local wildlife nervous with my comings and goings was an easy way to top up my supply of fear without being a jerk to anyone.

The air in the woods clung even more damply to my skin, but as soon as the trees closed around me, I reveled in the relative silence and solitude. No one watching me, evaluating me, deciding how they could use me or hurt me. Even in my bedroom, it was hard to feel completely alone with just that thin door between me and the common area.

A little melancholy crept in with the peace. The northern atmosphere might not match the one I'd grown up with, but it was hard not to remember the walks I'd taken with my parents on our periodic trips to this or that state park: Mom snapping photos, Dad chatting it up with other hikers we passed, me pulling out my sketch pad whenever we paused to make a quick pencil study of this flower or that interesting tree.

Never again.

That knowledge squeezed around my throat. I walked faster to outpace my grief as well as I could. It wasn't going to help me in this place.

I rambled through the brush until the uneven ground started to make my calves ache and a multitude of tiny quivers had filled the space behind my collarbone. As I turned back toward campus, a heavier crunch of a fallen branch froze me in my tracks.

A figure was picking his way through the trees toward me. It only took a moment for his coppery hair to stand out amid the vivid spring greenery.

Jude cocked his head as he reached me. "I thought I saw someone from the path. There *is* a path, you know."

"Sometimes I like to make my own," I said, my posture rigid.

He laughed, but it didn't sound as mocking as usual. "Fair."

"Well, now you know it's me. I'll be on my way."

"Hold on, Ice Queen," he said as I moved to walk away. His tiny golden dagger earring winked with the sunlight filtering through the leaves overhead.

I raised my eyebrows at him, unable to hold back the question. "I get to be queen after all?"

His mouth had settled into a lazy smile that only emphasized everything that was attractive in his boyishly wicked face. "After that little display the other day, I think you've earned the title."

That was unexpected. After my initial, rather pathetic attempt at freezing Malcolm in place to stop him from harassing some junior student, Jude had made a game out of calling me as many ridiculous ice-themed nicknames as he could. I couldn't tell what he was playing at now.

"Where are you headed?" he asked.

"Back to school," I said, because he'd figure that out soon enough just by watching me.

"So was I. I'll walk with you."

That would be a no. I raised my chin. "I wasn't looking for company. Anyway, I thought you preferred the path."

"Depends on who I'm walking with." He spread his hands in a gesture of appeal. "Can't we get along as fellow scions? You've proven yourself, beat the hell out of the assessment. I respect that. No need for us to be at each other's throats. We *are* going to have to work together someday."

I'd always had a hard time figuring Jude out, but he was outdoing himself today. Did he expect me to believe this white flag was genuine?

I shifted my weight. "Malcolm doesn't seem to think the war is over."

Jude made a show of peering around himself every which way, giving me an excellent view of his leanly muscled body in his dress shirt and slacks. "Just as I thought. The heir of Nightwood doesn't have me on a leash. Malcolm's a stubborn prick, I'll give you that. I see more value in flexibility."

And that would be great, except I don't believe you.

My skepticism must have shown on my face as I debated what to say. Jude waggled a finger at me. "Maybe I shouldn't be telling you about stubbornness. Was I really that awful to you?"

Oh, did he want a list of transgressions? I counted them off on one hand. "You ripped into me in Insight class and made sure everyone heard all the embarrassing memories you dug up. You made fun of me after I had to relive my parents' *murders* in Desensitization. You helped kidnap my familiar and did everything you could to convince me yours was going to eat it piece by piece. And that's only the things I know for sure." Who knew how much he might have helped Malcolm with one scheme or another along the way?

Jude hummed to himself. "It seems to me that my first crime came after you'd already taken a jab at me—"

"I was just completing the exercise!" I said. "And if you're going to get technical about it, *you* still took the first jab."

"—*and* insulted me and the other scions in front of most of your dorm, without any provocation I can think of."

"How about the provocation of you'd been acting like jerks the entire time I'd been around you?" I grumbled.

Jude ignored me, sailing smoothly onward. "I don't

recall making any snarky remarks to you after your desensitization session until you'd already insulted my intelligence. And your familiar wasn't the slightest bit hurt."

"It was still a horrible situation to put me in."

"We were testing you. Making sure you'd live up to your title. That's how things work here and out there." He motioned in the general direction of town, but I knew he meant the wider fearmancer community. "You rose to the challenge; I recognize that. It's done."

Was it really that easy for him and everyone else here to shrug off the way they treated each other?

"I didn't grow up like all of you did," I said. "Those aren't the kinds of rules I follow."

"But you're here now, and *we* didn't grow up the way *you* did. You don't join a symphony and get mad that no one will jam along with your ukulele."

I didn't want to "join" at all, I shouted inside my head, but it wouldn't be smart to say that out loud. I still needed to give some appearance of wanting to be here, or I'd never get enough access to figure out how to undermine the place.

"Fine," I said. "You were doing what seemed to you like normal things to do. That doesn't mean I have to like it—or want to see what the hell you might decide to do to me next. Do *you* honestly like living this way, always at each other's throats?"

Jude paused. For the first time, a more serious cast came over his expression. When he smiled again, the edges were sharper.

"Maybe I don't," he said archly. "Maybe that's why I'm here talking to you right now."

I *really* didn't know what to make of that. In my silence, he shrugged.

"Forget all of that, then. Let's make it simple. Your life would be easier having me as a friend rather than an enemy, if you get to choose, wouldn't it?"

"Is that a threat?"

He rolled his eyes. "No, it's just a question. Friend versus person-you-have-nothing-to-do-with, if you're going to get nitpicky."

"I guess it would," I said. If I could have trusted him to be an actual friend.

"There you go. Maybe you haven't developed the fearmancer taste for blood yet, but you're already as practical as one."

I bristled, wishing I could take back my answer, but to my relief Jude stepped back.

"You need some time to stew on it," he said. "I can take a hint. Think hard and well, Ice Queen."

With a jaunty salute, he strolled off toward the path.

I waited until he was out of sight, all my senses gradually easing off of high alert, before I continued toward campus. Had that been the opening to some new scheme from the scions? Or had he actually *meant* what he'd said?

It didn't really matter. I couldn't picture ever calling Jude Killbrook a "friend." But there was some truth to that old saying about keeping friends close but enemies closer.

The wind picked up as I reached the edge of the

campus, thick and damp. When I tugged my hair back behind my ears, the currents of the air yanked at the dark waves a second later.

A small group of mages—juniors from the look of them—stood farther down the line of the forest tossing birds I assumed were their familiars up into the air and laughing. To train them for bad weather? To drink in the animals' fear at trying to fly in the growing gale? Lord only knew in this place.

I'd taken three steps across the field when a wrenching groan filled my ears. I spun around in time to see a huge oak topple over right into the group of mages.

———

I looked up at the sound of footsteps where I was sitting on a stiffly cushioned chair in the reception area of the health center. Professor Banefield stepped inside, his gaze moving straight to me. He sat his barrel-chested form down on the chair across from me.

"I heard you were here," he said. "Did you know one of the injured students?"

I shook my head. "I just—I saw it happen. I wanted to make sure— No one will tell me if they're okay. Do you know if they're okay?" I'd been sitting here for two hours, waiting for news. One of the kids had walked out with a brace on her wrist and a couple bruises, but two others were still off in the inner rooms.

"I believe one has finished treatment and is simply resting as he fully recovers. The other— From what I heard, there was damage to her skull. A brain injury is no easy thing even with magic."

Especially not magic designed for tormenting people. My jaw clenched, but some of the anger in me snuffed out when I looked at Banefield. His shoulders were slumped, his expression as weary as if he hadn't slept in days.

He might have known at least one of the kids. He taught the junior Insight classes. Hell, he probably knew all three of them.

Maybe I did have a taste for blood after all, because I couldn't help saying, all the same, "That was the tree Shelby was talking about. The one she was worried had rotted."

"Yes," Banefield said. "Clearly."

He looked at me like a man before a firing squad, waiting for me to take the next shot. The killing blow. *If you'd just listened to me...*

No, I didn't really want blood after all. There was enough of it already on the ground under that fallen tree.

"They're still people," I said instead. "*We're* still people, not gods or something. Sometimes they're going to be right. Sometimes we'll make mistakes. That's all I was trying to say before."

Which the current disaster had proven amply true. A swell of guilt overwhelmed any remaining anger. I dropped my face into my hands. "I should have pushed harder. I should have gone to talk to the maintenance staff myself."

"Rory..." Banefield cleared his throat and shifted

forward on his chair to rest a hand on my head in an almost fatherly gesture. "This isn't on you."

I couldn't stop a little bitterness from leaking into my voice as I swiped at my eyes. "I guess this is just more of that weakness you talked about, caring about other people."

Banefield was silent for a moment. "No," he said. "I don't think it is."

He withdrew his hand. We sat there without speaking for a while as I gathered my composure. Then he got up. "There isn't anything useful either of us can do here. Why don't you go back to your dorm and take some time for yourself? We can talk more later. If you need to reach out to someone in the next day, you can speak to Ms. Grimsworth or any of your professors. I have to take a trip off campus."

A trip? Now—to go where? But he was already heading out the door. All I got was a glimpse of determination tensing his exhausted face before he was gone.

CHAPTER SIX

Malcolm

Taking a run with Connar was always a good challenge. He might be as big as a linebacker, but he could keep up a good pace for an hour without breaking much of a sweat. My own tee was sticking damp to my back by the time we started to slow as we passed the lake for the sixth time. My familiar, loping alongside us, pulled ahead and then glanced back at me with one of those wolf expressions that seemed to say, *Is that all you've got?*

The early morning breeze cooled the sweat on my skin in an instant. I swiped the workout towel over the back of my neck. The burn of the exercise had spread through my calves up into my chest, exactly the way I liked it. You couldn't keep up magical endurance unless you had the physical endurance to support it.

Shadow circled us with a huff. "You need more of a

challenge?" I said with a smile, and fished the rubber ball
he was oddly fond of out of my pocket. He twitched with
anticipation at the sight of it. I whipped it across the field
as hard as I could, and he dashed after it in a blur with a
joyful panting. My smile stretched into a grin as I
watched. He'd have run the whole day if he could.

Connar and I had fallen into the casual jog of our
cooldown, which made it easier to talk. "Sometime we'll
have to drag Jude and Declan along on one of these runs,"
I said, mainly for the snort I knew I'd get from him in
response.

"They'd fall over before we were halfway through," he
replied, but his amused smile only lasted an instant.
Insight might be the one area I couldn't claim a strength
in, but I thought I could say the guy had been even
grimmer and more taciturn than usual in the past week.

I could take a few guesses at the reason. The main one
was named Rory Bloodstone.

"All the more reason they should start working up to
it." I nodded to the triangle of buildings we were coming
up on. "At least Declan's making himself useful in other
ways. Sinleigh set him up as our Bloodstone scion's tutor.
That should get us some good material to work with."

Connar's jaw tightened. "She's picked herself up pretty
well since the assessment. And she was awfully hard to
shake before that too."

He didn't need to remind me. A prickle of tension ran
down my spine thinking of her dazed but triumphant
expression when Ms. Grimsworth had announced her
results, my brief encounter with her afterward when she'd

answered my threat with one of her own. The way she'd asked about the burn mark I hadn't been hiding well enough, my defenses momentarily lowered because I thought I was alone... I wasn't going to let her see another hint of vulnerability, that was for sure.

I waved my hand dismissively. "Maybe we came on too strong to begin with and that backfired a bit. There are plenty of subtle tactics that can do the trick. Don't worry, we've got this. No way in hell are we letting her spend the rest of her time here reciting joymancer philosophies and mouthing off at us."

I hadn't worked my ass off and endured everything I had to cement my position only to have this girl barge into our lives like a bolt of lightning and bring it all crashing down. She might be riding high now, but I'd seen how quickly currents could shift, especially when there was blood in the water.

Connar hadn't seemed all that concerned at first by the feud that had developed between the four of us and Rory, happy to lend support as needed and otherwise to let Jude and me lay our plans. Apparently her defiance had been gnawing at him underneath. I'd never seen him go off on someone out of the blue like when he'd ripped into her that one day while we'd been matching Declan's hawk against another senior's falcon. His temper could be explosive, sure, but you could generally see it coming with the lighting of the fuse.

Rory hadn't said a word to us, hadn't even been looking at us, as far as I'd been able to tell. He'd simply snapped at the sight of her.

Connar's expression didn't shift. "What plans have you got in the works now?"

"It starts with a slow build, and then we'll ramp it up fast once she starts to wobble. She's still a fish out of water here. She's not going to find much support. We make her feel completely unstable in all those righteous attitudes of hers, and she'll have to turn to the authorities for help. Who better to set her straight than her fellow scions? With Declan there, we've already got one foot in the door."

"She might just crash and burn on her own."

I grimaced. "It already looks bad that she's gotten away with so much crap in the first place. We need her in line before *she* undermines our authority in any permanent way. And the barons want her ready to join in the pentacle as soon as possible—with the appropriate respect in place."

Dad had given me a nice long lecture about that this weekend, along with the cut now scabbed over but stinging on the inside of my arm. As always I'd cast an illusion to hide the injury. More training. A Nightwood should never let anyone see he was wounded. A year after I'd started at Blood U, my parents had started dealing out those sorts of lessons with less care in the expectation that I had the skills to pick up the slack.

"Well, you know if you need anything from me…"

"Of course." I cuffed him lightly on the side. "We just want her to struggle… in quiet sorts of ways. Has she ended up in any of your classes?"

"One of my Physicality seminars," he said.

"Perfect. Even you should be able to do subtle in your own league." I shot him a teasing grin. "Funny how her conjurings will just keep falling apart for no reason she can see."

"Yeah. I can manage that."

He didn't sound all that happy about the prospect. I eyed him as we slowed to a walk, Shadow running wolfish circles around us. "Is something else eating at you?" If Professor Darksend had been hassling Connar about the stupid tourney again, I'd shove his head up his ass.

"What?" Connar looked momentarily unsettled, or maybe I misread that, because a second later he was smiling his usual quiet smile. "No. I'm good to go, whatever you need."

"There's nothing left to do for this bit. I set up this morning's move last night. We should be just in time…"

With a glance at the time, I motioned for him to follow me toward Ashgrave Hall. It was still so early that only a couple of students had ventured out onto the green. Most of the dorm room windows stood at least a little open to let in the fresh spring air. I expected we'd have heard Rory even without that factor, though.

We were about ten feet distant when the first shout carried from her room at the top right corner of the building, opposite mine. Rory's voice broke through the air hollering a wordless sound of frustration and then sputtered into a flurry of swearing. Connar gave me a quizzical look.

I chuckled. "She's still asleep. She doesn't even know what she's doing."

When I listened carefully, I made out the rasp of tearing fabric. Exactly as designed. Everyone in her dorm would be hearing that commotion. She wasn't the only person who'd think she was getting unstable.

Connar's stance had tensed, but he nodded to me. "Sounds like you got her good. I'd better shower before I have to get to class."

"If you don't mind missing the end of the show."

"I can tell there's lots more to come."

He disappeared into the building. Rory's voice had petered out. She'd have woken up by now. Given the state she should find herself in, I'd imagine it wouldn't take long before she made an appearance.

I whistled to Shadow and crouched down as he loped over. He dropped the ball at my feet and ducked his head for a scratch between the ears. I gave him a good one, his dark fur coarse but soft beneath my fingers.

Ms. Grimsworth had decreed that because of my familiar's size, he had to keep to the kennel during class hours. I'd campaigned against the idea, but I hadn't won that fight.

It wasn't right. Wolves weren't meant to be kept caged. Leaving him behind in that building on the edge of campus always jabbed a thorn of guilt into my side. When we left Blood U, I'd make sure he had free run all day wherever we ended up going.

"You've got another hour or so, boy," I said, extending the scratching to the crook of his jaw for good measure. "You want to give the woods another roam?"

His ears perked up, probably detecting my meaning as much through our familiar bond as the words themselves.

"I can't come with you," I added. "We'll go for a proper hunt tonight."

He trotted off, I straightened up, and the Bloodstone scion came striding out through the main door of Ashgrave Hall, just a few feet away.

Rory's hair was in disarray, clearly not combed with anything other than a swipe of her fingers since she'd woken up. Her blouse hung unevenly over her sleek jeans. And yet she still managed to look so stunning that fuck me if my pulse didn't skip a beat in that moment.

Of course, part of that was anticipation. "Hey, Glinda!" I called out before she'd taken two steps toward Killbrook Hall—off to see her mentor or maybe the headmistress, no doubt. "You don't look so hot. Wake up on the wrong side of the bed?"

Rory spun around. She might have looked flustered, but her dark blue eyes still flashed with that gleam of challenge when they met mine. Somehow that iron will rose up whenever the two of us faced off. Now that I knew to expect it, the sight sent a thrill through me alongside my resolve.

"It was you, wasn't it?" she snapped. "One of your stupid persuasion spells, probably."

I let my eyes widen and held up my hands. "I haven't got a clue what you're talking about. I just got back from an hour's run with my familiar around campus."

Her gaze flicked over me, taking in my sweaty shirt and the exercise towel tucked over my shoulder. Glancing farther, she'd have caught sight of Shadow just before he vanished into the forest.

She let out her breath in a huff. Her voice came out so fierce yet husky that it provoked a deeper thrill straight down to my groin.

"If you are doing something, I am going to find out, and then you're going to regret it."

"I look forward to it," I said with a cheery wave.

She made a face at me and hurried off. Her stride wasn't quite as steady as it usually was. I should have felt victorious as I watched her march into the other hall, but mixed in with the triumph was the same sort of jab as when I ordered Shadow into that godawful kennel.

Rory Bloodstone wasn't meant to wobble. It wasn't a good look on her at all. Why the hell did she have to cling to her pretentious joymancer ideas about heroes and villains so stubbornly?

If she would just fucking admit she needed us, then we could get on with the good parts of having the full pentacle of scions together at long last. And she *did* need us, whether she wanted to accept it or not.

None of us made it alone, not in the field of barons and heirs.

CHAPTER SEVEN

Rory

I stopped just inside Killbrook Hall to take a deep breath and take a stab at tidying my rumpled hair. It was possible I was going crazy, but I'd really prefer not to convince Professor Banefield of that before I even opened my mouth.

He had to be back, didn't he? It'd been two days ago he'd said he was leaving for his "trip." We were supposed to have a mentoring session in an hour and a half anyway. Surely he'd have sent a message along if he'd had to cancel it?

If he wasn't there, I didn't know who I'd talk to. Ms. Grimsworth didn't exactly put me at ease, even if she had warmed up a bit since discovering my many strengths.

Just remembering how I'd woken up turned my innards into one huge knot. The tips of my fingers still throbbed from where I must have dug them into the folds of my sheet, hard enough to wrench the fabric apart. Because that's how I'd found myself when I'd hurtled out of sleep with my throat raw and my ears ringing—tangled up in torn strips, bits of thread clinging to my skin and my pajamas.

I hadn't even been dreaming, as far as I could remember. I'd torn into the sheet for no reason I could imagine, and Deborah had told me I'd been yelling too. Nothing pleasant, from her hesitance in mentioning that part.

I couldn't wake you up, just like I couldn't last week when you got caught up in writing on that paper, she'd said with an anxious paw on my hand. *I couldn't get close as it was, the way you were... moving around. I peeked out into the dorm, but the other girls around all looked startled.*

I'd asked her if she could scurry through the walls to check Declan's room below mine, just in case. Even if I didn't want to believe he would mess with me like that after the tentative understanding we'd come to, one of the other scions might have been able to use his room to get close enough to effectively cast. But she'd returned to report that it'd been empty, no one around.

My dormmates who'd been up had still looked startled when I'd emerged a few minutes later after a hasty change. Even Victory, who'd been standing by the table, had stiffened as if she were wary of what *I* might do even as she'd arched her eyebrows. The other girls had averted their gazes and given me a wide berth, one of them flinching at the tap of my footsteps.

A whole lot of nervous fear had flooded me, but I

hadn't gotten any satisfaction from it at all.

And then Malcolm had been waiting outside with his goading comments. Maybe it'd just been an awful coincidence... but if he didn't have anything to do with my weird episodes, and my dormmates didn't either, then the problem was probably me, wasn't it? Something in my own head, nothing magical at all—or a response to the magic I wasn't used to that was now flowing through me more and more potently.

I swallowed thickly at that thought. None of the staff had mentioned any concerns that my time with my joymancer parents, the four or so years while my natural magic had been completely suppressed, might have any negative effects. Had they ever known any fearmancers who'd been stifled like that before, though?

A senior guy I vaguely recognized walked out of the hall that led to the staff wing. Someone with an official early morning appointment with one of the professors, I guessed. His gait slowed when he saw me, and my back automatically went rigid. He clearly recognized *me*.

I caught a flicker of anxiety, and then he was striding up to me, his jaw set. He bobbed his head in a weird almost-bow when he stopped in front of me. "Rory Bloodstone. I was hoping I'd get a chance to talk to you. I —I'm taking part in a challenge on the casting grounds this afternoon. It would be an honor if you'd watch my performance. I do intend to win."

I blinked at him. He didn't sound as if he were happy to be talking to me or he really wanted me spending any more time around him than was happening right now. At least the guy who'd tried to flirt with me the other day had seemed like he thought it was a good idea until I'd told him off. Or maybe this wasn't a come-on but some bizarre fearmancer custom that no one had bothered to tell me about.

"Why?" I said. I didn't have the energy to beat around the bush right now.

A sharper flare of fear shot into my chest. It felt a lot more like panic than nervous jitters. Why the hell was he talking to me at all if I made him this uncomfortable?

His hands fumbled in front of him as if he thought he could grasp onto an answer with them. "I—I think you'd be impressed with what you see. My family has a strong heritage in both Illusion and Persuasion."

Okay, I was pretty sure this was another attempt at dating me. Fearmancers just had really weird approaches to courting.

"Look," I said, as gently as I could manage around my already frayed nerves, "I don't give a crap about your family heritage. I mean, not just yours, but anyone's. All right? And I'm not really interested in having people impress me either. You'll probably do better with your challenge if you're not inviting people you're terrified of."

That last bit might have been a little too much honesty. His expression flickered, and his posture tensed more than it already was. "I didn't mean to offend you," he sputtered, and dashed off before I could tell him he hadn't really.

One of the juniors who lived in the dorms above had come into the front hall while we'd been talking. She glanced after the guy and then gave me a haughty look that reminded me of Victory, although this girl couldn't have been more than fifteen.

"Don't be mad at him," she said in a slightly sneering tone. "His parents probably put him up to it. Landing a scion would be a *big* step up for them."

"Thanks for the… tip," I said, feeling abruptly defensive of the guy. God, if he'd put himself through that conversation despite his fear of me, how much *more* terrified was he of his parents? "Maybe everyone here should practice staying out of other people's business."

At the sharpness in my voice, a flicker of anxiety rippled out of her. She took a step back. I restrained a groan and hurried off toward the staff wing before I could inadvertently terrorize anyone else.

The hall with the professors' offices—each of which led into their personal apartments, from what I'd gathered —was totally quiet. My steps sounded too loud despite the thick carpeting on the floor. I stopped at the door with *Prof. Archer Banefield* engraved on the bronze plaque and knocked, first softly and then, when I didn't get an answer, as hard as I dared.

I didn't hear anything from the other side. I was debating between trying one more time and just stewing in my worries until our actual meeting time when the lock clicked over.

Banefield opened the door looking rather rumpled himself, which was saying something when he never came across as all that neat to begin with. If possible, his light red hair was sticking out in even more directions than usual, his shirt buttons were off by one, and he was still in his socked feet.

"Rory," he said, managing his usual warm tone despite his disarray. "I wasn't expecting you this early. I was still in the process of, ah, getting myself together for the day."

Embarrassment flared in my chest. "I'm sorry. I can come back later. I just—this morning—I needed to talk to someone, but it can wait."

His eyebrows drew together as he took me in, concern shadowing his eyes. I guessed my attempt at composing myself hadn't been a total success. He motioned me in. "No, it's all right. You're here now. Why don't you sit down and tell me what happened?"

Once I was in his office, sitting on the rich brocade of the armchair where I'd spent so many mentoring sessions, I felt even more awkward. "I'm not even sure exactly what's going on," I said. "Whether it's me or someone using magic on me or... or what." Were there other possibilities beyond those two? I hoped not. "If it's someone else messing with me, I know I should deal with that myself. It's just—if it's *me*—I'm not really sure what to do. I thought someone should know, anyway."

Banefield leaned back in his chair with a puzzled frown. "What exactly *has* happened?"

I explained about the time last week when I'd gone into the daze and then how I'd woken up this morning, leaving out the parts about Deborah's attempts to intervene and her observations of the nearby students. When I'd finished, Banefield's frown had deepened. He looked almost... *angry*.

He'd never seemed all that perturbed by the treatment I was getting from the rest of the student body before, and honestly a lot of that had been worse than this, just easier to identify. I hadn't screwed up with how I'd handled the episodes, had I?

"You're right that an immediate casting generally requires close proximity," he said, setting his elbows on his desk with a thump. "Have you checked your room for any objects that might be holding a sustained spell?"

I nodded. Deborah and I both had the first time, and we'd done another quick sweep this morning while I'd thrown on my clothes. "I haven't found anything that I can tell has magic in it."

"You should be able to sense anything that could have that strong an effect on your mind. If there's anything you could have failed to check—clothing, or personal articles that often leave the room with you…"

"I checked *everything*," I said. "The last thing I want is for this to keep happening."

He rubbed his mouth. "Professor Sinleigh told me she arranged for you to begin additional tutoring in mental shielding with her aide. Has that started yet?"

"We've met up twice," I said. "It's definitely helped. I'm getting in the habit of maintaining a low-level shield without needing to constantly think about it—while I'm awake. I guess it'll take more practice before I can keep up that kind of security while I'm asleep. But if there isn't anyone or anything around working the magic, then maybe it's not coming from outside my head, right? I don't know—I never had any teaching or practice with this stuff, and then all of a sudden…"

I faltered before I forced myself to say my deepest fear, but Banefield picked up on the direction I was heading in. He met my eyes with a firm expression.

"There's nothing wrong with you, Rory," he said. "I'm sure of that much. Even if we haven't determined how, what you're experiencing… It will be the work of outside forces."

"How can you know that?" I said. "How often do long-lost scions turn up needing to figure out their magic years later than every other student?"

He paused with a twitch of his jaw. His gaze slipped away from me. His fingers laced together, his knuckles whitening as if he were grappling with something between them. When he finally looked at me again, his words came out low and rushed.

"I don't know how much I'll be able to say. They may have— But we need you, I can see that, and I can't let them— You *have* to stay on guard. There are plans being put into motion, and the—"

His voice cut off with a hitch. The color drained from his face as he pressed his hand to his gut. His mouth tightened into a thin line.

"Professor?" I said with a jolt of panic that was no one's but my own.

He opened his mouth and then doubled over with a violent retching sound. I scrambled to my feet. Before I'd even made it to his side, his body sagged over the arm of his chair as if all the life had gone out of him.

CHAPTER EIGHT

Rory

Will he be all right? Deborah asked from where she was cuddled next to my leg at the edge of my bed.

I ran my thumb over her soft fur, summoning the bits of hope I'd found beneath the heavy weight inside me. The sun was beaming outside the window, but it didn't brighten my mood.

"I'm not sure," I said—quietly, aware of the clinking of silverware as my roommates ate lunch in the common room. "The mages who work in the health center didn't want to tell me anything more this morning than they did yesterday. They did say he was improving, at least, and I think they expected he'd be going back to his quarters pretty soon. But they're talking as if it's just a bad stomach bug and he fainted because it came on so fast."

Hmph. Very convenient timing for a severe flu to kick in

suddenly when he was about to tell you something important for your safety.

"Yeah." I'd spent an awful lot of time thinking about that since Professor Banefield's collapse. I just wasn't sure how it could have been a purposeful attack. We'd been alone in the room and talking normally—I didn't think anyone outside could have heard what he was saying. After the way Banefield had asked about searching my room for spelled objects, I didn't think he slacked off in that area himself. But there was still so much about magic I didn't know.

He was the one I'd have gone to with a question like this, which obviously was out of question. Deborah had shuddered in horror at the idea of someone causing an illness like that—joymancers usually went around curing them, like my dad had during his volunteer hours at the hospital—so she wasn't any help. Who else could I talk to about it without potentially putting Banefield or myself in even more danger if it had been purposeful?

I was an official student now, with a place on campus no one could take away from me and powers everyone was starting to respect, but in some ways I was still as alone and adrift as I'd been when I'd first set foot on campus. Maybe even more so, now that I knew what horrors the people here were capable of.

"Keep listening at the walls," I said, "as far as you can safely go around the building without being seen." It seemed unlikely that any of the students would be involved in a magical assault on a professor, but it couldn't hurt to monitor things. "If someone is hurting him, I have to help him. He was obviously trying to help *me*—it seemed almost like he knew something about the weird stuff I've been experiencing, or at least who might have caused it. 'They' and 'them'...."

Could it be the other scions?

I frowned. "I don't think so. Banefield didn't step in even when Malcolm was being awful to me in front of everyone last month. Why would he suddenly care so much about ripped sheets and random writing? He said he was taking a trip somewhere—he was gone for at least a day—right before this... Maybe that had something to do with it. Or with whatever he found out that he wanted to tell me. I wonder if I should take a trip too."

Deborah nuzzled my knee. *What do you mean?*

"I don't know where he went, but my family—my birth family—has properties I've never seen yet. The Bloodstones could have enemies I don't know about. There might be information out there I can use. I just have to figure out how to get out to them."

Shelby had mentioned that there were buses that stopped by town, but who knew if they'd get me to the right places. Most of the students seemed to have their own cars, or else they had their parents or a chauffeur pick them up when they wanted to go somewhere. The school had a chauffeur or two of its own, but I didn't really want to call on one of those to take me on what could be a day-long road trip. Especially when I didn't know if I could trust *them* either.

"I'll have to talk to Ms. Grimsworth," I said. "I'd need

her to loosen up the tracking spell on me if I'm going that far anyway."

Are you sure venturing out there is a good idea? If your family has enemies, which they very well might given the way these people operate, they'll find it much easier to hurt you if you're out there on your own.

"I know. But I can't just sit around here hoping answers will drop into my lap." I gave her fur another stroke of my thumb. "Don't be a Debbie Downer. I've made it this far. I think I'll survive a little longer. It'd be good to have more room to maneuver." At the very least, I didn't think anyone wanted to outright kill the Bloodstone scion. What would happen to their rulership then?

———————

I had to wait for Ms. Grimsworth to finish a meeting before I could see her. She pursed her thin lips in a way that managed to look slightly sympathetic as she let me in.

"If you were hoping for news about Professor Banefield, I can tell you that he's doing well enough to have returned to his apartment. The health center staff have advised him not to engage in any work for the next day or two while he completely recovers, but after that, we have every expectation that he'll be available to you as usual."

"That's good to hear," I said with a rush of relief. "I don't suppose… He mentioned he was taking a trip a few days ago. Do you know where he went?"

The headmistress's beady gaze sharpened. In her fitted

dress suit—a deep forest green today—and with her graying blond hair pinned in its usual thick coil by her neck, she always gave off a strictly formal vibe.

"The recreational activities of my staff are beyond my purview," she said. "If the trip related to your studies in some way, I'm sure you can discuss it with your mentor when he's back in full health."

I hadn't really expected her to tell me even if she knew. Hell, maybe Banefield's illness *had* been non-supernatural, the timing simply a coincidence, Shelby had spent a week fighting off a flu not that long ago.

"If that's the only matter you wanted to see me about..." Ms. Grimsworth added, reaching for a notebook on her desk.

"No, actually, it's not," I said quickly. "I was thinking—I'd like to take a trip of my own to see my family's properties. Any of them that are close enough that I could go out there without missing any of my classes, at least. I could use some directions, and I'm not sure of my best way of getting out to them... and I'd need the tracing spell you have on me relaxed so the blacksuits don't go on the alert when I get that far off campus."

Or removed completely, if she was in a trusting mood. If I could have run off from the university without the fearmancers being able to trace my movements, I could make it back to California and the Enclave of joymancers before they managed to catch me, I was pretty sure. Of course, I'd have to be *absolutely* sure before I made an attempt like that. As soon as I revealed just how deep my loyalties to the joymancers ran, these people would never let me walk around freely again.

I wasn't sure I knew enough yet to prove those loyalties to my parents' people either. I should be able to direct them to the location of the university, but I hadn't figured out anything about taking down the wards or otherwise tackling the place. Still, not setting off alarms the second I walked farther than the neighboring town would be helpful no matter how much longer it took for me to work out the rest of my plans.

The headmistress was nodding, so the request must have sounded reasonable. "I can relax the spell's range. We still want to be sure you're protected after everything you've been through."

"Thank you," I said, hoping I didn't sound overly grateful.

"The main Bloodstone home is in Maine, too far to make a day trip of it unless you hire a private plane, but they do have a couple of properties closer by. I'd imagine your grandfather packed up most of your parents' personal items for storage before he passed on, but everything else has been maintained as it was. As for getting to them, we had someone bring by one of your family's cars a few weeks ago in case you wanted to make use of it. Let me get you the key."

I hadn't expected to discover I owned a car, although maybe I should have given the size of the bank account I'd inherited and the fact that there were multiple properties across the Northeast in my name.

Ms. Grimsworth tugged open a drawer on her desk

and riffled through it before handing over a car key on a worn leather fob. My fingers closed around it with a flash of uncertainty, but I wasn't sure I wanted to share my doubts with her.

"Thanks," I said.

"The vehicle has been kept in good working order, as with all your family's property, in anticipation of your return." She paused. "I hadn't mentioned it because it was so important that you focus on your studies leading up to your second assessment, but your other grandparents have been asking about seeing you."

I froze. "I thought all my grandparents were dead."

"On your mother's side—on the Bloodstone side. Your paternal grandparents are still much with the living." The hint of derision in her tone made me suspect she'd put these people off for more than just the sake of my studies. She didn't like them. "They have no particular authority among the barons, but they are relatives. It's up to you whether I accept their request and allow them to visit you here."

I had living family among the fearmancers. Maybe I was supposed to be leaping with joy at the idea, but instead I felt sick. Dealing with the expectations of my classmates and teachers had been bad enough. I wasn't sure I was ready to pretend I wanted to take on another family.

Since Ms. Grimsworth didn't appear to like the idea either, at least I wouldn't face any pressure from her. "I think I'd like a little more time to get my bearings first," I said. "It's going to be a little...awkward, meeting people who are supposedly family but are basically strangers."

"Yes. I agree. Better to wait until you're feeling secure in your role." Ms. Grimsworth nodded to the key I was clutching. "Your Lexus is in spot 39 in the garage. Let me see what I can do with your tracing spell while you're here."

I paid close attention as she came around the desk and walked around me, but the sounds she murmured were her own spell-casting words, indecipherable to anyone else. Most of the time she was behind me where I couldn't even see how she moved her hands, if that made any difference. Other than a faint quiver that ran over my skin at one moment, I wouldn't have known she was adjusting the magic attached to me at all.

I left the headmistress's office with several locations marked on my phone's map and a twist in my stomach. I didn't have any classes until late in the afternoon, so I went to take a look at my new acquisition.

This was the first time I'd had any reason to venture into the garage just east of the parking lot at the front of the school. The trim wooden building didn't look all that big from the outside, but then, that was in comparison to Killbrook Hall, which loomed over the south end of the grounds like a craggy Victorian mansion-slash-castle.

Clearly a lot of the students did have their own cars on hand, because it turned out the garage housed three long rows of parked cars with a lane looping around the middle, leading to a ramp up to a second floor that presumably held even more vehicles.

I found my Lexus just around the curve in the lane: a sleek sedan that shone pale gold in the sunlight streaming through the building's high windows. As I eased toward the driver's seat in the space between it and the neighboring Porsche, a flame-red Ferrari pulled out of a spot farther down and zoomed past me with a girlish whoop. I peered through the driver-side window of my car.

Well, I knew enough about cars to tell that it was an automatic, thank God. I tried to picture Mom in there—she'd done most of the driving back home. What she'd have grasped or pushed first. How she'd have set her hands on the wheel.

A lump rose in my throat. What I wouldn't give to have her or Dad here right now.

I squeezed my eyes shut against the flood of grief. Hold it together, Rory. Anyway, this was ridiculous. Of course I wasn't going to get anywhere like this. Maybe I could—

Footsteps tapped down the concrete ramp from the second floor. I glanced up, and my gaze locked with Jude's. His eyebrows rose slightly. I braced myself as he sauntered over.

He came to a stop by the rear of the car and let out a low whistle. "Is this yours, then? Bloodstones know how to make a statement, don't they?"

I didn't hear any mockery in his tone, only apparently genuine admiration, but it didn't set me any more at ease than his comments the other day in the forest had. "I can't take any credit for it. It'd have belonged to my—to my birth parents." I wasn't going to start calling the Bloodstones my *parents*, full stop.

"What are you waiting for? You should take her for a spin, make her yours."

"I can't," I said, figuring he'd connect the dots soon enough even if I tried to avoid the subject. "I don't have my license."

He laughed. "Half of us here never bothered. You can always magic up an illusion of one if you need to."

I shoved the key into my purse. "No, I mean I never learned how to drive." One more way Mom and Dad had ensured I'd stay close. There'd never been many places to drive to, with me being homeschooled and pretty deficient in social life. I'd asked about it a couple of times, and they'd made one excuse or another... I hadn't cared enough to push it.

Jude's eyebrows jumped a little higher. He propped himself against the Porsche's trunk. "Good thing I happened to be passing by. That's simple enough to fix. I'll teach you."

I gave him a skeptical look. "Yeah, that sounds like a brilliant idea."

"I'm not joking. Jump in, and we can get started right now. I enjoy living dangerously." He grinned at me when I continued to hesitate. "If that's not a good enough reason for you, consider it my way of starting to pay you back for the shit I put you through."

That framing did make the idea more palatable, but that didn't mean I trusted him to mean it. "I feel like I can find a driving instructor who didn't put me through shit in the first place."

I hoped I could, anyway. The list of people who fit

that criteria was depressingly short. It wasn't as if Deborah could teach me.

Jude's smirk suggested he realized how limited my options in that department were. He cocked his head. "What exactly do you think my evil plan is here?"

"I don't know," I retorted. "I just know there's a fairly good chance you have one."

"And there's no way I can convince you otherwise?"

"I can't think of any, and I doubt that's going to change. So why don't you just call it a loss and save us both a bunch more arguing?"

My frustration seeped into my voice despite my best efforts. Jude considered me for a moment, his smirk fading into a more thoughtful expression. Then he wet his lips.

"What if I gave you a free pass? One question, asked with insight, and I'll let you in. 'Do you have any evil plans?' or 'Are you trying to screw me over?' or however you'd want to put it."

For a second I could only stare at him. Jude who kept a wall up that felt solid as a mountainside, Jude who I'd never actually managed to get a read on through magic— the only "insight" I'd been able to glean had been through observations I'd made with my eyes... *He* was offering to let me inside his head? Did giving me driving lessons really matter that much to him?

How could I pass up the opportunity to take a peek at whatever was really going on behind those dark green eyes?

I turned to face him. "All right. Let me know when you're ready."

I'd need to pick my question carefully. Leave the wording open enough that he shouldn't be able to hide any ill intentions.

Jude's expression tightened for a second as if he was regretting the offer, but he exhaled slowly and tipped back his head. "Go for it."

I focused on his temple, the pale skin beside the fall of his dark copper hair, and coaxed some of the energy swirling behind my clavicle up my throat and into the words I spoke. "Why are you offering to help me?"

I caught a glimpse of Jude's mouth twitching, and then I was tumbling straight into a mass of sensations that overwhelmed the rest of my awareness, not even a sliver of a wall to slow my fall.

Images and emotions whirled past me. A glimpse of me standing beside Ms. Grimsworth as she announced to the curious onlookers that I was the only current or recent student with strengths in all four magical domains. A mix of irritation and admiration as Jude shook ice off his shoes. A chuckle at the thought of a pale-haired man sputtering with indignation.

And deeper, underneath all that but so vast and sweeping it rushed over me alongside everything else, a panicked impression of scrambling, of something crumbling away in his hands as he tried to grasp it. *Fear*— but not of me, or I'd have caught it before. The gaping size of it, the frantic fumbling to recover, jolted me back to the Desensitization room, to the metaphorical spire I'd watched disintegrate under Jude's feet.

All those sensations crashed through me in the space

of a couple seconds, and then a familiar wall slammed in front of me, hurtling my consciousness back into my own head.

Jude was staring at me, his face taut and his shoulders rigid, looking shaken for the first time I could remember. He shoved himself off the Porsche. His voice came out taut too. "Never mind then. Sorry I bothered you."

He was... walking away. What the hell? Apprehension gripped my chest. I'd obviously gone deeper into his mind than he'd expected, given the way he'd cut me off so abruptly, but maybe I hadn't gotten quite as deep as he thought.

"Wait!" I said.

Jude had already made it past the neighboring car. He stopped and swiveled only halfway toward me. "What?" he said flatly.

I crossed my arms, studying him. "Why are you giving up? What do you think I saw?"

His lips curled into a smile so tight it looked more like a grimace. "I'm aware that desperation is hardly an appealing quality. You don't have to rub it in. I'm going."

There wasn't anything else, then. Fearmancers did make a big deal out of anyone seeing them the slightest bit vulnerable. And maybe it shouldn't be a surprise that Jude would be worse than most, considering how hard he must work to maintain his usual blasé attitude when he had all that turmoil roiling around underneath.

I didn't know how to interpret every part of the insight I'd gotten, but I'd seen enough to tell he wasn't here to hurt me.

"I'm not trying to rub it in," I said. "I just want to understand. What are you so worried about?"

As he eyed me, his shoulders came down. His expression didn't exactly relax, but some of the defensiveness in it softened. "Is the price for giving you driving lessons the full baring of my soul?" he said lightly, his gaze still wary. "You've already gotten a better look than anyone else ever has. You dive in there fast, Ice Queen."

"You offered," I had to point out. "And I think I'd be good with just an explanation of why driving lessons are so incredibly important all of a sudden."

The corner of his mouth curled up, more of the tension seeping out of his stance. He took a few steps toward me again and stopped, still a safe distance away. I couldn't tell what was going on in that striking head of his *now*, but his attention brought a tingle of warmth to the surface of my skin.

"Would you believe it's simply that I'm starting to see I might have ruined my chances with the only person who's ever made me care if I did?"

No, not really. What I'd felt in him had felt way more fraught than I could imagine had to do with just me. "You hardly know me," I said.

He shrugged. "I'm not sure about that. You don't make much effort to hide who you are."

I supposed that was a fair point. I sucked my lower lip under my teeth, trying to sort through the jumble of emotions now residing inside me. My decision no longer felt so clear cut.

Lay out the pros and cons, my dad would have told me.

Pros: It would be really, really useful to learn how to drive so I could make whatever investigations I needed to without anyone looking over my shoulder. I wasn't sure who else I could ask. Jude might have been an asshole to me in the past, but at least I knew what I was dealing with. Everything I'd seen in his mind a moment ago and his reaction afterward told me he did care about getting this chance to make amends, even if the fact that he cared exasperated him. I hadn't caught any hint of a conspiracy with the other scions or anyone else.

And he could be a very useful person to have on my side here at Blood U if I happened to need a rule or two to be broken in pursuit of the justice I wanted to bring down.

Cons: I remembered the humiliation and horror he'd put me through with wrenching clarity. No matter what I'd seen, I wasn't sure I'd ever trust him.

But that might be a pro in its own way. If I never trusted him, I'd never make a mistake out of misplaced trust.

"I don't know about 'chances'," I said, "but I'll give you one. Where do we begin, Mr. Instructor?"

Jude blinked at me as if he didn't quite believe his ears. Then he smiled again, so brilliantly my heart fluttered even with all those memories front and center. He held up his hand. "Key? Garage navigation is an advanced skill. I think I'd better be the one to get us out to the parking lot if you want your car to stay in one piece."

I tossed him the key and moved out of the way so he could take the driver's seat. As I got in on the passenger side, he ran his hands over the wheel with a pleased sigh. "You did luck out with this inheritance."

I couldn't help snorting at his reverent tone. "Are you in this for me or my car?"

"Oh, don't worry, a hunk of steel is no competition. Although you should see the beauty I've got upstairs sometime." He revved the engine without waiting for my response and backed out of the parking spot fast but so smoothly my heart only leapt halfway to my throat.

We cruised out of the garage into the smaller lot just outside. Jude parked so we could swap seats, and I settled in on the driver's side with a flicker of nerves. It took me a few seconds to find the lever to adjust the seat so I could reach the pedals Jude's long legs had found so easily.

"Brake," I said, tapping one with my foot. "Gas."

"There you go," Jude said. "I barely need to teach you anything. One tip: Take the car out of park before you try to go anywhere."

"Um. Right. Obviously." I pulled the gear shift into drive and then, rethinking that move, into reverse. Then I slowly eased on the gas. The car edged backward inch by inch.

"Turning the wheel also helps for steering clear of nearby buildings," Jude said, watching my progress with amusement. "Left to go left, right to go right, even when you're heading backward."

I would have glowered at him if I hadn't been keeping all my attention on the movement of the car. I tugged the wheel to the side, and the Lexus glided around, leaving me with a clear path down the lot. All right, first challenge met. I stopped, switched to drive, and pressed the gas a little harder than before.

My pulse hitched with the lurch of the car, but the engine settled into a not totally terrifying pace.

"Nice," Jude said. "Take us down to the end and then turn around and go back. We'll go in a few circles before we aim for a longer straight line."

Was he thinking we'd leave the parking lot on my first time out? My gut twinged with nerves, and at the same moment someone's cat familiar came darting across the lot in front of the car.

I was going slow enough that it shouldn't have mattered. The problem was that in my jolt of panic, I jammed my foot down—on the pedal I'd already been pressing.

The Lexus surged forward. The cat's sudden terror flooded me. I let out a yelp and yanked at the wheel instinctively. The car roared around toward the edge of the lot.

Jude jerked forward, his hand skimming over my knee. A hasty word tumbled from his mouth, and the car screeched to a halt right at the edge of the pavement. He'd hit the brake with a smack of magic.

He pulled back as quickly as he'd leaned in, curling his fingers into his palm rather than letting them graze my leg the way he could have if he'd wanted to cop a feel, and casually shifted the car back into park. I exhaled my jitters, but my heart kept thumping double-speed. Shit.

Jude glanced over at me and tsked his tongue teasingly. "So ambitious. I know you like to carve your own path, but I think the staff would appreciate it if we avoid literally cutting one across campus."

An unexpected laugh tickled through my lungs and spilled from my mouth. Slightly hysterical, maybe, but it felt good. God, when was the last time I'd really laughed, not in a bittersweet or self-deprecating way but just because of the absurd humor of the moment?

Who would have thought when I did, it'd be because of this guy? Who'd have thought he'd be sitting there looking so happy about it?

I took a shaky breath and leaned back in my seat, adjusting my grip on the wheel. "Okay, let's give that circle another shot."

CHAPTER NINE

Declan

A show-off from the front row topped off the afternoon's Insight seminar with a sudden sprouting of thorns from the tops of all the desks. Professor Sinleigh took in the sight and the startled yelps, looking rather unimpressed by the display.

"I'll give credit to Physicality if you can remove those protrusions as quickly as you conjured them up," she said, and the guy whipped the desks flat again with a few mumbled words and a jerk of his hand.

Rory came up beside me as the other students headed out. "People are really starting to ramp up all the credit-seeking spells."

She wasn't standing particularly close, but my skin still warmed with the awareness of her presence. I directed my focus to slinging my bag over my shoulder. "This always happens as we come up on the end of term. We're halfway through now."

"You mean it's going to get worse?" Rory made a face.

"All part of school life." I couldn't resist glancing at her to raise an eyebrow. "You're an official student now. Better get used to it."

The wry smile she gave me in return reminded me why I should have resisted. It set off a flare of a sharper heat that brought our kiss in the library racing to the front of my mind. I averted my gaze and steeled my defenses to protect my own mind from my idiotic impulses. "Ready for your next lesson?"

"Absolutely."

She followed me down the tower staircase, keeping a couple of steps behind rather than staying beside me through some sort of unspoken agreement. I wasn't sure how aware she was of the delicate balance I was maintaining after the one piece of my struggle I'd confessed to her last week. I was aide and tutor and fellow scion, strictly professional, helpful but not friendly, available but not open.

I couldn't let her find out just how many pressures were attempting to yank me even farther in the opposite direction of my personal feelings. That could be disastrous for both of us.

"The pranks don't just become more frequent—they get bigger too," I said to fill the silence in which my thoughts seemed to blare. "Everyone's always trying to top the ones they've heard about from previous terms... There was a stunt for Physicality my first year here that I don't think anyone feels has really been beat yet—a girl who was adept enough to perform a full shapeshift took on her bear form and charged into the middle of this awards ceremony for the Nary students."

"You mean some people can literally turn into animals?" Rory said, sounding startled.

"No one's mentioned that to you yet?"

"I guess… My mentor did say something along that line, but I didn't really think it through. It hasn't come up in my seminars."

"It wouldn't," I said. "Pulling off a full shift is hard—unless you devote yourself to physicality, you're not likely to get there. Holding it for long enough to rampage around a gathering for several minutes is even harder. The students who practice shifting spells have special sessions devoted to that aspect."

Whatever had gone on between her and Connar, the transformative side of his studies mustn't have come up. I'd only seen him shift a couple of times. It was impressive, but also unsettling.

"More surprises to look forward to," Rory muttered.

"At least the better you get with the shielding, the more you can prevent the persuasive gambits from affecting you." I slowed as we came out of the tower, and she fell into step beside me as we crossed the green to the building that held the aides' office. "It'd be exhausting fully guarding against every possible spell all the time, but if you suspect someone might be going to cast, you can always prepare."

"And once you get particularly good, you can cut off

an intrusive spell even after it's gotten into your head, right? I think I did that kind of accidentally in my first Insight class."

I winced inwardly at the memory of the way Jude and Victory had torn into her that day. But she'd held strong, gathered the will to shove them back rather than crumpling under the attack.

That moment, watching her stare defiantly back at them while they realized they couldn't break her wall, might have been the point when I'd really started falling for her. She was a fighter, just like I'd had to be—more than anyone else here at the university had.

I yanked my mind away from those thoughts. "Once someone's in, it's harder to kick them back out. It's easier with Insight than with Persuasion spells, where they're not just looking through your mind but actively affecting your thoughts. But anyone who's a master at Insight can block everything if they're in good mental shape—not overly tired or similar. You just might have a while to go before you get there."

"Are you a master yet?" Rory asked in a lightly teasing tone. I didn't let myself look at her, but I heard the smile in her voice.

"Maybe journeyman at this point."

We'd slipped into this dynamic so easily: tutor and pupil, advisor and advisee. The two sessions we'd had so far, Rory had followed my lead, listened to my guidance, and avoided bringing up anything I'd shared during that uncomfortable moment in her room. I doubted she trusted me completely, but the fact that she was trusting me even this much left my gut in a tangle.

If I could see her through this without her taking any permanent wounds, I would. I just wasn't sure *whether* I was capable of it yet. The one thing I absolutely couldn't do was warn her. Someone would find out. My life would be over. A baron who betrayed the other barons didn't keep his title—or generally anything else.

They meant to betray her too, to break her down and mold her to their will. I didn't have the power to challenge three ruling families directly on my own, but maybe behind the scenes I'd manage to give her the chance she deserved to really fight for herself. I'd had my whole lifetime to prepare—she'd only had a month.

Imagine how she could shift the pentacle if she had just a little more time to find her feet.

During our previous sessions, one of the other aides had been working in the large office space that was about the size of one of the dorm common rooms: desks set up along the walls, a couple of tables and a cluster of armchairs in the middle. The chairs were more comfortable, but I preferred the built-in boundaries the tables provided. Especially when we walked into the still, faintly pine-scented air of the office and found the room otherwise empty.

That was fine. I had my own mental defenses built up, made up of the looming mass of responsibilities and goals and people I intended to protect. However much I was coming to admire and care about Rory, it was better even for her if I maintained this distance.

"Have you been practicing the exercises I gave you?" I asked as I sat down at our usual table.

Rory pulled out the chair across from me. "Of course. Pretty much whenever I have a few spare minutes and I don't think I'll be interrupted. They seem to be helping. When I was in class today and we paired off for that one assignment, my partner tried to get a sneaky read on me before we'd officially started, but I had enough of a barrier in place that I noticed it and built it up stronger before she got in."

"Excellent. I figured you'd pick it up fast." She was nothing if not a quick study. I rested my arms on the tabletop. "So far we've been focusing on defensive tactics. Today I want to do some work around active casting."

Rory knit her brow. "What does that have to do with shielding?"

"A lot. The moments when your own mind is most vulnerable are when you're attempting to tackle someone else's. Any time you're casting a spell that involves reaching out your consciousness—to peer inside someone's thoughts, or to influence their behavior with your will— you have to let down your guard. A solid shield wards off magic both ways. Once you get good enough that people know you're generally protected, anyone who wants to get at you will watch for when *you* cast a spell and use that as an opportunity to strike."

Rory's jaw set. She was always pretty, but I didn't think she ever got quite as beautiful as when that spark of determination came into her dark blue eyes.

"All right. How do I make sure that doesn't happen?"

I let myself smile. "You get good at casting as surreptitiously and quickly as possible, so you can have your wall back up before anyone even realizes it was down."

I gave Rory a few simple spells to practice to hone her subtlety and speed. As she launched into them, my pulse kicked up a notch.

This was the part I hated. I watched her concentrating on the exercise—and murmured a casting word of my own with the intake of my breath, so soft she wouldn't hear it.

All I took was a little dip inside her mind during the brief vulnerability in the midst of her casting. No aim, no depth, just skimming the surface for the first few random impressions I could catch. Her resolve to develop this skill as quickly as she had the others. A nip of hunger and a longing for the chocolate brownie waiting back in her dorm room. The image of a round, pale face—Professor Banefield, her mentor—with a ripple of worry.

Nothing all that private. Nothing that could be turned against her as a weapon. Just enough so that when the older barons questioned me, I could honestly say I'd continued working around her defenses, in case any of them happened to slip past mine to gauge the truth of that statement.

Still, if she ever noticed what I was doing, that would be the end of, well, everything. I couldn't imagine there'd be any coming back from it. So I'd better make sure I damn well kept it fast and subtle until I'd built up her defenses every way I could and no one—me, the barons, the other scions—could shatter them.

Just as I was pulling back, she glanced at me, and I caught one last impression. A flicker of a memory—a close dark space, her hand pressed against someone's chest, a mouth hot against hers. A matching heat shot through me. She was remembering our kiss, and with a waft of desire.

I jerked my awareness all the way back into my head and willed my blood to cool. It didn't do me any good remembering that myself—or thinking about what it might mean that she was. She was devoted and determined, unshaken in her convictions even after the battering she'd taken last month, and no matter how much desire that woke up in *me*, there was no fucking universe in which I could really have her.

Those glimpses into Rory's head weren't the only gambit I had to play here, simply the one I disliked the most. After I'd given her a few more pointers and she'd practiced some more, I pulled a sheaf of paper out of my bag.

"I thought you should have this," I said, which was mostly true. Technically presenting Rory with this kind of information had been Malcolm's idea, but I'd chosen the specifics. Whatever campaign he was attempting to wage against her now, I had to stay impartial. That feud, at least, was a clash between equals. I'd teach Rory every defense she asked me to help her with, but coddling her in that conflict wouldn't do her any favors.

Besides, I did agree with him on one point. Rory

needed to understand her past before she'd be able to completely accept who she was and what she was meant to do. Not all her convictions were based on reality.

Rory cocked her head as she studied the papers. "What is this?"

"The official report from the blacksuits on the altercation in which your parents were killed," I said. "I had to call in a favor to get it, but I figured you deserved the full story." She'd been horrified by the way the blacksuits had dispatched the joymancers who'd raised her. Would she understand their actions better if she saw just how the joymancers had ravaged our people before they'd taken her? There were photographs in that print-out that made my stomach turn.

Rory's gaze ran over the first paragraph. Then she met my eyes. "This will be the blacksuits version. They'll want to make themselves sound as justified as possible, won't they?"

I looked back at her steadily. "Our people may be brutal when they need to be, but most of us value accuracy. Our side took lives that day too, and the report doesn't shy away from that fact. We know what we are. It's important that you know what we—and the joymancers —are too."

"The joymancers wouldn't have—"

Rory cut herself off. From what Malcolm had said, she'd made her preference for joymancer attitudes quite clear to him, but she might not realize how much he'd told the rest of us. She was being careful, which did her credit, even if she hadn't been able to stop a familiar angry flush from coming into her cheeks.

She'd loved the people she'd called her parents. I wasn't going to blame her for that. The two of them might not even have been bad people as individuals. They'd still had a part in tearing her from her home and her rightful heritage.

"How many joymancers did you know?" I said quietly.

She bit her lip. "Only my parents," she admitted.

"You have to realize there are reasons they kept you away from the others. What you'll read in there will fill in some of those blanks."

Her hand still hesitated over the report, as if she were torn between taking it and shoving it back at me. My gut twisted tighter, but I played the one card I was sure would work with her.

"*You* care about knowing the whole truth, don't you? You've never seemed like the type to shy away from the facts even if they're painful."

"Of course I want to know the facts," she said, grabbing the papers and stuffing them into her purse. "I just wonder what the joymancer account says, that's all. In the interest of covering all the bases."

"Well, if I can manage to scrounge up that too, I'll pass it along."

She guffawed and got up. "Well, thank you again. Are you still good for the same time on Sunday?"

"I'll meet you here."

I lingered by the doorway as she headed down the hall, a hard, heavy sensation sinking through my chest. I'd done everything just as I'd planned it. As far as I could tell, I'd handled the balance just right. But watching her go with the image of her gorgeously resolute expression imprinted in my mind, I was filled with the sickening certainty that one way or another, I was failing.

CHAPTER TEN

Rory

A low, graceful melody carried from my dorm room. I stopped in the hall outside, taking it in as I reached for my keycard. The lilting strains had a mournful quality that seeped right into my chest with the ache of uncertainty that had been lingering there all morning.

The music cut off abruptly when I opened the door. Shelby's head came up with a swish of her ponytail where she was sitting in one of the common room armchairs with her cello propped in front her. She relaxed a little when she saw it was me, but not completely.

"Sorry," she said, getting up. "I can go back to the music rooms in the tower."

I waved her back down. "What are you talking about? I don't mind. You're really good. We should be glad to get the free concert."

She laughed stiffly. "Yeah, most of the other girls don't

feel that way. There's usually no one here for an hour or so this time on Fridays, so I stick to that. I like getting to hear how the songs sound in different spaces—you notice different elements."

I could almost see in the hunch of her shoulders the way Victory or her lackeys must have taken their jabs at Shelby over this like so many other things. The only thing they seemed to enjoy more than hassling me was intimidating the Nary students in every way they could.

"Well, don't stop practicing on my account," I said. "I'd love to hear more."

I must have said it emphatically enough, because a smile crossed Shelby's face. "Wait until you hear us all together," she said. "Just a few more weeks until the annual concert."

I grinned back at her and patted the phone pocket on my purse. "I've already got it written in my calendar."

She lifted her bow again. The delicate glide of it across the strings sent an appreciative shiver down my back. She must have worked her ass off to make it into the music program here, one of the special streams Bloodstone University offered just to their nonmagical scholarship students. According to Shelby, the opportunities anyone who graduated got were incomparable, which they'd have to be for anyone to put up with the crap the rest of the student body put them through.

I went to the kitchen to grab a snack. Surprise, surprise, one chunk of cheese and a couple of yogurts I'd left in my section of the fridge had gone sour and spotted with mold. After the second time I'd seen that happen, it'd been obvious someone was messing with my food as yet another power play. Now, with the fifth time, I couldn't even be bothered to get angry about it.

I chucked those items in the garbage and reached for the apples farther back that I'd cast a concealing illusion on. Victory and the others couldn't spoil what they didn't know was there. I had enough of a budget to afford to buy a few decoys. Not letting them get to me felt like the best possible revenge.

When I came into my bedroom, the smell of the cut apple brought Deborah out of the nest she'd built for herself in the wall. I set her half on the bed beside me and took a bite of mine while she started to nibble. The juice that flooded my mouth was perfectly tart, but the ache inside me expanded again with the cello song seeping through the door. My other hand crept up to curl around my dragon bead on its chain.

Courage and strength—that's what I'd told Mom it meant to me. I needed both right now.

"Deborah," I said quietly, "what do you know about the confrontation with the fearmancers where the joymancers took me?"

She paused, and I thought her little muscles tensed just slightly between her sleek white fur. *I didn't have any part in it. I didn't know the Conclave had taken in a fearmancer child at all until they extended the offer of getting out of my cancer-addled body. Those kinds of missions weren't general knowledge if you didn't work closely with the Conclave.*

"But it didn't surprise you that it could have

happened. That they could have killed fearmancers and taken one of their kids."

One of our duties as joymancers is to stand up against those who'd destroy the happiness people can find in the world. If we have an opportunity to interfere with a malicious plan, whether it's orchestrated by fearmancers or Naries, we take it.

That was exactly the kind of thing I figured she'd say. I let out a slow breath, my hand dropping to rest on my purse. My purse that contained the printed-out report Declan had given me yesterday. I'd read it at least ten times since then. It hadn't sat any better with me this morning than it had last night.

"According to the fearmancers' report on the fight... my birth parents and the other fearmancers in the building were just there to consider buying the place. That was why the joymancers were able to get the better of them—they weren't expecting any conflict. They hadn't brought along anyone to defend them. They brought *me* along. Obviously they wouldn't have done that if they'd thought they might be walking into a battle."

No doubt they would have used that building for some nefarious purpose, Deborah said. *These people don't know how to do anything* other *than nefarious.*

"I know," I said, even though I couldn't have said that was completely true. I didn't think Imogen was a bad person, even if she'd hurt me. The more time I spent with Declan, the more sure I was that he was doing his best given his circumstances. Like Jude had said the other day, everyone here had simply grown up with different priorities and a different way of looking at the world than I had. That didn't make every single thing they did evil.

Any more than every single thing any joymancer did was necessarily good.

"It just seems pretty... vicious to attack a bunch of people going about their business—with their kid right there too—when those people aren't hurting anyone right then, you know?" I went on after a moment's hesitation. "Shouldn't we be better than that?"

I don't know all the ins and outs of the situation. I'm sure there was more to it. Why don't you put that away, sweetheart? You've had enough to worry about without adding to it with events from years and years ago.

I knew what she meant. This morning I'd woken up again with a sore throat, a mug I'd left on my desk smashed, and nervous glances when I'd come out of my bedroom. Deborah had darted off as soon as I'd started yelling, but she hadn't been able to identify the cause. I wouldn't be surprised if she thought the episodes were my toxic fearmancer magic messing with me from the inside out and not an attack. I didn't really want to think too closely about that possibility.

"I'm not saying they didn't have any good reasons," I said. "I'm not even necessarily saying the joymancers are wrong to stop the fearmancers any way they can. I just— maybe it's not totally bizarre that everyone here hates joymancers as much as they do. If you look at things from their perspective."

And a warped perspective that is, Deborah muttered,

digging into her apple again. *Don't let them get in your head, Lorelei. You were raised to be better than that.*

She didn't say that I *was* better. Only that I'd been raised better. I looked down at her for a moment, my stomach rejecting the thought of eating any more of my own piece of apple.

Did she really trust me even now, or was she just as wary of me turning into some kind of monster as the joymancers who'd taken me must have been? She hadn't even liked the idea of me leaving campus to visit the places I'd inherited.

I didn't know how to bring up the other part that had stuck in my head: the pictures of my birth mother and father after the slaughter. And it had looked like a slaughter. They'd been burned to the bone, their skin and clothes crackled black in swaths across their bodies, my father's neck gaping open like a dark second mouth. The building's polished tile floor had been smeared with ash.

In one of the pictures, I'd been able to make out a tiny toddler footprint in that ash where two-year-old me must have stood next to my mother's charred body. The seared remains of her arm had been stretched toward that spot.

My real parents hadn't deserved to be murdered by the blacksuits, blood splashed all over our kitchen. But maybe that violence hadn't been automatic brutality so much as the fearmancers' idea of payback.

Declan's mother had been in those pictures too, her body just as ruined. He must be old enough to remember at least a little about her, even though my memory of the attack was a blank.

The cello music halted. I lifted my head to catch the voices that filtered in from the common room. That sounded like Imogen. I shook away the tension inside me. Now was my chance to dig a little deeper into the possible magical payback that might be happening right here.

When I stepped out of my bedroom, Shelby was just ducking out of the dorm with her cello. Imogen caught my eye and shrugged. "I didn't ask her to stop. I guess she's self-conscious."

And maybe Imogen hadn't always been the friendliest in the past. She'd been tentatively warm when I'd included Shelby in some of our conversations and outings, but she hadn't seemed all that enthusiastic about socializing with a Nary.

That fact served as a useful reminder to be careful how I treaded with her.

"Hey," I said. "I actually wanted to ask you about something... You said you're studying the medical side of physicality magic, right?"

Imogen nodded, curiosity mixing with the wariness in her expression. "Is this about— I know you having been sleeping all that well."

Was she going to be weird about my morning episodes, steering clear of me the way the other girls had even more than usual? Shelby hadn't withdrawn from me, but then, she spent as little time as possible in the common room, so she might not have even realized which bedroom the disturbance had been coming from.

"No," I said tentatively. "Well, maybe it'd be useful for that too, but I'm mostly thinking of someone else. Can a mage make a person sick using magic? And if they can, how would that work? Like, are there ways to tell whether it's magical?"

Imogen's eyes widened. She sat down on one of the sofas, and I followed suit. "Why are you asking?"

"The professor who's my mentor came down with something that seemed serious the other day, and I'm probably just being paranoid, but I can't help wondering about that possibility, after everything that's already happened. So it *is* possible, then?"

Thankfully, I didn't need to explain to Imogen why I'd be paranoid about people targeting someone who'd supported me. She'd been on the receiving end herself not that long ago. She brought her hand to her mouth as she considered.

"It's definitely possible. It's actually one of the most common methods of quietly... interfering with people someone wants out of the way but can't challenge openly." She paused. "You've heard about Connar Stormhurst's family, haven't you?"

An icy prickle shot through my stomach. "No, nothing to do with challenges or whatever. Why? What did he do?"

"Oh, it wouldn't have been him. It happened when I was, like, six or seven, so he wouldn't have been much older—no magic yet." Her gaze darted through the room and came back to rest on me. "I'm not saying this to criticize the baron, just to be clear. Everyone knows about it. There's no reason you shouldn't too."

"*What?*"

She swept her tawny hair back behind her ears, making her silver dragonfly clip bob. "His mother wasn't always the Stormhurst baron. Her brother was the one who inherited the position. But there was an... accident that killed him and injured his wife badly, and then their one kid, the scion, got sick... No one could prove it was magic, but she didn't respond to any regular treatments either."

"Their daughter died too?" I said, the chill congealing into a pool of nausea. "Connar's mom wiped out the competition so she could have the baron spot?"

Imogen clasped her hands in her lap. "Like I said, no one could prove anything. If they could, there'd have been sanctions. But everyone *knows*. It's happened before. And then there's the whole thing with Connar and his brother."

I braced myself. "What about them?"

"It's only rumors what exactly happened. But he definitely has a twin brother. I guess if things had gone by official policy, their performance here at the university would have decided who was named the scion. But before their magic kicked in, they had some kind of fight... No one's really seen his brother since then. He was messed up so badly he couldn't come to Blood U. Apparently he's still *alive*, but..." She worried at her lip with her teeth.

Connar had hurt his own brother so badly the guy was a permanent invalid? I restrained a shudder. I wouldn't have thought the guy I'd gotten to know was capable of that... but I wouldn't have thought he was capable of making the caustic remarks he had the day after we'd had sex. He had a brutal side, that was for sure. I'd let myself forget it when we were away from everyone else, but maybe he was the worst of my fellow scions.

"That's awful," I said.

Imogen shrugged stiffly, her expression still tight. "It's how things go. Prove your strength, hold onto your power —or grab it from someone else. Sometimes I wish my family was respected enough that people would care what I think… but a lot of the time I'm glad to pretty much fly under the radar."

Not an option I could take. Maybe my assessment had gotten the casual bullies to back off, but it'd clearly also pointed an even bigger spotlight on me than I'd already had as simply the long-lost Bloodstone scion.

Malcolm had told me once that the only real rule here was to avoid getting caught if you broke one of the other rules. It sounded like that applied to all fearmancer society.

"If no one could prove what happened with his cousin, then I guess that kind of spell isn't easy to identify?" I said.

Imogen shook her head. "Not from what I've read and seen. The magic usually kicks off the problem, but a… 'good' spell of that type will set in motion a bunch of effects that will feed off each other naturally once they're going. Unless you're there to catch the original spell when it activates the process, there's nothing to trace."

I sighed and leaned back on the couch. "Do you think even the victim would be able to tell the difference between a real illness and a magical attack?"

"Probably not. But it doesn't happen *so* often—or

leave people living and able to talk about it enough—that we've got a lot of examples. Sometimes you can guess based on the symptoms or the after effects, if they don't totally align with a regular illness."

That was something. I considered her. "Would you know what to look for?"

"I have a basic idea. Why?"

I motioned toward the door. "I was going to go pay Professor Banefield a visit—see how he's doing, bring him one of those double-chocolate brownies Shelby got me addicted to. It's the first day since he got sick I'm allowed to drop in. *I* don't have any idea what signs to look for, but if you're up for coming along… If only just to get my paranoia in check? I'd really appreciate it."

Imogen stared at me for a second as if she expected me to take back the invite. Then she got up with a flash of a smile, looking as pleased as if I'd offered to get her into the hottest party of the month and not to visit a still slightly under-the-weather professor. "Of course," she said. "If you think I might be able to help. I owe you about a thousand times over."

My violent morning episodes obviously hadn't stopped her from wanting patch up our friendship. She was happy I trusted her enough to bring her along. I hadn't actually trusted her enough to admit the full extent of my fears about what had happened to Professor Banefield, but she didn't need to know that.

I smiled back at her. "Let me just grab that brownie, and we can get going, then."

I'd given Banefield plenty of time to get back to his

office after his morning seminar. He answered the door immediately at my knock, looking pretty much his usual stout, messy-haired self if maybe a little paler than usual. His forehead furrowed when he took in Imogen beside me.

"It's good to see you, Rory, and... Miss Wakeburn, is it?"

"Good memory," Imogen said brightly. She'd told me on the way over that she hadn't had class with Banefield in over a year.

"We won't stay long if you've got catching up to do." I held out the brownie in its clear plastic bag. "I brought you a get-well treat. Or, I guess it's an 'I'm glad you got well' treat at this point."

Banefield chuckled as he accepted the brownie. "Really not necessary. I have to apologize for our last meeting. I'm sure I gave you quite a scare."

"It's not *your* fault," I said. "You're really feeling better?"

"Almost one hundred percent." He shifted his weight as if he were going to step back and invite us into the office, but then he stopped. "Has anything come up that you need my assistance with right now?"

I wanted to know what the hell he'd been about to tell me when he'd gotten sick, but I definitely didn't trust Imogen enough to bring that up with her around. Damn it.

"I didn't get to ask you before how your trip was," I said. "I was thinking of traveling off campus when I have the chance. Maybe you can give me some tips on spots to visit."

It was the best way I could think of to prod him to tell me where he'd gone without outright asking a question that was none of my business.

Banefield chuckled again. Was the sound terser this time? I itched to try an Insight spell on him, but the chances of my pulling that off without getting into trouble for working magic on a professor seemed pretty slim, given that Insight was his specialty too.

"It was more of an errand I had to run than anything like a vacation," he said in a tone that didn't invite further conversation. "I'd imagine your peers could advise you best on the most trendy leisure spots in the area. Thank you for coming by, Rory, and for the treat."

I'd been hoping for a bit more of a chat than that, but I wasn't going to hassle a guy I'd watched collapse just last week. Had he forgotten what he'd started saying? Maybe he'd only said it at all because of the sickness coming on— maybe it hadn't even been true, only some wild fever dream.

"I'll see you for our usual session," I said.

As we meandered back down the hall, I glanced at Imogen. She knew what I was wondering before I had to say the question out loud.

"I'm really not an expert on this or anything," she said, "so I can't make any promises. But I didn't notice anything that gave me a bad feeling. At least nothing to do with him being sick."

I stopped in the second floor landing. "What do you mean? Did it seem like something else was wrong?"

Imogen frowned. "I don't know for sure. Maybe he's just unsteady after that illness. I never got into any trouble when I was in his class, so I've got no idea what else it could be. A couple times when he looked at me, I felt…" She touched the base of her throat. "He was *afraid* of me."

CHAPTER ELEVEN

Rory

For mages who often objected to being characterized as villains, the fearmancers sure had a lot of material in their library on the various strategies for dispatching people you didn't happen to like. Whatever they might say about questionable things joymancers had done, I doubted the Conclave library had dozens of manuals of destruction.

I was paging through my fifth volume of the afternoon, several more stacked beside me, when a lean figure swooped in and plucked the top book off the pile.

"Hmm," Jude said, propping himself against the shelves opposite me as he flipped to the table of contents. "This looks very ominous. Suddenly I'm not so sure I want to be spending any more time in moving vehicles with you, Ice Queen."

I rolled my eyes as I looked up at him. "Don't worry.

So far I've decided you're useful enough that I'll keep you around."

"Ah, but what terrible fate will befall me when you no longer need my oh-so-generous instruction? So many terrifying options. An enchanted blade? Suicide by Persuasion? A portal into an endless void?" He considered me with mock seriousness. "You don't really seem the void type, I'll admit."

I held out my hand for the book. "Is that even really a thing, or did you just make that up?"

"Maybe a little of both. It depends on how you interpret the material." He tossed the book to me and eyed the rest of the stack. "No, really, dear heir of Bloodstone, what the hell are you plotting tucked away back here?"

I was tucked away in the back of the aisle because I liked it better here than sitting at the tables out in clearer view. Just yesterday, I'd had yet another of the senior guys attempt to impress me into dating him, this one by toppling a group of juniors with a miniature earthquake. I wasn't sure which was worse—that, or the increasingly nervous reactions I was getting from quite a few of the other students whenever they saw me.

I'd had another bad episode this morning, shouting and tearing up the sketchpad I'd bought last time I was in town. Word about the Bloodstone scion's volatility was clearly starting to spread.

"Maybe I didn't want to get asked a whole bunch of questions about my reading material," I said, giving Jude a pointed look. "Also, as you of all people should be able to figure out, who says I'm reading this stuff for offensive use and not for defense?"

Jude hunkered down on the carpeted floor across from me, stretching out his legs to rest just a few inches shy of mine. We'd come into fairly close contact here and there during the three driving lessons he'd given me so far, but only when absolutely necessary. The rest of the time he'd kept a carefully considered distance.

I still wasn't sure what exactly he was after from me, but at the very least, I really had been getting the hang of driving with his help, and he hadn't done anything horrible during that time. I'd actually found myself almost *looking forward* to seeing him when I'd gone out to the garage yesterday, which maybe was a little terrifying in itself. There was something about his don't-give-a-shit attitude—ever present other than that one lapse when I'd peeked inside his head—that made all the other problems I needed to tackle seem smaller.

"I'll admit this school isn't free of idiots," he said. "I may have informed many of those people of their deficiencies in the past. But I doubt there's anyone here quite idiotic enough to try anything in those books on you."

"Why not?" I said abruptly. A question had been creeping up in the back of my mind as I'd skimmed through the books, and Jude was as good a person to ask it as any. He was here, and, well, if I trusted him at all, it was to give me an answer without sugar-coating the way Imogen or Banefield or, heck, even Declan might have.

"I'm the last living Bloodstone. What happens if someone does decide to murder me?"

Jude's casual grin faded. "Deep dark thoughts in the deep dark depths of the library?"

"It seems like an important thing to know, as someone who'd rather take precautions against getting murdered if I need to."

"No one will try," he said, so matter-of-factly and firmly I believed *he* believed it. "It wouldn't be to anyone's advantage unless you really, *really* piss them off and they also happen to be extremely good at magic to cover their tracks. We tend to be a practical lot. Violence for gain. All anyone's going to gain from offing you is a death sentence for themselves for killing a baron."

I rested my current book against my raised knees. "From what I've heard, that hasn't stopped other barons from being murdered before."

Jude hummed. "Lines of inheritance. If you can get away with it and you're next in line, some will take that risk. But you don't have any next in line. It's just you. If you're gone..." He snapped his fingers. "The heart of Bloodstone power will leap into whatever fearmancer it deems most worthy."

Interesting. I'd rather have found out I was immortal until I had my own heir or something, but I'd take that explanation as well. "And what's to stop it from jumping into my theoretical murderer?"

"Nothing. It's just an awfully big gamble to make. The few times people talk about a final heir having been killed in the past, the person the heart picked wasn't at all who anyone would have expected. Even if you do really piss someone off, they'd have no guarantee that getting rid of you wouldn't land them with someone who pissed them off even more."

Yeah, I could see how that factor could work in my favor. So, my life should be fairly secure. All the things I cared about in that life... not so much.

"Hey, enough with the morbid thoughts. Bring on the sunshine and sparkles." Jude clapped his hands with a smirk. He must have cast a spell in his last comment, because an illusion rose up, so solid I might have thought it was a physical conjuring if I hadn't known his preferred area of expertise.

The pages of the book I was holding glowed, and a flurry of butterflies burst forth, their wings tickling my hair as they whirled around me. My gaze latched onto one for long enough to see Jude had gifted it with humanoid eyes and a mouth that stuck its tongue out at me. Another wiggled its body in a wobbly jig, its ass waving this way and that, before winking at me.

A snort escaped me. I covered my mouth to muffle a laugh that might have brought the librarian over to shush me. Mission accomplished, anyway. It was hard to think dire thoughts about my mortality when faced with cheeky dancing butterflies.

Jude wiped his hands together with a satisfied smile that beamed brighter when I met his eyes. The illusion vanished with the motion of his hand.

"Much better. I'll tell you what, Ice Queen. From what I've seen, anyone who *really* tries to mess with you will probably regret it." He paused and tapped his chin. "Unless saving yourself requires driving more than half a mile. Then you might be in trouble."

I gave him a light kick in the shin. "If that happens, it'll be your failing as a teacher."

"Oh, and now the natural fearmancer aggression comes out." He winked at me much like his butterfly had and pushed himself back to his feet. "Let's see if we can make it a mile next time."

He sauntered off, leaving me sitting there with a strange fizzing sensation in my chest, not exactly eager but not exactly uncomfortable either. He couldn't have known what I'd planned for my next class, but his interruption had given me a boost in confidence.

Damn right, no one had better mess with me. Malcolm had gotten away with too much already. Now I was going to mess with him right back.

My resolve continued humming through me as I walked to Nightwood Tower for my Persuasion seminar. If I'd had easy access, it was Connar's head I'd most want to open up. Physiological ailments were the domain of Physicality, and he had a family history of removing unwanted people using that sort of magic. But I'd also never seen Connar use the kind of spells that would give me a chance to slip past any shields he had up.

I didn't really know him, as much as I'd started to feel I did. I had no idea how to provoke him in the right direction… and the thought of finding out what he might do if I provoked him in the *wrong* direction made my stomach knot.

Malcolm's favorite trick was exerting his will on my mind. It shouldn't be too hard to encourage that impulse. And he'd been the ringleader from the start. I didn't think Connar would have gone after a professor without at least talking to the Nightwood scion about it.

If one of them was responsible for Banefield's illness, Malcolm should be able to tell me, whether he wanted to or not.

The classroom was half full when I reached it. Malcolm hadn't shown up yet, as I'd expected. He preferred to mosey in with just a minute or two to spare.

Ever since the day a few weeks ago when he'd nearly persuaded my feet to walk me right out of the tower, he'd always taken the same seat next to the window. Maybe to subtly remind me of that moment and the battle I'd have lost if Professor Crowford hadn't called an end to it. No one else touched it, leaving it to him.

Until today. I strode right over and sat myself down.

Cressida, sitting at the back of the class, let out a disbelieving chuckle. A few of my other classmates glanced my way but said nothing. The guy behind me drew back in his seat as if already retreating from a skirmish that hadn't started yet. Professor Crowford didn't give any of us more than a brief glance while he read over his lesson plan, his silver hair slicked down so the black streaks stood out even more starkly.

My heart thumped fast but steady as I waited. A couple more students trickled in. Then Malcolm's voice carried through the doorway, hollering a wry insult after whoever he'd been talking to on the way up.

He walked into the room, and his gaze shot straight to me. There were two empty desks left, both on the other side near the door. He strolled right past them to the desk I was sitting at, his eyes never leaving me for a second. I stared right back at him.

"I think you've gotten lost, Glinda," he said. "All that fresh air isn't so good for you."

The warm spring breeze wafted over me. I smiled mildly at him. "I'll take my chances with the window. Unless you really think you can move me again."

At the same time, I brought my mental shield into sharper focus: breathing into the image of it around my mind, feeling every inch of it solid and impenetrable, the way Declan had taught me.

Persuasion was Malcolm's league, and as he'd reminded me not long ago, he had way more practice at using his magical skills than I did. But I had a couple of advantages. One: I was a hell of a lot stronger than I'd been the last time he'd exerted his will on me, and he wouldn't be expecting too much of a challenge. Two: I was fast. Fast enough to dig deep into Jude's head before he'd realized how far I'd gotten and tossed me out.

Hopefully fast enough to leap into Malcolm's mind in the brief opening I'd get and set him off-balance before he could take another stab at me.

Malcolm let out a dark chuckle, a glint lighting in his dark brown eyes. "This should be fun. *Stand up.*"

He didn't slack off much. A jolt ran through me as his spell jabbed into my shield—but my defenses held. The instant I felt the impact, I spoke my first personal casting word under my breath.

"Franco."

I hadn't told even Declan what I'd picked. Maybe the word wasn't total nonsense, but using my former last name felt *right* for this purpose. It'd been my parents' name, and Mom and Dad had been the ones who'd taught me how important every kind of insight was—to understand what people wanted and needed and to bring them joy.

Malcolm had let down his own shield to cast his persuasive spell. My awareness soared straight into the jumbled impressions of his consciousness. I hadn't had enough time to risk going for a targeted question with my spell, but he was focused on me right now, so any larger intentions he had for hurting me shouldn't be buried too deep.

Banefield—was there anything at all to do with my mentor in his thoughts? I dove deep as quickly as I could, getting just a glimpse of emotions and images.

I caught a flicker of triumph, not just for the victory he assumed he was going to win right now, but something else—my chaotic appearance when I'd dashed out of Ashgrave Hall the other morning—a small object with a cool smooth surface he'd held in his hands—a tang of something almost like longing—Connar's stern face—Malcolm's wolf familiar loping off into the woods —me sitting right here at this desk, a rush of exhilaration at the challenge—an impression of Crowford's voice saying, *Credit to Persuasion* as Malcolm strode out of the room while the rest of us bowed down so low our foreheads touched our desks—a prickling hint of frustration—

Wham. The force of Malcolm's mental wall flung me out of his head so violently I jerked in my seat, my spine jarring against the hard back of the chair. My own thoughts spun.

Malcolm glared at me, looking all devil and very little divine in that moment. He opened his mouth to aim another persuasive spell at me, and I knew I probably wouldn't be able to hold up my own defenses now that he was pissed off.

I groped through the bits and pieces I'd seen in his mind for something to throw him off balance. That scene with the classroom—that hadn't happened. It had to be something he was planning.

"Everyone had better keep their mental walls up at the end of class," I blurted out, pitching my voice to carry through the room. "Malcolm thinks he's going to have us all bowing to him on his way out."

The anger in Malcolm's eyes flared even hotter. His voice came out even but taut, splitting straight through the barrier I'd yanked back up as solid as I could. "*Get your ass out of—*"

Professor Crowford cleared his throat loudly, cutting the Nightwood scion off. My muscles released where they'd seized to follow the command.

Malcolm spun toward the professor, barely holding back another glare. Crowford was watching us. Was there a hint of amusement in his heavy-lidded eyes? The rest of his expression was so inscrutable I wasn't sure.

"I think Miss Bloodstone has proven she can handle her chosen seat," he said. "Credit to Insight. There are other fine chairs you may sit yourself down in, Mr. Nightwood."

Malcolm's jaw worked, but he lifted it rather than arguing. He shot me one last look before retreating to the other side of the room, full of smoldering promise. My body stayed tensed.

The sense of triumph I'd seen in him and the images connected to it—I was pretty sure I'd just confirmed that he'd had something to do with the weird episodes I'd been experiencing. I hadn't dug up enough to figure out how, though. And there hadn't been any sign that he knew or cared about any scheme involving Banefield.

I'd better be able to figure out what he *was* up to fast, because that glare had promised payback.

CHAPTER TWELVE

Connar

The Physicality classroom took up nearly the entire half of the third floor of the tower. It held broader desks for conjuring work and room for twenty students, although it was rarely full. We'd generally had eighteen until Rory had started turning up a couple weeks ago.

She had her back to me today, like she usually did. I'd started sitting toward the far end of the room where I could more easily keep an eye on her without her noticing, and she'd always picked a spot that gave her plenty of distance from me. But while I watched the fall of her dark hair and the delicate movements of her hands as she shaped her magic, the memory of her walking in on the first day hovered in the back of my mind.

Her expression when she'd seen me—the tensing of unexpected pain, almost as bad as when I'd laid into her the other day on the green. It'd only been there for a second before her face had hardened and she'd turned away, but I hadn't been able to forget it.

I couldn't dwell on that. I couldn't think about before, about the smile I'd been able to bring to her lips or the tenderness in her eyes when she'd looked at me or the way her body had felt against mine. None of that had really been mine anyway. I'd pretended to be someone else with her, someone who hadn't done the worst of the things I'd done.

I was someone who hurt people. Better she found that out now, before we'd gotten any closer.

My hand dropped to my pocket, to the lump of the metal dragon she'd conjured from the earth for me. For the man I'd managed to briefly convince her I was. But even my friends couldn't really trust me, could they? I'd hidden the fact that I was seeing her from them. I'd told myself I was doing it to help Malcolm, but how much had I really been thinking that plan through and how much had I just been making excuses so I could have her?

He thought we needed to break her before she'd finally accept what she was and let go of all the joymancer ideas in her head. And when she'd come around to our side, he wanted her, if she'd have him. I'd stepped right in the way of both of those goals for my own selfish reasons...

I could make up for that part, at least. I'd screwed up, but I was fixing my mistakes, like Malcolm had fixed so much for me over the years. If I couldn't even do that, then I deserved every wary look the rest of the students directed my way.

So, as Rory conjured a rising patch of fire in the clay

bowl on her desk, I kept half my attention on my own elemental assignment and half on picking away at hers. For each murmur I put toward building my flames up, I aimed another at making hers falter. A little chill to dull the heat. A snuffing out of this spark and that one.

The fire wavered and vanished. Rory brushed her hair back behind her ear, and I made out the edge of her frown, the movement of her lips as she tried to work the spell again. Professor Viceport came to a stop in front of her desk. I was watching closely enough to notice the fraction Rory's shoulders came up at the professor's attention.

My stomach balled. I curled my fingers under my desk and sent another murmured spell her way. Subtle and slow but steady. Draining the energy from her conjuring. The new flames in her bowl died.

"I'd expect better from you after that assessment," Viceport said in a cool tone, and walked on.

Rory didn't reply, but her jaw tightened, and the knot of my stomach tightened even more at the sight.

It didn't matter in the long run. I wasn't outright hurting *her*. Just adding a little uncertainty until she gave up on standing apart from us. When she was ready to add her strength to ours, we'd shore up hers in return.

If she'd met Malcolm in some secluded clearing away from the jostling of school politics, she probably would have liked him too. She'd never gotten to see the guy who, at seven, had waved my brother and me over to climb trees with him and the others while our mother joined her first meeting of the pentacle as baron. Who'd smiled at us even as Jude and Declan watched uncertainly. He'd come ready to accept us even if we'd only just been named scions, no matter what whispers were going around about what our parents had done to make that happen.

Rory hadn't been here for my first couple months at the university when I'd been shell-shocked with grief and guilt—for all the times when senior students who'd known the former Stormhurst scion or juniors just looking to stir shit up had tried to provoke me into a fight, and Malcolm had diffused the situation with a few cutting words and his unshakeable confidence. For all the times since then when I *had* lost my temper, and he'd come 'round to find me right afterward and ramble on as if nothing odd had happened until I felt grounded again.

He'd always believed I was worthy of his friendship even when I wasn't so sure of it myself. The least I could do in return was believe that he knew what the hell he was doing. He pretty much always did.

I focused on those memories as I snuffed out yet another of Rory's conjured flames. I couldn't let anything distract me from the loyalty I owed.

By the time class wrapped up, my stomach might as well have transformed into a rock. I ducked out of the room before Rory had even left her desk and strode across campus. I wasn't really thinking about where I was going, but my feet knew where to take me when I was in a twisted-up mood like this. The cool breeze washing over the lake brought the scents of moss and spring flowers.

I was just passing the building that carried my family's name when a voice hollered out. "Connar!"

Declan was just coming out of the building, his hair damp from the pool. I stopped as he walked over to me. He swept a few stray strands away from his forehead and peered at me with his intent eyes. Even if I hadn't known insight was his specialty, he'd have given me the impression he could see right inside my skull. Not that he was in the habit of testing our mental walls. He knew what loyalty meant too.

"We haven't had much chance to talk in a while," he said, which sounded strange to me.

"We were all hanging out in the lounge a couple days ago," I pointed out.

"I mean just you and me." He took a breath, and the wariness *he'd* never totally lost around me flitted through his expression. I'd seen it way too many times on too many faces to need any of my insight skill to recognize it. "What happened with you and Rory?"

Shit. My pulse stuttered with instinctive panic, but I knew how to keep my expression impassive. Just pretend you don't know about it, pretend it didn't happen. That approach had gotten me through plenty of clashes in the past.

I hadn't had to use it with one of the other scions before, though.

"What do you mean?" I said. "What did she say?"

Declan kept studying me. "Not much. Just enough for me to know the two of you got friendly without the rest of us noticing—and that the way you tore into her the other day really shook her up."

I ignored the first part of his statement. "Isn't that what we're supposed to be doing—shaking her up?"

"Sure," he said. "Her attitudes. Her faith in the joymancers. Whatever's getting in the way of her being able to do what she needs to do as a leader here. But she's still a scion. She *is* one of us. She deserves better than cruelty for cruelty's sake. And she's never going to warm up to us if we've been encouraging her to see us as allies and then yanking the chair out from under her when she's willing to."

"I didn't set out to yank any chairs out," I said, which was true enough. The whole situation was an epic fuck-up, one I hadn't intended or anticipated, and that was on me. Declan didn't need to know all the details.

Maybe my expression turned even sterner or some flint came into my gaze, because the Ashgrave scion eased off. "Fine. Just keep in mind that if you break her more than we can build her back up, we lose as much as she does. We need her on our side."

He stalked off, leaving me twice as tense as before.

I tried to put all of it—the conversation, the sabotage in class, the expectations I'd failed and the ones I wasn't sure I could meet—behind me as I pushed into the forest. Finding my way to the clifftop was as easy as breathing. I'd found the little rocky clearing overlooking the lake years ago when I'd stomped off into the woods, purposely veering into the thicker underbrush to give me a distraction from whatever I'd been steaming about. The moment I'd stepped out into that quiet space, nothing but trees and water around me on all sides, the emotions inside me had stilled.

It always worked. Somehow, looking out over the lake made me feel as far away from the rest of my life as if I'd taken a jet across the ocean. Maybe the rest of my life was still there when I returned to the rest of campus, but it didn't weigh on me quite as heavily right after.

At least, that was how it'd always been before. Now, when I emerged from the trees to the glittering expanse of the lake and the frame of trees all around it, a fresh wave of emotion rolled over me.

I could remember exactly how Rory had sat on the log that stretched across one end of the clearing, the way she'd held herself with all the confidence she could exude, determined not to be scared of me. The awe on her face when we'd looked out over the reflected stars. The heat of her mouth. The smell of her hair—

I closed my eyes and shook my head. No. I wasn't going there. I didn't want to go back to any of that. Anything I'd shared with Rory was in the past, far away, like the rest of the weight I carried.

No matter how much I told myself that, though, the impressions of her still lingered. I sat down with my back to a pine and couldn't help thinking that I'd been sitting exactly two trees over when she'd first ventured into this space. When my hand came to rest on the earth, it was with the sensation of how I'd laid her body down on the ground just over there, under mine.

The natural magic of this place had to come back, didn't it? If I just gave it enough time?

Today, I waited it out for half an hour before I was sure I couldn't shake the memories completely. My heart sank as I stood up.

The clifftop wasn't just mine anymore. Rory had come and made it hers too. How could I leave every uncomfortable thing behind when she was tied up in so much of that uneasiness, and she lingered up here in ways I couldn't erase?

I didn't want to erase her. I wanted to sit with her, talk with her, kiss her all over again. What the fuck was wrong with me?

Gritting my teeth, I marched back in the forest without any real sense of destination. If I walked far enough, maybe the crunch of my footsteps would drown out everything inside my head for at least a sliver of time.

CHAPTER THIRTEEN

Rory

Jude showed up in the garage carrying a cloth bag filled out in a vaguely rectangular shape. He tossed it in the back seat when he got in—on the passenger side, because last lesson I'd graduated to maneuvering, very very slowly, out of the parking spot myself.

"What's that?" I asked, settling myself behind the wheel. Faint mingled smells reached my nose: bready and sugar sweet and a tart scent that made me think of fresh strawberries.

Jude stretched his legs out as far as the space allowed and flashed me a grin. "Since we *are* going more than half a mile today, I brought a reward for if you make it to the intended destination. I picked out a picnic spot a little ways outside town."

We'd only driven into town and then back last time. My pulse sped up at the thought of taking the car farther, but I'd managed not to run into anything so far, with no further magical interventions from Jude needed.

"We're going to have a picnic?" I said with skepticism I couldn't disguise.

Jude raised an eyebrow. "They're not really a fearmancer sort of thing, I admit. I was under the impression they were a Nary thing, so maybe you'd appreciate it considering you spent most of your life mingling with them. If I'm wrong and picnics aren't anybody's thing, I can always find something else to do with a tasty lunch."

"No, no, picnics are good." And from the smell continuing to seep through the car, that one was *very* good. "Just unexpected."

He made an extravagant flourish with his hand. "I aim to be inexplicable."

"Well, you definitely do a good job of that," I muttered as I started the engine, and he laughed.

I managed to make it out of the garage and down the road into town with only a few momentary panic attacks. After I pulled off the left-hand turn at the main intersection that would lead us out into the country, my hands started to loosen where they'd been clenching the wheel. Driving really was a pretty simple process once you got used to the basics, at least out here where there wasn't much in the way of traffic or any such thing as rush hour. I didn't think I'd want to brave city streets quite yet.

As we left the last of the houses behind and cruised on along the country highway Jude directed me to, he rolled down his window. The wind ruffled through his floppy copper hair and tossed my brown waves back from my face.

A sly smile curled his lips. He motioned to the farmland around us. "It's awfully flat out here. No blind turns, no pedestrians. I think you can push that engine a little faster."

I glanced at the speedometer. "I'm at the speed limit."

He made a dismissive sound. "*Everyone* drives at least ten over. On a stretch like this, more like twenty. Common rules of the road." His smile curled a little higher. "Show me you've really got control over this hunk of steel, Ice Queen. I wouldn't want to think you're scared of a little asphalt."

My heart thumped even faster, but I knew what he'd said was true. My parents used to complain about how fast they had to go to stay with the rest of traffic rather than getting in the way, which could be even more dangerous than speeding. And that *was* in the city. Better to get used to it out here.

No problem. Just ease a little more weight onto my foot on the gas pedal. There we go.

The engine growled louder. A few pebbles rattled against the undercarriage, and I restrained a wince. The wind warbled past us.

"Not so bad," Jude said. "I think you can handle at least a bit more than this. Don't you?"

I adjusted my grip on the wheel. It felt the same as it always did. The tires sped across the pavement, and the road ahead was clear. But still I hesitated.

Jude's voice came out in a coaxing tone. "Come on, Rory. You've got this."

I did. What exactly was I scared of? I could see for myself there were no obstacles ahead.

I pushed on the gas harder, and the car raced down the road. A jolt of exhilaration ran through me. I'd been so tense and careful while I was driving up until now, I couldn't say I'd really enjoyed it. Right now, like this, it felt like flying.

I *was* in control. This vehicle and the power of its engine responded to my command without needing any magic at all.

Jude didn't prod me for more. He tipped his head back with the wind coursing in from the window and closed his eyes as if losing himself in the sensation.

Only for a few seconds. Then he straightened up again and pointed to a crossroad up ahead. "Just past that road, we're going to want to make a right. Do with that information what you will."

I slowed as we passed the intersection, the thrill of flying along the road deflating. But the reduced speed did mean I was able to spot and pull onto the dirt track a hundred feet farther without any screeching of tires.

The track led through a sparse stand of trees and petered out at the edge of a sunny field dotted with wildflowers. It was about as perfect a picnic spot as I could have dreamed up. I glanced at Jude as I put the car into park. "Are you sure you're new at this whole picnicking thing?"

Jude beamed at me and snatched the bag out of the back. "I'll take your amazement as a compliment."

It turned out the bag wasn't actually a bag but a sheet of cloth folded and tied around a wicker basket. Jude unfurled the sheet over the grass as our picnic blanket and started laying out the basket's contents. He peered up at me when he realized I was still standing there in the grass, staring.

"I can't take credit for the trappings," he admitted. "I just told the family chef I wanted the fixings and food for a picnic, and she sent all this along with the week's meals."

Somehow, that made me feel a little better. "Good," I said, sitting down on one corner of the cloth. "Otherwise I'd have to worry that you'd been possessed or something."

"By a picnic-loving spirit? You should be so lucky."

"You'll have to give my compliments to your chef." The food looked as amazing as it had smelled. There were turkey sandwiches on rolls I could tell were home baked, deviled eggs sprinkled with paprika, a fruit salad of assorted berries, lemon tarts, and bottles of fizzy lemonade. When I lifted one to my mouth, the liquid prickled over my tongue with the perfect blend of sour and sweet.

I didn't know what to say after that, so it was a good thing I had plenty to stuff my mouth with to avoid talking altogether.

When we'd polished off most of the main dishes, Jude sprawled out on his back with his elbows propping him up, squinting against the sun and looking so pleased with himself I couldn't hold my tongue.

"How did you find this spot, anyway? Or did you send your chef to do that too?"

"I am capable of doing some work for myself. I spent a few hours driving around checking the likely sites. The ones not too far away from campus, obviously. I did want to be reasonably sure you'd make it." He smirked at me.

It was hard for him to imagine Jude Killbrook going to that much trouble to set up a picnic—for my benefit, no less. "So where's the catch?" I said. "There's got to be more to this, right?"

"Because I can't enjoy a pleasant afternoon with good company unless I have ulterior motives? I'm wounded." He sighed dramatically and plucked a few berries out of the salad bowl. With a flick of his wrist, he tossed a raspberry in a perfect arc up into the air and down into his mouth. A blueberry careened after it.

"You're going to end up choking like that," I had to point out.

"Concern for my well-being! I'm making a little progress."

I resisted the urge to stick out my tongue at him. "I didn't say I'd *care* if you choked. I just thought you might like to know."

"So chilly, Ice Queen." He mock-shivered and tossed up another raspberry.

I leaned forward and snatched it out of the air in mid-arc, then popped it into my mouth instead. Jude pushed himself upright with a sound of protest. "Just saving you from yourself," I said at his glower, but I couldn't help smirking right back at him.

"In that case," he said archly, "I find I'm suddenly deeply worried that you might choke on that tart." He scooted over to snatch at the last of the lemon tarts that I'd been saving for when my stomach felt a little less full.

"Hey!" I grabbed it first and yanked it out of his reach. "You already had two. Where's your hospitality?"

"Says the woman who just literally stole the food from my mouth." He feinted left and shot out his hand to the right, and I jerked the tart away just in time.

His fingers closed around my wrist. Heat spread over my skin from that point of contact, and my body snapped into awareness of how close we'd gotten to each other, his arm across my abdomen, his knee against my thigh.

His head bowed just a foot away from mine, the sunlight catching in his dark green eyes. His stunning face filled my entire field of view. A momentary dizziness washed over me despite myself.

This was Jude Killbrook. No matter how charming he'd been the last few weeks, I'd seen how cruel he could be. He'd been that cruel to *me*.

In my distraction, he slipped the tart from my grasp and set it back on its plate. "I'm not sure this is what I want after all," he said, low and soft. He let go of my wrist, but he didn't pull back, his gaze searching mine. "I'd like to kiss you, but I'm a little concerned you might punch me."

My pulse hiccupped. I willed my voice to stay steady. "Is there any particular reason why I *shouldn't* punch you?"

"You could give kissing me a try first. I've gotten excellent reviews from multiple sources."

I made a face and gave him a shove to propel him backward, careful not to let my hand linger on his lean chest. "How romantic. Consider working on your sales pitch."

He shifted at my push, but his gaze stayed on my face. "Is the idea really so horrifying?"

"I don't know about *horrifying*, but..." I let out an exasperated sound. "I appreciate your help with the driving, okay? And the picnic. And I'll admit I've actually had fun. But you can't expect me to just forget the whole first month I was here. You've never even apologized for the crap you put me through. You can't just pretend it never happened and expect me to play along."

Jude blinked at me as if startled. As if he *had* thought he could pretend the taunting and the pain away.

"What if I don't know how to be sorry about that?" he said after a moment. "When I think about the way we came down on you, I remember how you rose to the challenge. Every tactic we tried, you pushed back harder. You were fucking brilliant. Do you think I'd be here otherwise?"

A lump rose in my throat. He sounded so sincere, but at the same time I didn't know how to wrap my head around the perspective he was offering.

"It still hurt," I said. "*You* still hurt me. I didn't ask you to put me through hell so I'd learn how to be 'fucking brilliant.' You can't pat yourself on the back for that and not take responsibility for every other part. And don't tell me that's just how fearmancers do things or whatever other excuse."

"I wasn't—" Jude's lips twisted. He lowered his head for a moment and swiped his hand through his hair as he raised his eyes again. "You're right. I hadn't thought about it that way, and I should have. I'm sorry for the pain you went through because of anything I did."

The resistance inside me softened. I hadn't really thought he'd apologize at all. But then, how much did he even mean it?

"Malcolm is still trying to come down on me," I said. "Do you know anything about that?"

When push comes to shove, will you be throwing me under the bus to make him happy?

Jude shrugged. "Malcolm's going to Malcolm. He's said some stuff about going for an indirect approach and finding more subtle ways to shake you up, but nothing specific I could tell you to watch out for. I think he's waiting to make sure whatever he's planning works before he starts bragging about it. I'm pretty sure you already know to watch out for him in general."

"If he did say something specific, would you tell me?"

"Would you want me to, even if I knew you could handle it on your own?"

"I might be able to handle it more easily with a heads up, so yeah."

Jude made a sweeping gesture with his arm. "Then consider it done."

I wasn't quite satisfied yet. Another question spilled out. "What does he think about you taking me on picnics and all this?"

"I haven't seen any point in giving him a play-by-play

of our time together," Jude said. "He probably assumes I'm working voodoo on you for the cause. Easier for both of us if he keeps thinking that."

That might be true. If Jude was being sincere in wanting to make amends and separating himself from Malcolm's campaign against me, I couldn't imagine how furious the Nightwood scion would be when he found out, and he'd definitely take it out on me at least as much as his supposed friend. But only if Jude didn't have any sway at all there. Only if he assumed nothing he said would make any difference to what Malcolm did anyway.

Or if he couldn't be bothered to find out whether he could stop Malcolm, with all the trouble that the attempt would stir up.

Exhaustion washed over me just thinking about it. Maybe what he'd just said was all the answer I needed.

I started clearing the blanket, sticking the dishes back in the basket. Jude joined in with glances my way as he grabbed the last few things. He lifted his chin toward the plate by the edge of the sheet. "You still have your tart."

My stomach tightened in resistance. "You know," I said, "I'm not really hungry anymore. You can have it."

Jude didn't look particularly happy to have won that battle. Instead of eating it himself, he tucked the tart into the basket with the rest of the picnic remains. He set the basket on the grass and moved to shake off the sheet as I stepped to the side. His gaze stayed on me as he folded it up.

"I think I should be clear about something," he said abruptly. "The other girls—there aren't any other girls now. That I'm kissing. Or whatever else. There never was anyone else I really wanted anyway. I didn't know what I wanted until you. So I'm in this just for you as long as there's any chance at all. I can make up for what happened before. I *will*. However long it takes."

I stared at him. "Why? What's so special about me?" What could possibly have prompted the desperation he'd acknowledged that first day in the garage?

He dropped the folded sheet onto the basket and gave me a crooked smile. "Weren't you just lecturing me not that long ago about how you're not like us?" He waved in the general direction of the university. "Everyone in that place is so busy fighting over who's got the biggest dick— or whatever it is the girls fight over—that they haven't got room in their heads to think about anything else. You don't give a shit about any of it. You rise up above it all like an angel over the battlefield."

"I wouldn't have thought you wanted an angel."

"One who can go head to head with me, mouth off right back at me, sure." He took a step closer to me. "You know what you want. You say what you mean. You don't let anyone shake you. You're going to have assholes lining up around the block trying to get with you just because of your last name, and none of them will have a clue what really matters about you, and that's a fucking disgrace. You should at least know it."

He said every word so emphatically, his eyes holding mine, that the dizziness I'd felt earlier tingled through me again. He took another step, close enough to touch my cheek now. A jolt of fear ran alongside the heat it provoked, but he didn't go in for a kiss like I'd expected. At least, not that kind of kiss. He eased up on his feet just slightly and brushed his lips to my forehead.

My breath caught, my whole body flushing as if it'd been a much more intimate gesture. Jude dropped his hand. "However long it takes," he repeated. "I'll wait. You're more than worth it, Rory."

Part of me wanted to follow him, to grab him by the collar and find out what those lips would feel like pressed against mine. I held myself in check.

I'd rushed in with Connar. I'd let myself get swept up too quickly, and I'd obviously missed the warnings I should have noticed before. I was *not* going to let another of these guys rip my heart out like that.

"Okay," I said. "I—I guess we should get back to campus."

Jude didn't argue, just carried the picnic stuff back to the car. He sank into the passenger seat with every appearance of serene patience. I inhaled and exhaled slowly before starting the engine, willing the chaotic mess of emotions inside me to chill out.

My heartbeat had evened out by the time I'd gotten the car back onto the highway. Gazing down the empty road ahead of me, I eased my foot down on the gas pedal, inching us faster and then a little faster still. Jude made no comment, but a smile crossed his lips.

His words echoed in my head, though maybe not the ones he'd have expected to stick the most. I knew what I wanted. I didn't let anyone shake me.

I couldn't let myself be scared.

I made it into my spot in the garage without any scraped paint. Jude bobbed his head to me after he got out. "Until next time?"

"Until next time." I could agree to that much.

Outside, he set off toward our dorms, and I turned toward Killbrook Hall. There were answers I wanted, answers I *needed*, and I hadn't pushed for them because I'd been conscious of my mentor's recovery—and the fact that he might have been targeted because of me. Imogen's comment about feeling his fear had lingered with me.

He was perfectly fine now, though. He'd been going to tell me something, whether it'd been feverish nonsense or not. I had to find out what.

I'd have been willing to wait if it'd turned out Banefield was in a seminar, but he answered my first knock on his office door. "Rory," he said with a bemused expression. "You look like a girl with a mission. What can I help you with?"

I waited until he'd shut the door behind me, and then turned to him with my arms crossed. "That's what I need to ask you. What can you help me with? You were about to say something important right before you got sick. Something you were worried would happen—someone you think I should watch out for...?"

His mouth pressed flat before he answered. "That's not — I don't know how much I can tell you. I *want* to help in every way I can. But maybe that's not it."

So there was something real. I caught a flicker of fear from him now too, sharp and quavering. It made my throat close up.

"I don't want to put you in danger over this," I said. "I just want to keep myself out of danger too. Did someone *make* you sick?"

Banefield waved his hand dismissively, but he didn't look startled by the suggestion. "You don't need to concern yourself with that."

"Of course I do, if it's because of me—because you tried to help me." My heart sank. "But you aren't, not really, are you? In case it happens again."

Could I blame him for not taking the risk? Maybe not. But as the realization washed over me, I felt completely alone even with him standing right there in front of me.

Watching me, a resolute expression came over Banefield's face. "I'm so sorry, Rory. This is ridiculous. I'll try—I should at least be able to warn you that the—"

He choked on the next word. "Professor!" I yelped.

His body was already doubling over like it had before with the same sputtering retching sound. I tried to grasp his shoulder, but he fell to his hands and knees before I got a grip. With a shudder, he vomited onto the carpet. His arms gave.

I managed to catch my mentor before his face smacked right into the puddle of puke, my arms straining at his slack weight. I eased him down onto his side, my gut twisting at the smell and the sight of the sweat already dappling his lolling head. Then I scrambled to the door to call for help.

The certainty chased me there, digging deep into my chest. The health center could try to call this a regular relapse if they wanted, but they'd be wrong—or lying. It wasn't some virus or bacteria making him sick. It was me. Somehow my presence and his attempt to talk to me about that particular subject was setting off a magical bomb inside him.

What the hell did he know? And who had gone to these lengths to stop him from sharing it with me?

CHAPTER FOURTEEN

Rory

There were a lot of places I'd rather have been than in one of the Stormhurst Building's gyms while the rest of the members of the Insight league mingled and muttered around me. Unfortunately, league meetings were compulsory even if you didn't give a damn who won the term competition. I just hoped it wouldn't take too long for them to hash out whatever they wanted to hash out.

Declan had turned up a few minutes ago, giving me a slight nod but going to stand at the other end of the room. Keeping everything professional. That was fine. I preferred his distance to the glare Victory's friend Sinclair was shooting at me every time my gaze happened to pass over her. You'd have thought she was offended I'd shown up at all, as if I had any choice in the matter.

It was hard to pay much attention to either of them when my mind kept returning to yesterday's meeting with

Banefield. Every time I remembered his collapse, my gut twisted with a queasy mix of guilt and apprehension.

He'd known he'd get sick again if he tried to tell me… whatever he'd been trying to tell me. That was why he'd balked. But he'd tried anyway, done his best to spit out his warning before the spell grabbed him.

Maybe I shouldn't have pushed for answers. But considering how viciously someone was punishing him for talking, I had to think whatever he knew could make the difference between my surviving here and becoming a victim myself.

I had to figure out the spell that was targeting him and how to stop it, for both our sakes. It was my fault he was sick. The staff at the health center hadn't been able to give me even vague reassurances about his recovery when I'd stopped by this afternoon. Would whoever was targeting him go even farther this time?

What if they killed him?

A bellowing voice cut through my worries. A big guy with bristly brown hair had gotten up on a chair at one end of the room so he could see over the entire crowd that had gathered—some fifty or so of us. "Insight League!" he said. "Let's get down to strategy. We've only got one month left in the term, and we're behind all the other leagues."

"As usual," a girl near me said under her breath.

"We've got *two* scions on our team now," someone near the front of the group said, pitching his voice to carry. "That's got to give us some advantage."

"Sure, let's hear what they have to say about it." The

guy who seemed to have appointed himself leader of the
league scanned the crowd.

"You know I can't make recommendations while I'm a
teacher's aide," Declan said from his spot near the wall.

"Where's our Bloodstone?" The guy on the chair
spotted me and beckoned me over. "If you've got a fresh
perspective, we'd love to hear it."

As I hesitated, the gathering parted to make way for
me. Sinclair let out a not-quite-surreptitious snort.
Everyone was watching me now. Shit. I'd come because I
had to, not because I had any interest in leading the
discussion.

Now that the guy had put me on the spot, I couldn't
get out of contributing without looking like a total ass. I
forced myself to walk over to join him. He went as far as
to hop off the chair to offer it to me. Wonderful.

I climbed up and looked uncertainly over the crowd of
figures who, other than Sinclair with her sour expression,
were looking at me as if I'd shown up at Villain Academy
to lead them to victory. It wasn't as if my assessment results
had come with a league competition strategy guide.

"Ah, as I guess everyone knows, I haven't been here at
the university very long," I said. "I'm not sure what our
not-so-fresh perspectives on the league competition are.
When was the last time Insight won?"

A murmur that sounded half disgruntled, half amused
rippled through the gathering. The leader guy beside me
let out a dry chuckle. "Can anyone here remember us ever
winning?"

Heads shook all around the room. Declan spoke up

with a pained smile. "It's happened a few times, but very rarely—the last time was almost a decade ago. Insight can give us an advantage over the other skill areas in all sorts of ways, but it's not particularly flashy. It's difficult to use it in ways that are both effective and grab the professors' notice. I don't think we should fault ourselves for that."

"We've got to at least try to win," a girl in the middle of the crowd said.

"Okay." I resisted the urge to bite my lip. "I guess no one here knows how we managed to win those times before, then…"

"Why are we listening to her?" Sinclair's crisp voice cut through the continuing murmurs. "She can hardly figure out how to use her magic for herself."

My hackles rose. I hadn't asked to be looked to as some kind of advisor. And I *had* used my magic pretty effectively in the last few weeks, thank you very much. As the murmurs rose, my mind leapt to the other day when I'd managed to get one over on Malcolm Nightwood himself. A spark of inspiration lit in my mind.

"I might still be getting the hang of things, but I'm a fast learner." I didn't give Sinclair my direct attention, focusing on the less familiar faces around me instead. "Maybe we can't do flashy tricks, but we *can* catch on to the tricks the other leagues are planning before they can go ahead with them. Call them out so people around will be on guard and they won't be able to pull it off. I've already gotten credit for using Insight like that."

"Go around acting like a bunch of narcs?" a guy said. "I don't know."

No, it was perfect. For the first time since I'd watched Professor Banefield crumple yesterday, the sense of control I'd had racing my car along that country highway came back to me. I'd earn a little more faith from my league while stopping some of the chaos the other leagues were spreading around campus. I just had to frame it in a fearmancer-appealing way.

"We won't be narcing on them." I let a slow smile cross my face, thinking of Jude's smirk for inspiration. "We'll be getting the jump on them. Showing we know them too well for them to get away with any crap. Reminding them that even what's in their head isn't safe while we're around."

Putting it that way made me feel a little sick, but matching smiles sprang up throughout my audience.

"We could give it a shot," the leader guy said. "Scan everyone around you, looking for schemes. If we're all keeping watch, they won't be able to get much by us."

"Yeah!" a girl said. "Take away the element of surprise, and anything they're plotting falls flat. How're they going to fight back when we can see all their plans?"

I'd done enough here, right? I stepped down off the chair, and after some more enthusiastic conversation, another guy got up to make suggestions about watching for gaps in the professors' mental walls so we could find the best ways to butter them up. No one seemed to mind when I drifted toward the back of the group without commenting on any other strategies.

"We've got a month to turn this around," the leader guy reminded us before we left. "Not a word about any of the ideas we've discussed once we leave this room! You know the other leagues are always hanging around hoping to get a jump on *us*."

I slipped out of the gym ahead of most of the crowd. Outside the Stormhurst Building, the lights mounted over the door cut through the thickening dusk. Several figures were hanging around just outside the building, making an effort to look casual. Spies for the other leagues? They weren't hearing anything from me, anyway.

In California, it would have stayed warm all through the night by this time in May, but here in northern New York, a chill had already crept into the air. I hurried toward the glowing windows of Ashgrave Hall.

I hadn't made my escape quite fast enough. I'd just reached the main green between the halls and the tower when Sinclair caught up with me. "You really think you're so smart, huh, Bloodstone?"

I paused and turned to look at her. She crossed her arms over her chest, the ends of her black bob swinging along her jaw as she raised it at a haughty angle.

What the hell was her particular problem with me today? I hadn't seen her offering any useful comments during the meeting.

Most of the other students had been heading in the same direction as us. A bunch of them came to a halt rather than continuing on, watching the confrontation. My skin prickled. I just wanted to go up to my room and get away from all these people for a while, but I didn't think it'd be wise to turn my back on Sinclair while she was fuming like this.

"People asked me for ideas," I said evenly. "I gave them one."

"That's not what I'm talking about." Her lip curled with a sneer. "Miss Super Special with her four strengths, expert at Insight, and you can't even tell when you're being taken for a ride."

Had someone been messing with *her* head? I knit my brow. "I don't have any idea what you're talking about."

She guffawed. "Of course you don't. Jude wrapped you around his finger so easily, didn't he? Do you really think you're anything more than a challenge for him? He'll play you and then he'll ditch you when he's proven that he can."

My stomach tightened. Jude and I hadn't spent much time together on campus, but he hadn't made any effort to hide our little ventures in my car either. Of course other people had noticed.

Maybe she was telling the truth, or maybe she was just trying to get under my skin. Either way, she obviously wasn't looking out for my best interests, only to jab a knife in. I kept my voice steady.

"Thanks for the warning. I'll keep it in mind."

"You don't believe me. Just you wait. Please tell me you haven't fallen for the whole charade that easily. You can't think he actually *wants* you."

As she spat out the last sentence, a door behind me squeaked. Sinclair's gaze darted to the space beyond my shoulder, and her mouth snapped shut.

"And how exactly would *you* know what I actually

want, Sinclair?" Jude asked in a darkly languid voice as he came up beside me.

Her stance tensed. "I was just... I—"

"You were just trying to screw me over and harass Rory at the same time. Although I'm not sure why you'd care so much who I associate with when you clearly have such a low opinion of me."

Sinclair flung a hand toward me. "You can't really like *her*. I know you. That's not who you are."

Jude folded his arms over his chest. "Maybe I'm trying out being someone else for a change. You should give it a shot. It's very refreshing."

Sinclair glowered at him for a second before shifting her gaze back to me. "It isn't going to stick. He'll be back to—"

"Fuck off, Sinclair," Jude interrupted, his voice gone flat and cold, so unlike his usual tone that Sinclair faltered completely. Her hands clenched at her sides, and then she stalked away with a toss of her hair.

Jude swiveled on his heel, taking in the other students who'd assembled to watch. The glow of the overhead lights streaking through the darkness turned his copper hair even darker and his angular face even paler. His eyes had narrowed.

"If anyone else is thinking about taking on the Bloodstone scion, I'd suggest you think again—because you'll get your ass kicked not by me but by her. And if any of you have any problem with *me* or where I choose to bestow my affections, feel free to tell me all about it now." He spread his arms as if offering himself up.

No one spoke. Several figures slunk away into the dusk. Jude clapped his hands together.

"Good. If you have any problems you *don't* want me taking you to task for, consider making sure that I'm definitely not within hearing when you start spouting off about them, and we'll all be happier." He turned to me and gave me a slanted smile. "Sorry to barge in. I'm sure you could have defended yourself, but it sounded as if my honor was at stake too."

"It's all right," I said, a little dazed. Not so dazed that an automatic retort didn't tumble off my tongue right after, though. "I guess you don't have a lot to go around, after all."

Jude barked a laugh. "And now it's under attack from both sides." He set a careful hand on my shoulder and leaned in to press the softest kiss to my cheek. There, in the middle of the green, with at least a couple dozen students still watching. Shock fluttered up through my chest.

"You are all right, aren't you?" he murmured by my ear, and I realized the kiss hadn't even been the point. He was giving me the chance to let him know if I was more affected than I was letting on without having to admit it in front of our peers. Because I was a scion, and scions weren't supposed to show weakness. Because any vulnerability these witnesses observed might be turned into a weapon against me.

With everything he'd said from the moment he'd come out, he'd been careful not to imply I'd needed saving.

"I'm fine," I said quickly under my breath, and he

straightened up. His hand lingered on my shoulder for a moment longer before he withdrew it. As the warmth left my skin, it occurred to me that other than Malcolm's pompous welcome my first evening on campus, this was the first time any of the other scions had shown any public kindness to me at all, let alone a declaration of "affection," however Jude expected people to interpret the word.

How long would it take before Malcolm heard about this and figured out Jude hadn't really spent the last few weeks harassing me?

CHAPTER FIFTEEN

Rory

T he woman who'd come to the front desk at the
health center frowned at me with a pinched
expression. "I'm sorry, Miss Bloodstone, but as you've been
told before, we don't allow anyone other than family to
visit patients undergoing treatment."

I'd come fresh from a morning holed up in the library,
hoping I could try out a few strategies to understand how
the spell was working on Professor Banefield. Considering
all the fuss everyone had made about me being a long-lost
scion, you'd think it would at least get me visiting rights.

"He's my mentor," I said. "He's the closest thing to
family I have here."

It was true, and saying it sent a pang through my
chest. If my real family *had* been here, Dad would have
been doing everything he could to save Banefield, like he'd
done for so many critical patients at the hospital where

he'd volunteered. I didn't think the fact that my mentor was a fearmancer would have stopped him.

The woman in front of me wasn't so flexible. I could tell that gambit hadn't worked before she even opened her mouth. "I'm afraid that's still against policy. I assure you we've giving him the best treatment available."

I grimaced as I turned to leave. Their treatment wasn't good enough for them to have figured out he was under some kind of spell. Maybe if I told them more about how it'd happened—but if I revealed what he'd managed to say to me, that might put him in even more danger.

If I could find something more definite in those goddamn library books, the staff might listen to a suggestion or two even if I couldn't see him. I just had to be as sure as I could get. Before I spent any more time in the library, though, I had to get through my next Desensitization session.

My shoulders came up as I left the Stormhurst Building and started toward Nightwood Tower. My private sessions with Professor Razeden hadn't been *horrible*, and with his guidance I'd actually managed to crack through the illusions inspired by my fears the last couple times, but I doubted I'd ever look forward to those ordeals. They were designed to prepare us to stand strong against any attack an enemy might throw at us—not much fun in that.

I was about halfway to the tower when the ground suddenly tipped beneath my feet. I stumbled, and the path shifted again, rolling as if propelled by waves.

Every time I tried to catch my balance, the ground

swayed in a different direction. My stomach roiled. I stared at the path ahead of me, which rippled and dipped.

What the hell was going on? I'd experienced earthquakes and smaller tremors plenty of times in California, but they hadn't felt like this. A few other students had been crossing the green, and their steps looked steady enough. As I stumbled again, the two closest to me glanced my way and started to stare.

Great. Now word would go around campus that on top of her regular screaming fits, the heir of Bloodstone had been tottering around on a Saturday morning like a drunken sailor.

The problem wasn't affecting them too—so it wasn't the whole ground. Maybe it wasn't the ground at all, only my impression of it. An illusion messing with my equilibrium.

I dragged in a breath and closed my eyes, focusing on the bits of my surroundings I knew were real. The hard surface of the paved path under my shoes. The crisp bite lingering in the spring air. The hint of roast chicken carrying in the air from the junior cafeteria where the staff would be preparing lunch for the younger students.

The lurching beneath me faded and then stopped completely, so suddenly I knew I hadn't cut off the illusion's effects myself. I adjusted my feet against the ground as I opened my eyes. A smooth voice cut through the air from behind me.

"Not so sure of your feet today, Glinda?" Malcolm sauntered around me, cocking his head as he considered my face, and my mental shield snapped into place twice as strong automatically. "You look a little seasick."

He was switching up tactics, playing with illusion as well as his main speciality. I didn't intend to give him the satisfaction of showing I was any more unsettled than he'd already seen.

"Mostly just sick of your stupid games," I said.

"Oh, don't blame it all on me. You know you're still in over your head. You're just too stubborn to admit it. Those bad dreams aren't lying, though, are they?"

I raised my chin even though my pulse had lurched. "How do you know what my dreams are like if you're not messing with them?"

"Come on, Bloodstone. Hasn't anyone told you?" He shook his head, his eyes intent on mine beneath the gleam of his golden hair. "You yell so loud I'd bet the whole hall can hear you all the way down to the library."

I swallowed, remembering the now-familiar rawness in my throat this morning. "Fuck off," I said.

The dismissal had sounded a lot more powerful when Jude had shot it at Sinclair last night. From my mouth, it fell flat. I pretended not to notice and moved to stride on past the Nightwood scion along the pathway.

"It doesn't matter how many friends you rope in or how fast you run, not when the problem's in here." Malcolm shifted forward to tap my head, so quickly I couldn't jerk out of the way in time. When I whirled around, he'd already backed up, that cocky smile still curving his lips. "I'm ready to help whenever you're ready to beg for it. Let's see how long it takes you to *wake up*."

His last words had a hint of a casting lilt, like when he was using a persuasion spell. But I hadn't felt any tap at my mental defenses—and he couldn't persuade me to wake up when I was already awake, right? I hesitated, waiting to see if any of my limbs would move without my consent, but as far as I could tell, I still had full control over my body.

I was letting him get to me, reading more into his taunts than was there. "When you beg for forgiveness for being such an asshat, then maybe I'll consider it," I retorted, and marched on.

My legs moved perfectly normally under me, but as I hurried on, a brief wave of dizziness washed over me. A blurry movement at the edge of my vision brought my head jerking around. No one was there, just the empty field leading out to the forest.

Malcolm was watching me act jumpy. I pushed myself onward to the tower.

I stopped again at the top of the stairs leading down to the basement room. The shadows that filled the crevices around the steps and the stone walls unfurled and reached toward me with filmy fingers. My heart hiccupped, I blinked hard, and they snapped back into place.

Okay, Rory, Malcolm's nowhere near you now. Get a grip on yourself.

Professor Razeden was waiting for me outside the desensitization chamber, his tall gaunt figure a little like something out of a nightmare itself. He gave me a subdued smile when he saw me, even though I was giving him extra work on his weekend.

His dry, even voice had guided me enough by now that it centered me pretty much instantly. "Miss Bloodstone, right on time. Are you ready for another go?"

"Absolutely," I said, ignoring the niggling uneasiness that had followed me down. "Let's see if I can make it through with a little less coaching this time."

"There's no shame in needing the instruction," Razeden said as he ushered me into the black walled room with its arching ceiling. "Your peers have had years to build up their defensive strategies. Believe me, I had to talk every one of them through plenty of sessions. Get into position to begin."

I stepped into the middle of the room beneath the artificial glow of the overhead lights. What lovely horror was my mind going to conjure up this time? The spells on the chamber, when triggered by the professor, worked with a combination of Insight and Illusion, delving into our minds and projecting our greatest fears around us in terrifyingly vivid clarity. People who'd gotten more practice tended to end up with more metaphorical situations, apparently. So far mine had all been disturbingly literal.

"Slow, steady breaths," Razeden reminded me from his post near the door. "Start out calm and it'll be easier to stay there. Whatever comes, remember that you're stronger than it. You're real, and it's only an illusion."

Right. Easier said than done when you were staring your worst nightmares in the face in full living color, but at least I hadn't crumpled into a ball sobbing recently.

"Go ahead," I said.

The room went pitch black. Then a different space

wavered into view around me, the lines solidifying with a blink.

My pulse thumped faster as I recognized the scene. There hadn't been many details of the building in the photos from the report on my birth parents' deaths, but a couple sessions ago my mind had constructed its own version of a vault-ceilinged grand hall where a force of joymancers had burned them to a crisp.

Like before, I found myself standing between the two groups of mages, staring up at them from a great height, as if I were a helpless toddler again. The joymancers shouted at the fearmancers, who shouted back. Even though I didn't think they'd been a part of the actual attack, my real parents stood with the intruders, Dad's face flushed an angry red, Mom's hair flying wild. My birth mother jabbed her hand at them accusingly.

I opened my mouth, but I couldn't force out more than a babble of sound. When I waved my arms, they didn't seem to see me. I took a wobbly step and fell to my knees.

No, no, no. I didn't want to go through this whole thing again. Last time I'd had to watch them slice and sear each other until bodies had littered the floor. My only victory had been willing the images to disappear after the fact rather than needing Professor Razeden to end the illusion for me.

His voice reached me as if from far away. "Don't try to interfere with what they're doing. Accept that you can't stop the confrontation. Focus on walking away."

Walk away. Don't let myself care what they did to each other. It was already done anyway.

I pushed myself back up. One careful step, sliding my foot across the polished hardwood with my shaky toddler balance, tuning out the words whipping back and forth even more viciously around me.

"You fucking bitch!" Mom yelled, sounding like herself and yet like a stranger at the same time, and one of the fearmancers cried out. My arm shot up despite my best intentions as if I could ward off the spells they were starting to hurl at each other.

My hand had been empty a moment before. As it snapped out, the air twitched around my fingers, and a glimmering shape darted from them as if *I'd* flung something.

It whipped across the room and hit one of the joymancers right in the throat with a spurt of blood. A razorblade, metal gleaming amid the scarlet flow.

My stomach flipped. What the hell? *That* hadn't happened last time. I hadn't been able to affect either side at all.

"Don't pay attention to them," Razeden said. "Keep your eyes on that door."

Apparently he didn't have any tips related to my sudden affinity for weaponry. I guessed the same strategy still made sense. Clenching my jaw, I tore my gaze away from the illusionary man whose throat I'd just slit.

One step. Two steps. Someone screamed. My balance swayed, and my arm jerked as I tried to catch myself.

Another razor flashed from my fingers, into the

fearmancer side this time. It sank into my birth mother's belly. She flinched and bowed over the wound, blood spreading across the fabric of her dress.

"No," I whispered, curling my fingers into my palms. "No—"

My protest cut off with a gasp of pain. I stared down at my hands, at more razors digging through my palms as if I'd shoved them there. The throbbing echoed up my arms. My head spun.

Razeden's voice sounded even more distant now. "One foot after the other. You can do this."

No special tips for stabbing myself? My next step sent a fresh jolt of pain through my body. Sweat trickled down into my eyes.

A fiery spell whipped past me with a flare of stinging heat. I ducked, my hand bobbed down, and a blade plummeted from it right through my foot. It pinned me to the floor with another spear of agony.

"Keep walking," Razeden said, and a laugh sputtered out of me that turned into a groan. Every part of me ached, and the smell of burnt flesh coated my mouth. My stomach heaved as if to propel what remained of my breakfast up my throat.

I hunched over to pull the razor from my foot, but I couldn't use my mangled hands. The pain radiated deeper, thumping inside my head.

"I can't," I gasped out. "I can't! Make it stop!"

The sounds and smells of the carnage vanished. The pain leached from my body, leaving me simply trembling there crouching on the floor. Fuck, fuck, fuck.

At least I wasn't sobbing. I swiped at my eyes and looked up. Professor Razeden had walked partway over to me, but he stopped at my movement.

"What happened?" he said in his usual even tone. "You looked as if you had a good grip on yourself at first. What threw you off?"

Hadn't it been obvious? I motioned to my hands. "The razors. They just came out of nowhere, and I couldn't stop them, and the illusion of the pain got so intense..."

Razeden's normally impassive expression had turned befuddled. "Razors?"

They hadn't exactly been subtle. "Yeah," I said, frowning. "They hit a couple of the other people, and then they stabbed my own hands... You must have seen them."

The look Razeden was giving me made my stomach churn all over again. "I didn't see any weapons at all—definitely not any on or around you. Are you... are you *sure?*"

"Of course I'm sure. I couldn't exactly imagine—" I stopped. That was what I'd done, wasn't it? They hadn't been part of the room's illusionary effect, the one that projected out for everyone in the space to see. They'd only appeared to my senses. Like the undulating of the ground outside right before Malcolm had taunted me.

How the hell could he have done *this*, though? Even if he could have cast from all the way outside the tower, which from what everyone I'd ever talked to had said was doubtful, there was no way he could know what the desensitization chamber was showing me to make his illusion fit. If it'd been one of the times when he and the other scions had appeared to harangue and assault me, I'd have happily shredded his fake self with a handy pair of knives.

Razeden was still eyeing me as if I'd started talking in tongues. "It was a separate illusion," I said quickly. "It must have been. I swear I saw them—I *felt* them—but if you couldn't, then it wasn't part of the exercise."

"There's no one here who could have cast an additional illusion."

"No one could from outside the room?"

He shook his head. "It's warded. No one wants outside magic influencing the process we go through in here, even accidentally."

But then—

The memory rose up in my head of Malcolm's last ominous remark, the lilt I thought I'd heard in his voice. The ghostly flickers that had crept into my vision when I'd left him behind to head down here. My throat constricted.

He couldn't have known exactly what I'd see, how the shadows would lie on the floor, on my way here either. It was as if my mind had generated those illusions just like it fed into the spells on this room.

"Is it possible to cast a spell on someone's mind that'll kick in when you're not around?" I asked abruptly. "Or, I don't know, that you can quickly trigger after the fact even if they're shielded right then?" Malcolm definitely hadn't broken through my defenses. I knew what that felt like.

Razeden frowned. "I wouldn't say that's unheard of, but it's uncommon. To embed a spell that securely and effectively takes sustained casting over a long period of time while the subject is vulnerable. Even from within the dorm rooms, it'd be difficult for anyone at a student's skill level to direct a powerful enough spell through one of the walls. I assume you've kept your bedroom secure so no one else would have access."

"As far as I know, I have." Deborah would have noticed if anyone was sneaking in and casting spells on me for 'sustained' periods while I slept, anyway.

"There's also a certain level of magic that can be transmitted via a person's familiar," Razeden said, "if the caster has access to the animal and not their intended target."

Yeah, no. Even when the scions had kidnapped my mouse, they'd only had her for an hour at most. Since then, she'd stayed more out of the way than I did.

"I don't know," I said. "Maybe I'm making excuses." Maybe Malcolm had managed to slip past my shield without my noticing? My head was starting to ache just trying to figure it out. "I guess it doesn't really matter in the end. Today was a bust."

"You've made progress. Every attempt teaches you something." Razeden paused when we reached the door. "If you believe someone is interfering with your training, Miss Bloodstone, you must do whatever you can to push back, just as you push back against the illusions in here."

Not, "Come tell me about it and I'll help." Not, "Take it up with the headmistress." Push back. Because that was all part of the Villain Academy training too, wasn't it?

I restrained myself from making a face, but the

comment stirred something in me, connecting to the thing Razeden had said about familiars.

I'd been so focused on learning to defend myself and figuring out what was happening with Professor Banefield that I'd set my most important mission aside. No matter what else happened, I still needed to figure out a way to push back against this entire university and the people who ran it like a battle royale.

Almost every mage here had a familiar. All of the scions did, as far as I knew. I might not be able to get into the mindset of a fearmancer all that easily, but animals were animals. How much could I influence what went on here if I made the sort of "friends" no one would expect?

How much could I unsettle the guy who was making a career out of unnerving me?

I walked back to Ashgrave Hall tentatively, watching for new illusions, but if Malcolm had sparked some effect in my head before, it appeared to have faded away. The uneasiness still coursed through me despite my best efforts to tamp down on it. Setting my jaw, I stopped by my dorm room for just long enough to grab some leftover chicken out of the fridge. Then I headed out to the small wooden building at the far edge of the eastern field.

The door wasn't locked. The inside of the building looked bigger than the outside, with a hall and just three doors leading into the inner rooms. Right now, only the one closest to the door had a name tag on it. *Shadow*.

There was a little barred window at waist height. I knelt down and peered into the space on the other side. A dry but distinctly doggy smell tickled my nose.

Nails clicked against the concrete floor on the other side. Bright eyes gleamed with the light filtering through the window on the wall inside the wolf's stall. Malcolm's familiar peered back at me with a huff of hot breath.

"Hey, boy," I said softly, remembering how Malcolm had talked to the wolf after he'd sicced it on me weeks ago. "You must get pretty lonely cooped up in here all day. Thought I'd come keep you company for a little bit. I brought a snack."

The wolf started to growl low in its throat, but the sound cut off the second I poked a piece of chicken through the bars. It snatched the chunk up in a flash and gulped it down. Its muzzle sniffled against the window for more.

"Are you going to be nice?" I asked it. "No more of that growling?"

The wolf let out a thin whine instead. I smiled. "All right, all right. I've got plenty."

After I'd fed it the rest of the chicken, the wolf licked its chops, looking immensely satisfied. My heart thumped as I held my hand up to the bars, braced to jerk it back if need be.

Shadow sniffed my fingers. He bared his teeth for a second before he seemed to think better of that move. Instead, he nuzzled the bars.

"Good boy," I murmured, and dared to give the wolf's snout a quick rub. Shadow held still and even nudged a little closer to accept the contact.

A sense of satisfaction filled my own chest. I wasn't ready to interact with the animal—and all his teeth and claws—without bars between us for protection, but I'd taken a step in the right direction. I'd have to keep wolfish tastes in mind on my next grocery shopping trip.

As I watched Shadow prowl around his stall, another implication of the familiar connection clicked into place in my head.

Did *Banefield* have a familiar? What if his enemies had conjured his illness through it so they couldn't be tracked directly?

I just hoped I could keep my mind steady enough to find out.

CHAPTER SIXTEEN

Jude

I'd known the reckoning would come. It was only a matter of when. Word didn't take long to travel around campus. Less than twenty-four hours after I'd put Sinclair in her place, one of my dormmates knocked on my bedroom door.

"Malcolm's asking for you," he said hesitantly.

I sighed and got up from my desk. Fucking Sinclair letting her fucking claws out. As if she had any right to think I owed her something more than our occasional casual interludes between the sheets when she'd been hanging all over Chandler Viceport last week and who knew how many other guys before that.

Things could have been just fine going as they were until Rory was more sure of me, but no, now we were going to have explosions.

There were a lot of insulting things people could have

said about me, and a decent number of them were true, but I wasn't going to be a coward. After all the faith I'd asked Rory to have in me, I owed *her* better than that. So I headed out to meet the self-appointed king of the scions.

Malcolm was waiting in the hall outside, his expression impenetrable, but it was fair to say it wasn't happy. "Come down to the lounge?" he said, his voice as emotionless as his face. He didn't want an audience for this hashing out. Any sign of division between the four of us would only reflect badly on all of us.

"Sure," I said with forced cheer. "I could use a drink."

Malcolm didn't say anything on the way down. When we came into the basement lounge, Connar was at the pool table, taking what looked like an aimless shot at the scattered balls. He straightened up at the sight of us, his jaw tightening. He might not be the sharpest tack in the box, but he knew this conversation wasn't going to be a pleasant one.

Declan hadn't graced us with his presence, but he was no doubt busy with aide business or baron business or whatever other responsibilities he'd added to his plate now. Sometimes I wondered if the guy had started to thrive on stress the way the rest of us were fueled by fear.

I walked straight to the bar cabinet and went about mixing myself a Jack and Coke. Malcolm stopped by one of the couches, folding his arms over his chest.

"What do you think you're doing, Killbrook?"

The temperature of his tone had dropped by about fifty degrees. Between that and the switching to last names, he might as well have aimed the tip of a sword at my throat.

"Making myself a drink," I said breezily. "I'd have thought that was obvious." I lifted my glass as I turned to face him, giving the dark liquid a little swirl.

Malcolm glowered at me. "You know what I mean. What the hell is going on between you and the heir of Bloodstone? We're supposed to be shaking her up, not cozying up to her. And I told you to keep your hands off."

My smile hardened. "You told me not to 'hit and split', if I recall correctly. I'm not planning on splitting. And shaking her up was *your* plan, not mine. It's gotten rather boring, don't you think? I'd rather appreciate who she is than rearrange her into something else."

"*Who she is* is a joymancer-sympathizing, feeb-loving party-crasher who thinks we're all assholes and is doing whatever she can to stick it to us."

"Has it ever occurred to you that maybe we *are* assholes?"

Malcolm tossed his hands in the air. "Fine. We're assholes, which we need to be because we've got a whole bunch of other assholes to keep in line when the time comes. She's chipping away at all the authority we've had here, all the authority we're going to need when we're barons."

I grimaced. "Is that your father talking or you?"

Maybe that hadn't been the wisest jab to make. Malcolm's eyes flashed, and his voice came out even tighter. "We should want the same things. She doesn't give a shit about the pentacle or everything they've built. She'd probably be happy to see it all come crashing down, the way she talks."

He might be right, but then, I didn't think we'd given Rory much reason to be happy to stand beside us either. I took a sip of my drink, the mix of sweet and sour tingling over my tongue. "Well, so far she hasn't seemed very impressed by the authority we've managed to exert over her. I'm comfortable with changing my own approach. You feel free to do you."

"It's starting to work," Malcolm said. "It might have already worked if you'd been holding up your end. We're in this together. We're supposed to have each other's backs."

A sudden surge of anger welled up inside me, hot and prickling. "Are we? And when exactly have *you* ever done anything for *me*?"

For a second, the Nightwood scion just stared at me. "What the hell are you talking about? I'm looking out for the rest of you all the time. I got us this room we're standing in right now, didn't I?"

"Which you enjoy just as much whether we're here or not."

"That's not— Fine. How many times did I get the seniors you kept mouthing off at to back down when you first got here? Or smooth things over with one teacher or another because you'd had one too many of those and couldn't keep your snark to yourself." He motioned to my glass.

My shoulders tensed. I might have hit the alcohol a little heavier than had been smart my first year here, but

I'd had plenty of shit I needed to drown. Shit I never could have told the guy in front of me about, because he'd have tossed me out of here faster than I could blink. He was loyal to a fucking concept, not *me*.

"You like playing the big man who has everything under control," I said. "Back then, I let you. I could have handled all that myself like I do now."

"If you believe that, you don't have a very good memory."

Connar stepped closer to us with an appeasing gesture. "Guys, I don't think—"

"How about this?" Malcolm barreled on. "I probably saved your fucking life that one night, making sure you didn't choke on your puke when you downed that whole bottle of scotch. I was the one who found you. The three of us sat there for *hours* working out how to conjure some of the alcohol out of your system to make sure your heart didn't stop beating. Or do you think you could have handled that on your own too?"

I'd shoved that night into the deepest depths of my memory. It came back at his words with a sickening rush of cold. My tongue flew before I'd had time to think about my response. "I'd bet I could have. I wouldn't be the first freshman to ever get blackout drunk. And were you even thinking about me or only the fact that if you'd had to go to Ms. Grimsworth about it, she'd have kicked us out of here and you'd have lost your precious lounge?"

Malcolm's voice came out in a snarl. "You—"

"*Guys.*" Connar stepped between us, shoving us back from each other, his own expression tensed. I'd heard him snap at plenty of other people, but never at any of us. He looked from Malcolm to me and back again. "Just stop. We shouldn't be arguing like this."

"*He* should remind himself what loyalty is," Malcolm muttered, but he turned away with a rough exhalation. Because of course he could get himself back under control just like that. How much could a guy who held himself in that rigid a fist ever care about anyone but himself?

I downed the rest of my Jack and Coke and resisted the urge to toss the glass at Malcolm's head to see how he'd respond to that. "I suppose I'll take my leave, then. Have a wonderful night."

"Jude," Connar said as I stalked to the door, but I ignored him. His first loyalty was to Malcolm, always. I didn't need to hear him explain to me how wrong I was too.

All the buried emotions the fight had stirred up churned in my gut as I climbed the stairs to the main floor. The thought of shutting myself away in my bedroom made me sick. I hesitated in the hall outside the library and then strode out across the green to Nightwood Tower.

The main music rooms for orchestra practice were on the lower floors of the tower, but there were a few smaller ones for private practice tucked away near the top. I'd often thought the layout had been planned that way on purpose to give the scholarship students' lungs an extra work out on the way up. You couldn't really play until you could breathe the music.

No one was in the tower at this time in the evening. I didn't pass a soul on the way up to the piano room, which was exactly the way I preferred it. I'd come to Mr. Hackov, the main music professor, for further instruction beyond what I'd taught myself, but he was the only one in the school who'd ever heard me play. He was the only one anywhere who'd heard me play. I could only imagine what Dad would make of *this* little hobby I'd picked up.

I closed the door, sat down on the bench, and rested my fingers on the keys. My hands moved automatically, falling into the patterns of the Beethoven sonata that was one of my more recent acquisitions.

The muscles in my fingers stretched, and as I leaned into the melody, the world narrowed down to just me and the instrument and the rising song. The notes spilled out around me and through me, washing over everything else and covering it back over much faster and more thoroughly than anything in a bottle had ever been able to manage.

I wasn't quite so lost in the song that I missed the squeak of the door. My body froze, my head jerking up.

Rory was standing there by the door that was just a few inches ajar, her fingers curled around its edge. She froze too, with a guilty expression. "Hey," she said warily.

If she'd walked in on me getting out of the shower, I'd have felt less naked. And not the kind of naked I'd imagined getting with this girl. Fuck.

I dropped my hands to my lap and cast about for my composure, pulling my mouth into a smile I hoped look casual. "Hey, yourself. What are you doing up here?"

She eased inside and closed the door gently behind her, but she didn't come any farther into the room. Her dark eyes searched mine with an intentness that made my mouth dry up. She'd seen more than I'd have wanted her to, that was for sure. A reoccurring theme with the heir of Bloodstone.

"I was in the library—I saw you and Malcolm going downstairs. I figured when you came back up, we might be able to talk."

I raised an eyebrow. "And instead of talking to me right away, you followed me over to the tower and up to the fourteenth floor without saying a word."

She bit her lip. "You seemed to be in a hurry. I wondered where you were going."

"So you snuck along to find out." I laughed without needing to force it, finding a little comfort in teasing her. "Hell, you must have used magic to stop me from hearing you. You're getting the fearmancer tactics down pat, aren't you?"

A blush colored her cheeks. "I'm sorry. I didn't mean to intrude."

"Sure you did. That's okay. I like seeing the sly side of you." Maybe if we focused on that, we could forget whatever side of me she'd seen before I'd noticed her.

No such luck. She hesitated and then said, "Are you all right? You looked— I know Malcolm can't be happy."

"Which is why it's a good thing I don't much care what he thinks of me. I've got to get my practice in sometime." I tapped the keys gently.

"I didn't know you played."

"It's not something I widely advertise. People would be

lining up demanding I put on concerts and so on, you know. It'd really be too much hassle."

The corners of her mouth twitched upward. Score. Making light of a situation always allowed it to go down so much easier.

"You're good," she said with a teasing note in her own voice. "Maybe you *should* put on concerts."

I made a dismissive sound and shifted over on the bench. "It's not all that hard once you get the basics down. Come here. If I can teach you how to drive, I can teach you piano."

She lowered herself onto the bench leaving a careful few inches between us, but there weren't the built-in barriers the car provided. My arm brushed hers as I leaned over to grasp her hand, positioning it over the keys. Her soft skin warmed my fingers. I focused on that and not how close the rest of her body was to mine.

"You can play the chords. That's C major. This is G major. A minor. F major. Again?"

She repeated them with a couple of adjustments from me. After the third run-through, I gave her an approving nod. "Perfect. Play them in that order, and I'll handle the rest."

"That's a song?"

"It will be."

She started playing the chords at a steady rhythm, and I let my fingers trip over the keys, improvising a melody to match the simple pattern. I could hardly call myself a composer, but my spur-of-the-moment invention wasn't half bad, really.

I sped up, making the song more intricate and adding a flourish here and there, and Rory laughed. In the middle of that, she lost track of her progression and fumbled with the keys.

"Ack," she said. "I ruined it."

"Can't ruin what's just noodling around. You kept up just fine."

She looked down at her lap and then, with a determined air, reached out and took my hand in hers, twining our fingers together as they came to rest on the bench between us. My heart skipped a beat. I was abruptly afraid to say anything in case whatever fell out of my mouth destroyed the moment.

I'd never worried like this with any other girl. I'd just gone for it, and most of the girls I'd gone for had been happy to have my attention for however long I felt like giving it, which I'd admit was generally not very long. But Rory wasn't like any other girl I'd known.

I'd thought, when I set this friendship or whatever it might become in motion, that I was mostly being strategic. How had I become this marshmallow of a guy who simply wanted to see her smile at me, who got giddy over her holding my hand, for fuck's sake?

I didn't know, but I wasn't sure I minded either. I just wished I could be sure I wouldn't fuck things up. This was all unfamiliar ground.

"Malcolm was angry with you," she said. It wasn't a question.

I shrugged, running my thumb over the back of her

hand. "He told me to fall in line. I told him to go fuck himself. It was a very productive conversation."

"I don't suppose he mentioned anything about what magic he's been working—or trying to work—on me?"

"No, unfortunately he didn't reveal any of his evil plans. I'm sorry—I should have pushed harder on that." I should have prodded him about exactly what he had going to "shake up" Rory before I'd laid into him. There was no way he'd cough up anything he wouldn't want her to know to me now. Damn it. Thinking before I spoke wasn't a particular talent of mine.

"That's all right. I guess it's a little much to hope that he'd hand you everything I'd want to know just like that." She paused. "I didn't get a chance to thank you for last night."

I looked at her with half a smile. "For what? I told you, I was simply defending my own honor."

She gazed back at me with so much compassion in those deep blue eyes I wanted to drown myself in them. "There were a lot of ways you could have done that. You made a statement. I realize that—and I appreciate it."

Had she leaned a little closer to me? I thought she had. I took a gamble.

"I did get a kiss out of it." I ducked my head to brush my lips against her cheek. Her breath came out with a slight hitch. She didn't pull away. No, she was definitely easing toward me with a tightening of her fingers around mine.

I dipped lower and pressed another kiss to the corner of her jaw, the caramel sweet smell of her skin flooding my lungs. I wanted to taste her everywhere, but this would do for now. I trailed my mouth down to the side of her neck. Her pulse thumped against the gentle flick of my tongue.

"Jude," she said, her voice rough. I pulled back, with only a minor pang of disappointment since I hadn't been sure she'd welcome my affection even that much. I was about to make some flippant comment to carry us through any awkwardness of the moment when she traced her fingers over my cheek and drew my mouth to hers.

Yes, thank God. I could have kept waiting, but Lord knew I hadn't wanted to. I ran my fingers into her silky hair as I kissed her back, reining in the urge to claim her mouth with everything I had in me. Her lips were even softer than the rest of her and just as sweet, and when they parted, the breath that met mine was searing hot.

My Bloodstone scion. My Ice Queen. My avenging angel. Mine, mine, mine. The thought rolled through me with the pounding of my heart, but I wasn't really aiming to make her mine. I was aiming to be hers. Her ally, her friend, her lover, her whatever-the-hell-she-needed-me-to-be, as long as it meant she'd have me, one way or another.

I'd assumed I'd have to fall one way or another, sooner or later, but maybe not. Not if she'd hold me up here with her.

I released her hand to slide my arm around her back, tucking her closer against me. Rory let out a hungry sound and kissed me harder. I could almost feel the power of her magic thrumming through her as if her body were a live wire. It turned me on like a shock of electricity straight to my groin.

My fingers teased through her hair, over her shoulder, and down the side of her chest, just barely skimming the curve of her breast. Rory's breath stuttered—and not entirely with desire. A flicker of anxiety passed from her to me.

I rested my hand on her waist and forced myself to relinquish her mouth. "We don't *have* to do anything." I murmured, our faces still so close together my nose bumped hers. "If it's too much—if you want to stop—"

"I'll let you know," she said before I had to keep going. She gave me a shyly sly smile. "For now... The kissing is good. Please continue."

I chuckled and caught her mouth again.

Yes, the kissing *was* good. This girl was good—good enough to stake my entire future on.

CHAPTER SEVENTEEN

Rory

"Do you think it's possible?" I asked Imogen, leaning my elbows on the dorm room table on either side of my now-empty lunch plate. "Could a sickness spell be passed on through someone's familiar?"

She tapped her spoon against the bottom of her bowl. The sweet tomato-y smell of the soup she'd eaten still laced the air. "Like I told you before, I'm not an expert at this stuff yet. And offensive magic isn't what I'm specializing in anyway. But from what I do know, I don't see why it *couldn't* be possible. It can't be what's going on with Professor Banefield, though."

I frowned. "Why not?"

"He doesn't have a familiar anymore," Imogen said. "Someone asked him about it in one of my classes with him. He got a little sad-looking and said the one he'd had for a long time had passed on, and he didn't plan on taking another one." We'd already been speaking quietly even though we were alone in the common room, but she lowered her voice even more. "I heard from one of my dad's coworkers that it's because of his wife."

"How so?"

"It's really tragic. She was in a car accident down by New York City years back. A drunk driver came out of nowhere. She was hurt so bad she couldn't call for anyone to help, and the Naries who showed up couldn't do enough to save her. The worst part is, she was pregnant, but not far enough along that they could rescue the kid either." She grimaced. "Anyway, he and his wife got their familiars together—cats that were sisters. I guess for him it was one last connection to her. When his cat died, he didn't want to get another one."

"That's awful," I said. "The whole thing about his wife, I mean." A pang of sympathy ran through me. Banefield had always seemed so warm and easy-going with me— other than when I'd gotten on his case about Shelby and her tree, anyway. The poor guy.

My mind slid back to my own parents with a flash of memory: Mom's defiant face, blood on the kitchen tiles. I closed my eyes for a second as my own grief welled up the way it did here and there without warning. Breathe into it and breathe it out.

I was going to get justice for them. That was the only reason I'd stayed here at the university. Maybe Banefield would help me, whether he realized he was doing it or not —if I could help him first. I owed him either way.

"What about—" I started, and cut myself off at the

squeak of the door. Shelby slipped into the dorm room, her face brightening at the sight of us. My jab of resentment at the sight of *her* was chased by a pinching of guilt. It wasn't her fault I couldn't talk about anything magical in front of her.

"One more week until the concert," she said, coming over to the kitchen with springier steps than usual. "We're going to knock your socks off."

I had to laugh. "I can believe it, with all that practicing."

She peered into the fridge and sighed. "I should have gotten more food yesterday."

"I've got some sandwich fixings left if you want," I said. "Although then I should probably get some groceries too." I checked the time on my phone. "I've got class in ten minutes, but when I'm out at two, you want to make a trip of it?"

"Sure." Shelby beamed at me, and even the little bit of resentment I'd felt faded away. Maybe I couldn't talk to—or around—her about one important part of my life, but she was a good friend, and she obviously appreciated my friendship a lot too.

I glanced at Imogen, who would have been an even closer friend if betrayal hadn't soured the pot. She gave me a wry smile as if she suspected my internal dilemma.

She had answered a lot of my questions about the whole magical illness thing, even been willing to look Banefield over herself. And she hadn't acted too weird about whatever commotion I'd been making during my repeated sleep episodes. Maybe we weren't going to be best buddies now, but I could still enjoy her company without giving away anything too personal.

"Do you need anything in town?" I asked. "We could make it a group trip."

She hesitated, and my gut clenched. Her gaze darted away from me. Oh. Apparently she was starting to rethink associating with me, at least outside this dorm room, after all.

"I stocked up not that long ago," she said, getting up. "But thanks."

I tried not to let her retreat faze me. Maybe she really just didn't want to make the walk. Shelby hummed an energetic tune at perfect pitch while I cleared my dishes and retrieved my sandwich materials from behind the illusion that concealed them, careful not to let the Nary student see. I focused on that upbeat sound as I headed out for my afternoon seminar in Illusion.

So, the sickening spell couldn't be coming through a familiar. I'd have to find another angle. If I could have at least seen Professor Banefield... I'd heard he'd been moved to his quarters for comfort but was still too sick to even think about returning to regular work.

An idea tickled up in the back of my head. Maybe it didn't need to be *me* who saw him.

I wasn't so distracted by working out logistics that I forgot my duty to my league when I stepped into the classroom. My gaze darted across the faces of the five students already in the room as I murmured "Franco" with the intake of my breath. I got a burst of imagery from an argument with the parents here and hit a wall there, but the girl in the middle of the room gave me a flash of a scheme to shift into mountain lion form and leap through the room the moment we were all focused on the lesson.

I caught her eye and stepped up to her desk, bringing the best authoritative tone I could to my voice. If I was going to cut down on the chaos at Blood U, I needed to do it in a way these people would respect.

"I'm usually a cat person, but I think you'd better stay in human form," I said, loud enough for the whole room to hear. "No credits for Physicality today."

The girl shrank back in her chair with a stutter of fear to my chest and a glitter of frustration in her eyes. Professor Burnbuck looked up from his desk and tipped his head to me as I sat down in the corner. "Credit to Insight."

A guy who'd been at our league meeting caught my eye from across the room and let out a short but appreciative whoop. I was proving my strategy worked. At least I'd made progress in one area, no matter how minor, today.

———

Declan's smile when he greeted me at the aide's office door looked weirdly stiff, and everything he said as we got started on our tutoring session was a little more abrupt than usual, as if he were getting it out quickly before he accidentally said the wrong thing. At first I thought maybe it was because one of the other teacher's aides was consulting with a student at the other end of the room. But even after they left, he didn't relax.

"Is something wrong?" I asked.

His gaze jerked to mine, with a tensing of his jaw that told me something definitely was. "No, everything's fine," he said.

I eyed him for a second and then pretended to let it go. But a few minutes later, I said casually, "Can you test my wall right now? Give it a good shove? I think it's strong enough, but it's so hard to tell."

"Of course." Declan fixed his gaze on my head and murmured his casting word that I still hadn't been able to make out. At the same time, I whispered my own.

He had to let down his defenses to try to attack mine. Maybe he'd get a glimpse inside my head while I did this, but that was a fair trade for a quick peek at whatever was pinging around at the front of his.

I fell into his mind with the rush of sensation that was becoming familiar. Only a few scattered images flitted by before he launched me back out again with a slam of his wall—Declan wasn't any slouch—but I'd seen enough: a sliver of a memory of Jude leaning in to kiss my cheek in the hazy light outside Ashgrave Hall.

I hadn't known Declan had been in our audience the other night, but he must have been with the bunch of Insight league-ers who'd been heading back to the dorms. Apparently the moment had stuck with him.

"What was that about?" he said, not just abrupt but sharply now.

"You're acting strange, and you wouldn't tell me why. I'm just practicing my skills. Isn't that what a good fearmancer would say?" I gave him a tight little grin.

"Do you have a problem with me and Jude being… friendly?"

Declan ran his fingers through his hair, but he looked as if he'd relaxed a little having the subject out in the open. "It's not really any of my business, is it?" he said, and looked up at me again.

The brilliance of those hazel eyes sent an uncomfortable shiver through my chest. It wasn't any of Declan's business, and I shouldn't have cared whether it affected how he thought about me, because he'd made it abundantly clear that nothing anywhere near that friendly was ever going to happen between him and me. I couldn't deny that I was still attracted to him, though.

How greedy was I? The memory of kissing Jude the night before, alone in the piano room, came back with a rush of heat—I didn't regret that for a second. But I wasn't sure I'd have turned Declan down if he'd gone for a kiss himself. Imagine having both of them. Two mouths on me, two sets of hands traveling over me…

Okay, Rory, back to reality. Clearly that interlude with Jude had woken up all kinds of desires that weren't happy about being kept bottled up. I wasn't going to throw myself into an orgy. Not that Declan was offering in the first place.

Another, much more unnerving thought struck me. "Do you think he's being real with me? He hasn't— You guys have your meetings in the basement all the time. If he's said something—"

Declan cut me off with an emphatic shake of his head. "I don't know what he's thinking or why he decided to change his, er, approach, but he hasn't said anything when I've been there that makes me think he's got ulterior motives. It's not part of any bigger plan, anyway. Malcolm is definitely very pissed off about the whole thing."

That matched up with what Jude had told me. He'd *sounded* like he was telling the truth. And the way he'd looked when I'd first peeked into the room, when he'd had no idea I was even there, his expression so lonely and lost... That hadn't been the face of a guy celebrating the culmination of a plan. That'd been the face of a guy who'd crossed a line with his friends he wasn't sure he could ever cross back over.

And he'd done it for me.

"You know," Declan said tentatively, "no matter how much he means whatever he's said to you right now... He doesn't have any siblings. There's no immediate family for the barony to pass on to. It'd cause a whole lot of chaos if he threw his position away—and I've never seen any indication that he'd want to do that."

Oh. I hadn't thought about that angle—I'd barely accepted the idea that I wanted to kiss Jude, so I sure as hell hadn't been considering future marriage plans. It'd actually been kind of a relief to know that he wasn't making some kind of play because of my status, since he had the exact same clout.

He had sounded awfully serious when he'd talked about what he admired about me, about being willing to wait for me, for a guy who only expected this to be something temporary, though.

"I didn't realize that," I said. "I guess that's something I should talk to him about."

"Yes. Talk to him." Declan let out a dry laugh. "It *isn't* my business, and I've no claim here, but… I don't want to see you get hurt. Not like that." He paused. "How do you feel about him?"

"I—" I brought my hand to my mouth, inadvertently stirring up kissing memories again. We hadn't gone much farther than that, but just the kissing had been thrilling enough to burn into my mind.

With Jude. Jude Killbrook. Another part of me still balked at the idea.

"Confused," I settled on. "Very, very confused."

Declan's mouth shifted into a pained smile. "None of us has made it very easy for you, have we?"

"Well, at least I know for sure Malcolm hates my guts. That's pretty straight-forward."

"I'm not so sure about that," Declan muttered. I guessed Malcolm's maliciousness could be plenty complicated.

Being the guy in charge obviously mattered a lot to the Nightwood scion, and I wasn't surprised that Jude might enjoy that kind of authority, but…

The question tumbled out. "Why is it so important to you? Being baron—ruling over people? Or are you just worried about causing chaos too?"

Declan stiffened. "It's not that. It's—" He paused, his gaze sliding across the room. "I have a little brother. He's seventeen now—he was practically a newborn when our mother died."

I didn't need to ask to know how much his brother meant to him. It was written all over his face. "He could take the barony, then, couldn't he?"

"Maybe. I haven't put him in a position where he had to consider it." Declan looked at me again. "My aunt—my mother's sister—took over as regent baron when I was younger. She wants the position for herself and her family."

I cringed, remembering Imogen's story about Connar's parents. "Has she tried to attack you?"

"So far she's stuck to undermining me in ways my father and I have been able to overcome, and she hasn't risked making too big a move out of fear of being caught, but the older we get... As long as my brother and I are alive, we're the primary heirs. We're a threat to her goals. As long as I'm holding onto the barony, I'll be her main target. She'll leave Noah alone. I've put everything I have into making sure I hold onto my position so she never has any reason to set her sights on him."

Something he'd said in our tense moment in the library came back to me. *Everything I have, I had to fight for.* I'd accused him of taking the easy route, of not caring enough to put in a real effort. No wonder he'd been angry.

He'd made himself a shield to protect his brother. Anything I asked from him beyond the requirements of a job might as well be an attempt to crack that shield.

A deeper emotion stirring beneath the constant flickering of attraction. The fearmancer world must feel as much like a war zone to him as it did to me. All the strictness and the attention to rules that had frustrated me weren't just for his own gain but a set of defenses he no doubt needed to survive.

And he'd done it. He'd kept his position and shielded his brother for how long, without an elder baron to really guide him?

Because the joymancers had killed the baron who should have been there for him, to shield *him* from his aunt's machinations.

"When did you take over the barony?" I had to ask.

"Six years ago," he said, which in my quick mental calculation put him at fifteen. At that age, all I'd had to worry about was finishing my latest homeschool assignments. "I started insisting on sitting in on meetings a few years before that. I'm still not full baron, though. My aunt has the right to stay on as my 'advisor' until I finish my education here."

"So this has basically been your whole life." Had he ever gotten to really be a *kid*?

"It's what I was born for. I'm doing my best with it." His smile came back, small but genuine. "You don't need to worry about me, Rory. I'm happy with my choices."

He just hadn't had very many. I dropped my gaze and rubbed my mouth, abruptly lost for words. "Are we okay to keep going with the tutoring?"

Declan blinked, startled. "Of course. I'm sorry I let my concerns about Jude interfere with our work. I'm not allowed to be jealous—can't get much more straight-forward than that."

It didn't sound easy to me, but I wasn't going to try to argue him out of helping me. Especially not when there was a specific way I'd been hoping he could help me deal with whatever crap Malcolm had brewing.

"Good," I said. "There's something else I'd like to focus on for the rest of our time today. We went over some techniques before for basic defenses during sleep, but I'm... not sure they're totally doing the job. Any more intensive strategies you know, let me at them."

CHAPTER EIGHTEEN

Rory

I glanced up and down the hall of wooden doors and murmured as quietly as I could, "Are you *sure* you're up for this?"

Deborah adjusted her position in the loose sleeve of my blouse. Her fur tickled against my wrist. *It feels good to be getting out of that dorm building for once. If I can help you more than I've been able to so far—this is what I'm here for.*

"Okay." I pushed down the twinge of guilt. I wasn't putting her in that much danger. The health center mage who was coming by a few times a day to check on Professor Banefield had left ten minutes ago. I'd watched him exit the building. No one else should be in Banefield's quarters except the professor himself, who I didn't think was alert enough right now to notice one little mouse.

I curled my fingers so my familiar could drop down

into them and peek around the hall herself. "Do you see any gaps you could squeeze through? That's his door, the next one on the right."

There's a gap at the bottom of the frame I should be able to manage. I'm discovering the best thing about old buildings is they've had lots of time to warp. Her dry chuckle tingled through my head. *Let's do this, Lorelei.*

I stopped just outside Banefield's office door and knelt as if to adjust the strap on my shoe. Deborah darted from my hand and squirmed through the gap under the door in two seconds flat. My pulse hiccupped as I straightened up again, but I couldn't linger there. I had to give her time to make her investigations and then pass by again when she'd be waiting.

Thankfully, I had a perfectly good excuse to go calling on the headmistress. I hadn't talked to Ms. Grimsworth since Banefield's second collapse, other than briefly right after I'd called for help. She couldn't blame me for having questions now that he'd been sick for more than a week.

I'd made an appointment, so the headmistress was expecting me. To my surprise, she answered the door and immediately ushered me out into the hall instead of welcoming me into her office.

"You're coming by with excellent timing, Miss Bloodstone," she said. "I would have requested your presence later today if you hadn't gotten in touch. Given the uncertain state of your mentor's health and how new you still are to the school, I've decided it's best if I assign you a temporary substitute mentor while Professor Banefield continues to recover."

He was that bad, then, that she didn't think he'd be able to offer me guidance again any time soon? I swallowed hard. "*Is* he recovering? That was actually why I wanted to see you—I know the health center let him return to his apartment here..."

"He has shown progress," Ms. Grimsworth said with a grim expression that suggested it hadn't been much. "They don't feel he's in critical condition at the moment, and he's more comfortable in his own space." She motioned me down the hall.

"Do they know what exactly he's sick from?" I ventured. I wasn't sure it was safe to outright ask about the possibility of malicious magic being involved, but it made sense for me to worry in general. "I saw him in between the two episodes—is it something contagious?"

"From what they've told me, there's no apparent threat to the rest of us. If there was, we'd have him taken to his home off campus." She stopped in front of one of the doors down the hall and rapped her knuckles against it.

I hadn't had a chance to ask her who she was assigning as my new mentor, but the plaque on the door told me in an instant. *Prof. Isla Viceport.*

Oh, shit. The Physicality professor had been chilly with me from my first seminar with her, for no reason I could figure out. When I'd asked her if there was anything wrong with my performance in class, she'd brushed me off with a cutting remark. And since I'd started my new schedule with two Physicality seminars a week, I'd been struggling to keep up. My conjurings and transformations kept falling apart even as I tried to build them up.

Professor Viceport had not been impressed. Her cold disapproval hadn't exactly helped my concentration or confidence.

"I—" I started, fumbling for a protest that wouldn't sound pathetic, but it was too late. Viceport opened the door and peered at us through her rectangular glasses. Stick-thin, her tall frame looked as if it'd been made out of sinew and wire, but she managed to hold it with a certain elegance that made me feel small under her gaze.

"You're already familiar with each other," Ms. Grimsworth said briskly. "I'll let you two discuss how you'll proceed with Miss Bloodstone's mentorship until such time as Professor Banefield can return to his post."

She nodded to Viceport and headed back down the hall, leaving me stranded there with the teacher whose gaze had only gotten icier as she'd studied me.

"Well, come in," Viceport said in a clipped voice, and spun so quickly her ash-blond pixie cut fluttered around her head.

Her office looked a lot like her: sleek, pale, and elegant. She had the same built-in mahogany bookshelves as the other staff offices I'd been in, but her chairs were modern white leather, her desk glass-topped. A light peach rug covered most of the hardwood floor.

I sank into one of the chairs opposite the desk automatically, my hands coming to rest on the cool leather arms, but Professor Viceport stayed standing, her lips pressed into a pinched frown.

"I will assist with any issues you have beyond your classwork as need be. I trust you are mostly up to speed and settled in at this point." She lifted her phone from the desk. "Let's determine the best time for our weekly meetings, and that should cover it for today. Will Tuesdays at four work for you?"

"Um, I have a seminar then. I was seeing Professor Banefield in the morning on—"

"I can't keep to your original session time. Five on Tuesdays or three on Thursday?"

"Three on Thursday should be okay." I reached into my purse to make a note for myself, and Viceport stepped back to the door. She really didn't want to spend any more time with me than she absolutely had to, did she.

I got up as she rested her hand on the doorknob, but my nerves jittered. I'd expected to be able to maintain a decent conversation with Ms. Grimsworth to give Deborah the time she needed. I didn't think she'd have finished her investigations yet. I couldn't just stand around in the staff hallway for minutes on end waiting for her to emerge.

There had to be ways I could stall. I fumbled for another topic—the one I'd brought up with the headmistress should work. Viceport specialized in Physicality, after all, which was the domain any health-related magic fell under among the fearmancers.

"Have you seen Professor Banefield since he got sick?" I asked. "I don't know if you've done much work on the medical side of Physicality…"

Viceport gave me a flat look. "I haven't seen your former mentor. What exactly do you think I could tell you if I had?"

"I just wondered if you had any idea what's wrong. He does seem to be pretty sick—it's hard not to worry."

The professor sighed. Her voice came out not just chilly but frigid now. "Miss Bloodstone, I realize you've gotten much fanfare for your return and your assessment, but regardless of your family, the world does not revolve around your desires. The health center staff are looking after Professor Banefield. He will recover on his own time regardless of how much you'd prefer to continue consulting with him rather than me. His needs come before your own at this particular moment."

My face flushed. "That's not—that wasn't what I meant." Why did she have to take a totally normal expression of concern and turn it into something horribly selfish?

"If you insist." She turned the knob to open the door.

She might have been a professor, but there was only so much of that cool, cutting tone I could take before my temper flared.

"What exactly is your problem with me?" I said. "We're going to have to see each other even more than usual now. Whatever it is, you might as well tell me so I can at least try to do something about it."

Viceport stared down at me, just a hair shy of a glare. "I know Bloodstones well," she said. "The apple rarely falls far from the tree, and I haven't seen any reason to believe it did this time. I will teach you. I will not be your friend."

She tugged the door wide. I wavered for a second and then walked out with no idea how I could answer that. She'd known Bloodstones? Great. I hadn't known any of them. I couldn't even be totally sure whether being like my mother and whatever other relatives I had on that side was a good thing or a bad one by my definition.

I ambled down the hall as slowly as I could without my hesitation being obvious. To my relief, as Professor Viceport's door clicked shut behind me, I caught a glimpse of a tiny nose peeking from beneath Banefield's door.

The hall was empty, but I bent down like before to collect Deborah, making a show of adjusting my other shoe. She scrambled up my sleeve to nestle at the crook of my elbow. The billowing of the blouse hid her small shape completely.

I didn't dare say anything knowing Viceport might come back out at any moment, but my familiar didn't need prompting.

He was in his bed. His breathing sounded hoarse. He tossed and turned a few times, but he seemed to be asleep. I went through the whole apartment and didn't sense any harmful magic. No sign of a new familiar either. She paused. *Every time he turned over, he scratched at his knee. I'm not sure if that's a sign of anything.*

I didn't remember anything in my reading specifically about knees. Maybe Imogen would have some idea, if she was willing to entertain more of my increasingly odd questions about magical illnesses.

At least Declan's latest tips had seemed to work to keep my mind shielded last night. I'd had a nightmare, but only the regular one about the morning my parents died. I'd woken up sweating but with my possessions intact and my throat feeling normal. I didn't think I'd done any shouting this time.

We'd see how long it took my dormmates to forget how ill *I'd* started to appear to be.

As I came up on the dorm building, I spotted my least favorite of those dormmates. Victory Blighthaven's auburn hair gleamed a little even in the shadow around the side of the building, where she was saying something to a guy I'd seen around. From the wave of her hand and her fierce expression, I got the impression they were arguing. As I slowed to watch, she gave him a little shove and disappeared around the back. The guy headed my way.

I wouldn't have given the moment much thought except when the guy saw me, he sped up. He caught up with me before I'd reached the doors and held out a hand for me to wait. I stopped, all my senses going on high alert.

"Rory," the guy said with a smile that was probably supposed to be smooth. "I hear you're a hard one to impress."

"Are you planning on trying? Because really, I haven't asked anyone to, and you should probably save yourself the trouble."

His mouth tightened, and then he barreled onward. "If you saw what I'm thinking about, you might not say that. I also hear you're quite the pro at Insight."

Was he daring me to try to delve into his mind? A wary prickle ran up my back. I didn't like this at all.

"All right, I'll take a peek then," I said, but I kept my mental shields tightly in place.

Either the guy didn't have enough insight skill to tell whether I was prodding his mind, or he was too focused on his scheme to pay attention. "*You want to go on a date with me*," he said, in a raspier version of the sort of tone Malcolm took on when he was working a persuasion spell. "*You're going to walk with me over to my car right now.*"

His effort pinged right off my defenses, but that didn't make me any happier about the attempt. I drew my posture straighter, ready to tell him off, when a brawny form jumped in, grabbing the guy by the arm.

"What the fuck do you think you're doing to her?" Connar demanded, his fingers squeezing the guy's bicep so hard the guy winced.

My stomach lurched. I'd been pissed off at the guy, but I was even more pissed off at the scion who'd intervened.

"I'm fine," I said. "He didn't manage to do anything. Let him go."

Connar frowned, but he released the other guy's arm. I glared at my supposed suitor. Had Victory put him up to using that spell on me? "Get the hell out of here. You try something like that again, and I *will* dive into your head, and I'm sure I can find all kinds of things in there you wouldn't want anyone finding out."

Being caught between two scions had obviously rattled the guy pretty badly. He hustled away without a backward glance—or an apology. I guessed that would have been too much to ask.

I turned to Connar. My gut knotted all over again. "You can get the hell out of here too. I don't know why you bothered stepping in, but I didn't need it. I'm *never* going to need any help from you."

He didn't budge, so I veered around him and strode into the hall. After a moment, footsteps thumped after me. I ducked into the stairwell, but Connar could cover a lot of ground fast. He caught up with me halfway up the first flight. I stopped before he could come up beside me, bracing my hands on the railings on either side, taking a little extra strength from standing a couple steps higher than him. For once, I was looking down at him.

"What?" I snapped. I might have the advantage of height, but being alone in a relatively enclosed space with the Stormhurst scion made my skin want to leap off my body and run away. Deborah was still crouched against my inner elbow, but she couldn't do anything to help.

Every part of me ached with the memory of the tenderness Connar and I had shared and how brutally he'd torn all that to shreds. The words he'd hurled at me echoed in my head.

You don't mind getting down in the dirt, do you? You can start begging any time now.

Connar hesitated, uncertainty sitting strangely on the planes of his chiseled face. The dim light of the stairwell turned his pale eyes from blue to a misty gray. A hint of his familiar scent, musky and smoky like vetiver, touched my nose, and I gripped the railings harder. I was not going to feel sympathy for any supposed vulnerability he showed.

"I don't *like* how this all happened," he said finally in his low voice. "But it's better this way. Okay?"

I bit back a harsh laugh. "No, that's not okay. What would have been okay is if you'd figured that out before you strung me along. Do you expect me to forgive and forget just because you've decided it's 'better'?"

He shifted his weight, his mouth twisting. "It's complicated. Everything here is complicated. You should know that by now."

"There was nothing complicated about us. You convinced me to trust you and then you stabbed me in the back, plain and simple."

A shadow flickered across his face. "You never would have trusted me anyway if you'd known everything about me."

"Is *that* your excuse?" I did laugh then, short and choked. "I know now. I heard all about your parents and how you supposedly destroyed your brother. But you know what? If I'd heard it back then, I would have asked you about it first. I would have listened to what you told me about it. And if I'd still seen the good in you that I thought I did, I'd have trusted you anyway. So don't blame me for judgments I never even made. This is all on you. And I guess your good friend Malcolm too."

Connar's expression hardened at that last comment. "You have no idea who *Malcolm* really is either. I've stood with him because he's earned it."

"And I didn't earn any of that loyalty?"

"It's not— You don't know. He's been there for me for *years*."

"Fine." I eased up a step. "Then go tell him how wonderful he is, and leave me alone."

"Rory..." He reached into his pocket and held up a small glinting shape that sent a bolt of nausea through my center. "I kept it. I remember what you said. Everything I've done, it's just trying to be—"

Fuck that. As I looked at the little dragon figurine I'd conjured for him out by the cliff, that I'd given to him telling him he could be his own person apart from the other scions, tears pricked at my eyes. That right there was the faith I'd had in him—the faith he'd burned to the ground.

"*No.*" That one syllable carried all the power I needed it to. I flicked my hand with a clench of my fingers before he could get any further with his justifications, and the little figure crumpled into the specks of metal dust that had formed it.

Connar let out a rough sound. His fingers snatched after the dust as if he could hold it together.

"If you want credit for being the person I thought you could be, then you need to make it happen for yourself," I said, not caring that my voice was shaking, and spun to hurry up the stairs.

This time, the Stormhurst scion didn't follow.

CHAPTER NINETEEN

Rory

"Credit to Insight," Professor Crowford said with a slightly bemused expression. My fellow student from the Insight league gave a little bow and smirked at the guy whose spell she'd just pre-emptively diffused by revealing his intentions. Then she glanced at me with an expression I wasn't so used to around here—looking for approval.

I gave her a thumbs up, because why not? I was glad not to have to watch the dude cast his nauseating illusion —no doubt the maintenance staff would really have appreciated the clean-up afterward—and she'd gotten the drop on him at the last minute. The other leagues were becoming more guarded at the beginning of class now that they knew we'd be scanning them. I hadn't read anything from him in my quick skim coming in.

Malcolm hadn't said anything during the whole

exchange. It wasn't his league the girl had interrupted anyway. He lounged casually in his seat with a bored expression. But when Crowford motioned for us to get up and go, I felt the Nightwood scion's attention on me.

Fortunately, I'd picked a seat closer to the door. I hustled out and down the stone steps, looking forward to the warm spring air outside. The music department's concert was starting in ten minutes. If Malcolm wanted to hassle me, he could wait until after I'd seen the performance Shelby was so excited about.

Unfortunately, I didn't make my getaway quite fast enough. Maybe the other scion had lent a little magic to his feet. Somehow or other, I'd only come up to Killbrook Hall when his voice rang out just behind me.

"Where are you off to in such a hurry, Glinda?"

I guessed I'd have to get this over with now. I spun around, throwing as much focus as I could summon into my mental shields. "What do you want, Malcolm?"

He prowled around me with a predatory vibe that made me tense up even more. I had to turn to keep facing him. His handsome face stayed calm enough, but a spark of what I thought was anger already glittered in his dark brown eyes.

"I'd like you to answer my question," he said, cool with just a bit of edge.

I set my hands on my hips. "Where does it look like I'm going? The end-of-year concert is happening now. I'm going to listen to some music. So sorry if that offends you."

Malcolm's lips curled, but it was hard to tell whether

that tight shape was more a smile or a grimace. "It *is* offensive how quick you are to run off to see what the feebs are going to do."

"I was under the impression most of the school goes to listen. They're here because they're freaking good musicians, aren't they?" I sighed and moved to walk past him.

He caught my wrist, jerking me to a halt. "You really still think you can just ignore me."

I glared right into his eyes. "It's been working all right so far."

"Then you haven't been paying attention. I can still play you like a puppet. You were born for this, but so was I, and I've been *living* it while you were off playing house with the joymancers who slaughtered your real parents."

The words brought back the images from the battle I'd unintentionally summoned up in the desensitization chamber. The screams, the violence on both sides. My stomach lurched.

I gritted my teeth. "I know who my real parents were, and I'm not afraid of you. As you should be able to tell. Not feeding your magic one little bit right now, am I? So let go of my fucking arm before I have to make you."

Malcolm released me, but he laughed as he did. "I've gotten plenty from you, Bloodstone. You just never know where and when. You're never going to make it, here or anywhere else until you throw in your lot with the right side." He lifted his chin in the direction of the pavilion where the concert was being held. "You might not want to go over there. Things could get dangerous."

My body stiffened. "What are you talking about? What are you going to do?"

"What have I *done*, you mean. It's already in motion. You'll be just fine back here, though. It's not as if there's anything you can do to help."

For fuck's sake. There would be if I knew what the hell he'd planned. I eyed him while he gave me that cocky smile of his. I'd gotten past his own mental defenses before, but I didn't think he'd fall for the same trick twice. Maybe, if I dove in there sharp and fast...

I turned as if I were going to head toward the pavilion anyway. Malcolm chuckled. As the sound reached my ears, I whipped back around and aimed my gaze at his forehead with a hastily whispered word. "Franco."

My magic surged up my throat. My awareness shot forward as fast and narrow as I could focus it—and sliced into the barrier I'd been expecting.

Not quite far enough. I jarred against Malcolm's internal wall before a single impression reached me from his mind. Just as my effort fell away, he spoke the command he must have been holding at the ready.

"You will do as I say. Stay out of my head."

The persuasion spell flitted straight into my mind past my own lowered barrier the instant before I yanked my defenses back up. The commands jangled through my thoughts. Shit. I opened my mouth to try to catch him now that his mind was vulnerable, and my tongue faltered.

He'd ordered me to stay out. The persuasive power of that order was wriggling through my brain behind my mental shields now. I couldn't force the casting word to launch my Insight spell out.

"Give me a little curtsy, Glinda. Let's see how well you can bow if you have to."

My legs swayed despite myself. He hadn't even needed to add the lilt of magic to those words. The impulse to obey him was embedded in my mind as well. I dipped my head to him with a scream of frustration locked in my throat.

Malcolm was outright grinning now. "Not bad. We can work on that. How about a spin?"

My body swiveled in an awkward twirl. I wasn't going to add any more grace to it than I was compelled to. I closed my eyes, shutting him out, trying to train my attention on the energy of his casting moving through my head. All I could sense was a faint quivering through my nerves.

It was almost impossible to diffuse a persuasive spell once it'd hit its target. You either waited for its power to fade on its own—or you put up obstacles to fulfilling it.

I'd done that before, when he'd tried to walk me out one of the tower windows. I could do a more elegant job of it now. "Wall," I murmured, picturing the air hardening into an invisible barrier fit right against my body.

"Come back here," Malcolm said. My muscles shifted and strained as my conjured wall held them perfectly in place. The Nightwood scion sighed. "What have you done to yourself? There's no professor around to intercede just because you tried hard. You know I can break whatever you conjured up."

"Go ahead and try it," I shot back.

The faint strains of orchestral music carried across the field and past the building behind me. Damn it, the concert was starting. I didn't know if Shelby would even notice I hadn't turned up, but if she did, I might lose the one person who'd been there from me since I first got here. The way the other fearmancers treated her, she'd probably assume I'd been faking my appreciation for her musical talent.

My expression must have shown my worry. Malcolm stepped closer, cocking his head. "Getting a little scared now, Bloodstone? I don't even *have* to break whatever armor you've put on. You still can't get to your precious feebs like you wanted to. And you can't stop up your throat. Why don't we have a chat? I'll tell you want I want to know—and you'll answer any question I ask."

Oh, fuck, fuck, fuck. If he started prodding me, he could stumble on information that'd put me in deep shit not just with him but the entire administration in a matter of seconds. Unless...

"What would—" he started, and I jumped in.

"Not if I shut you up," I said, urging my magic into a physical punch of energy to jam Malcolm's mouth closed. I trained all my will on muzzling him. If he couldn't talk, he couldn't activate the persuasive spell any more.

Malcolm's jaw clenched as he attempted to open his mouth, but I was plenty strong in Physicality, and today my efforts appeared to be holding just fine. Fury blazed in his eyes. He looked down, humming to himself, and shook his head with a snap and a crackle in the air. My muzzle shattered.

"Don't you dare—" he said with a rasp.

"Shut up," I snapped again with another burst of magic, and his lips smacked together. He glowered at me as he moved to free himself again.

I didn't know how long I could keep this up. The magic churning behind my collarbone was starting to burn and fray. I'd accumulated a lot simply by existing and being Rory Bloodstone, the unpredictable new-found scion, but I'd thrown all I could into each of these castings.

I drew in a breath to try another spell before he'd even broken through this one, and a shriek split the air from the direction of the pavilion.

My heart skipped a beat. More shouts and screams rose up in a wave, punctuated by a clatter of thumps and clangs. My gaze jerked to Malcolm, who'd just wrenched his mouth open again. "What did you *do*?"

To my surprise, he looked momentarily bewildered, staring in the direction of the pavilion where it lay out of our view beyond the hall. Then his expression molded back into his usual arrogant mask. "I haven't got a clue, Glinda. Didn't you realize? I only said I'd messed with the concert to get you to try me. Whoever's having their fun over there, it's got nothing to do with me. You'll have to blame some other villain."

A metallic-sounding crash made me wince. I believed him, if only because of that brief unguarded reaction—and because I couldn't imagine why he wouldn't be rubbing his triumph in my face if the chaos across the field *was* his doing.

I hesitated for just a second, long enough for a pained cry to pierce my ears, and then I smashed the wall I'd conjured around my body with a click of my tongue. The second the pressure left my body, I dashed along the path past the Killbrook Building. If Malcolm called after me, I didn't hear him.

A crowd of at least a hundred students and various teachers had gathered around the open pavilion at the far end of the field. They'd scattered now, some of them running back to the main buildings, some of them holding their ground and staring warily toward the stage. The stage where the orchestra set-up lay in a jumbled mess.

Instruments were strewn across the high wooden platform beneath the pavilion's arched roof, music stands tipped on their sides, chairs toppled. The performers lay sprawled between them. As I dashed over, I spotted one girl clutching her scraped elbow. A boy hissed as he moved his leg, his ankle twisted at an unnatural angle.

A familiar face emerged in the dispersing crowd—Imogen, her freckled face pale. I veered toward her. "What happened?" I said, breathless. "What's going on?"

She hugged herself. "Three bears," she said quietly. "They charged right past us and onto the stage. We could all guess they weren't really bears—you don't get ones that big around here anyway—but the Naries panicked."

Someone trying to top that bear-shifting prank Declan

had told me about. My hands clenched at my sides. "Where'd the 'bears' go?"

If I found the mages who'd put on this performance... I'd find some way to make sure they never did it again, that was for sure.

"They charged off into the woods," Imogen said, and another thought raced through my head with a jolt of fear rather than anger.

"Where's Shelby?"

"I don't know. I saw—she was near the back—I think she might have fallen off the platform."

Oh, no. I took off again, heading around the back of the building.

Two students had taken the four-foot tumble onto the grass, alongside a couple of chairs. One, a boy, was picking himself up on wobbly legs. The other sat slumped with a hand pressed to her temple, her other arm tucked close to her chest. I didn't need to see her face to recognize Shelby's mousy brown ponytail.

One of the staff had already knelt down beside her. "People are coming from the health center right now," he reassured her as I came to a stop a few feet away.

"My arm," Shelby said raggedly with a sound like a swallowed sob. She shifted, and I realized her arm wasn't just tucked against her. It was bent wrong at the wrist, the joint already swelling and red.

A tear streaked down her face. She tightened her jaw. "I'll be okay," she insisted. "It's nothing. Nothing that bad." But I could tell she didn't believe that any more than I did.

CHAPTER TWENTY

Declan

I'd never really enjoyed sitting at my spot around the table of the pentacle of barons, but over the last several weeks, the meetings had become increasingly uncomfortable. Mainly because the other barons—and my aunt Ambrosia, whom I was stuck with here until I could be named full baron—were spending increasing amounts of time interrogating me.

They pretended it wasn't an interrogation, of course. Baron Nightwood, Malcolm's father, smiled the confident smile he'd passed on to his son as he asked one or another prodding question. Baron Stormhurst, Connar's mother, didn't ask anything at all, just made pointed statements framed by huffs of breath. Baron Killbrook, Jude's father, had a perpetual furrow in his forehead as if he were questioning me only out of well-meant concern.

The fifth chair, at the Bloodstone point of the

pentacle, stood empty still. They hadn't wanted to bring Rory in for a meeting until they were sure they could count on her carrying the party line. And that was exactly why so much focus was turned on me.

"You've been seeing the girl twice a week for how long now?" Baron Nightwood said, leaning back in his chair at a casual angle as if he didn't know the answer already. "I'd have expected more progress by now, Ashgrave."

"Not much good having a baron inside the university if he can't get done the things that need doing," Baron Stormhurst muttered.

Aunt Ambrosia shifted beside me, always eager for a chance to make me look bad. "He has taken on so much." She patted my arm with her cool hand. "Perhaps it's more than he's able to handle all at once."

"The Bloodstone scion has a defiant mind," I said, ignoring her remark and keeping my voice even. You couldn't show any emotion around these people if you didn't want them pouncing on it. I had never been so glad that I was the only one of the present barons who'd focused on Insight as a speciality. The others might have decades more experience than me, but my mental wall could keep out their habitual prodding.

As long as they never decided there was grounds for a real interrogation from the inside out, I was safe. I wouldn't be able to stand up to all three of them making a concentrated effort—and blocking them in that case could be considered as treasonous as whatever they'd accused me of.

So I had to make sure they had no reason to accuse me.

"It's taking time, but I've unsettled her with the information I've been able to pass on about the joymancers. I've seen the toll the other scions' efforts are taking on her. She's weakening."

Not really, not hardly, but I had seen bits of pain and worry in her mind here and there, so I could say the words genuinely enough.

"Her mentor has been ill and unable to advise her for quite a bit of the past month too," I added, watching the faces around me. "That loss of support has clearly put an additional strain on her."

None of them gave any indication that this was a surprise to them or that they knew more than I'd just told them.

Baron Killbrook shifted in his seat. What had Jude told him about *his* activities involving Rory, if anything? He didn't jump in to crow about how his son was pulling one over on the Bloodstone scion, so I supposed that was one more bit of proof that if Jude had some agenda beyond simple affection, it was only his own, not for us scions or the barons.

"You could pay her another visit if your son's efforts are failing in potency," Killbrook said to Nightwood. "You said your mere presence frightened her last time."

Nightwood cut him a dark glance. "From the gossip circulating around the school enough to reach many parents, we've gathered Malcolm's influence has had a rather large impact, actually. The girl has been giving the increasing impression of instability. Some of the families have encouraged attempts at wooing her anyway, but whatever social support she stood to gain in the aftermath of that assessment has greatly deteriorated."

I stayed silent. Rory could build her support back up. The exercises we'd gone through a few days ago should have strengthened her defenses even while unconscious. However the hell Malcolm was managing to affect her from across the building, his influence was going to diminish. Better if they thought it was the result of her own practice and research than my intervention, though.

That thought came with a sharp little pang and the memory of Rory challenging me that same day about my devotion to the barony. If she *had* been here and disagreed with something the others were talking about, she wouldn't have kept quiet. She'd have told them exactly what she thought of their smugly callous attitudes.

And then probably they'd have found a way to beat her down completely, despite her being the only Bloodstone left. I didn't have even that security. I was easily replaceable.

Still, in that moment, I missed her straightforward, no-nonsense approach. Maybe her priorities and loyalties weren't all the most sensible, but fuck, she knew how to take a stand.

"Besides," Nightwood added with a haughty air, "how would it look to the community if we spent our time negotiating with a teenager? Let the boys do their work, and when she's as wobbly as they can get her, we can bring her in and sort her the rest of the way out here."

Stormhurst nodded with a blunt grin. My stomach clenched, but I forced a smile as I tipped my head in supposed agreement.

I didn't know if I could save Rory and myself, but I'd do whatever I could to make sure she was strong enough not to be crushed when that day came. She deserved to take her place here as she was, ready to divide and conquer, lit up with determination to follow what she felt was right. She deserved the chance to come into her own without these jackals who were supposed to be our leaders tearing her apart.

Maybe I couldn't *have* her, but seeing her in the pentacle unbroken would make this job I'd taken on ten times more tolerable. I might even start looking forward to the meetings.

The discussion turned to a recent business venture that needed our approval, but tension lingered in the room, thick enough that it itched at my skin. I wasn't sure how much more time the other barons would give Rory. They were restless to get on with the plans they'd been making before I was around, the ones I was starting to suspect they weren't going to share with me at all until they believed they could browbeat me out of any complaints I raised four to one.

I left the meeting to a dreary spring day outside, warm but so overcast only thin sunlight penetrated the layer of gray clouds. After I'd sunk into the driver's seat of my car, I let out my breath fully for the first time since I'd walked into the pentacle building.

Like all the baronies, the Ashgrave estate never wanted

for money. I could have had a chauffeur drive me to and from the meetings like the other barons generally did. I liked the feel of the steering wheel beneath my hands and the sense of control that came with revving the engine, though, especially afterward.

I had another tutoring session with Rory tonight. Another hour of tightrope walking between my various loyalties. Another hour of tamping down every other feeling her smiles and wry remarks stirred up in me. All the same, thinking about it, my pulse increased its tempo in anticipation. I couldn't deny I'd enjoy her presence even with the difficulties it brought.

Back on campus, I had a quick dinner and headed to the aides' office. I'd gotten there early, but Rory was already waiting by the door, her face drawn. My heart squeezed at the sight of her.

"Hey," I said carefully. There wasn't anything unprofessional about asking after a student's wellbeing when they looked so obviously distraught. "What's wrong?"

"Everything. This place. It's so—" She cut herself off with a sound of frustration. "I know *you* can't do anything about most of it. I just wanted to get on with the parts you can help with. If I'm too early—if you had something else you needed to get to first—"

"No, it's fine." I had been going to look through the archived records involving joymancers for another to add to the growing collection I'd been offering her—for background, for broadening understanding, for recognizing that those people she held in such high esteem *were murderers too*—but that could wait. "Come on in."

She strode past me when I opened the door. Rather than taking a seat at one of the tables, she paced from one end of the room to the other between them, her shoes tapping against the hardwood floor. A chill had crept into the room with the absence of sunlight. I flicked on the switch for the gas fireplace on the wall, and its faint warmth started to seep through the room with the wavering of the flames.

"He got in my head again," Rory said abruptly, coming to a halt. "Malcolm. He managed to mess with me, and I could hold him off but I couldn't completely *stop* him. If I had, if I'd been able to get over there in time like I meant to..." She exhaled in a rush. "I know he's your friend. I know you can't pick sides or whatever."

"Yes, I'm supposed to stay out of conflicts between students as long as no official rules are broken. That doesn't mean I *like* everything I see."

What had Malcolm done to her now? Despite all the confidence I'd had in her strength behind the report I'd given to the barons, she *did* look rattled, more than I'd seen in a while. The urge rose up in me to march right over to wherever Malcolm was and throttle him until he came up with some other strategy.

He kept doing this kind of thing because it was working, slowly but surely. It would keep working unless I could give her the tools to keep the essential parts of herself steady.

Rory made a dismissive gesture. "It doesn't matter

anyway. I'm a scion. I'm going to need to know how to stop *everyone* from messing with me. That's what anybody here would say, right? I have to learn how to kick people out. I have to be able to cut off a persuasion spell if someone manages to sneak one in. There's got to be more you can teach me, more I can do."

"Of course there is." I stepped closer to her, holding up my hands as if she were a wild animal in a snare that might bite me even if I meant to free it. "Some of the techniques will be beyond me—things you'll be able to work on with Professor Sinleigh when you move up to having sessions with her, but I do know a few additional strategies you can try."

"All right." She shuddered as if shaking the tension out of her body. "Let's get to it then."

Rattled and frustrated but ready to leap to the challenge all the same. I girded myself against the twinge of desire that ran through me.

"Cutting off a spell that's already inside you is tricky," I said. "The most important factor to start with is a deepened awareness of your mind itself, so you can sense where the magic is working and interrupt it. Close your eyes, and see if you can shift your focus through the different areas in your head—the ones that activate when you breathe, when you move your hands or adjust your posture, when you focus on the tastes in your mouth or the sounds that reach your ears."

Rory let her eyelids drop, her fingers curling into her palms at her sides. After a few moments, her mouth pressed into a tight line.

"I can't sort it all out. I'm *thinking* too much. It's like the thoughts and feelings keep churning around getting in the way of everything else."

"That just means you have a fully functioning brain." I hesitated and let myself walk right up to her. This was what I'd have done for any other student. I just had to keep any of my own feelings out of it.

I rested my index fingers against her temples, just a light pressure. "Focus on my touch. Then spread your attention just a little farther into your mind from there. See what those parts light up to. Let the rest of the clutter fade into the background."

Her skin was warm and smooth beneath my fingertips. All of me warmed up standing this close to her. It took a conscious effort not to trail my gaze over the slant of her nose, the curve of her cheeks, down to those delicate pink lips that parted just slightly now.

"Okay," she said, her voice slow and distant. "I think I see what you mean. How do I go deeper than that?"

"Slide your awareness back." I eased my fingers across her head, into her soft hair. "Push the thoughts back with it. Can you do that?"

Her expression tensed with concentration. Then a little light came back into it. "Yeah. It feels easier when you put it like that. Not completely *easy*, but…" She opened her eyes, gazing into mine. "Thanks."

Her hand came up, probably intending to replicate the pressure point herself, but it ended up settling over mine. She hesitated and then let her fingers slip around my palm to give my hand a gentle squeeze of gratitude.

Her gaze darted down to *my* mouth, and in that moment she was barely shielded at all. I hardly needed to reach to absorb the thought at the front of her mind. She was thinking about kissing me. Wanting to kiss me, with a longing I could taste. It echoed through me, drawing out my own.

She didn't, though. Just as easily as I'd gleaned that first impulse, I felt her clamp down on it and hold herself back.

For my sake. Because I'd told her I couldn't, and she had too much honor to cross that line. Fuck, that only made me want her more.

She had more self-control than I did in that moment. I couldn't quite force myself to pull back from her. My other fingers came down to brush over her hair, the most innocent of caresses. Rory swallowed audibly, her eyes locking with mine again.

No one was here. No one would know if I gave in just this once. If I offered what Jude no doubt already had. Whatever the hell he was up to when it came to Rory, I didn't trust his intentions to be totally pure. Up until now, he'd gone through girls like daily specials.

If I showed her she could have me that way after all, maybe she wouldn't fall for him. Maybe it'd be just one more way I was protecting her.

I wanted to believe that, and that was the problem. I couldn't trust my judgment. I was just looking for excuses.

I lowered my head, not to bring my mouth to hers, but just to bow it next to her, my cheek brushing her temple where my fingers had rested a few minutes ago. My hands came down to rest on her shoulders.

"I can't," I said hoarsely.

"I know," Rory said. "I wouldn't—I wasn't…"

She didn't seem to know how to go on. Suddenly it seemed very important to make one thing clear, to let her know she wasn't alone.

"It's not just for me. What we're doing here—it's the only way I can protect you. I don't want anything else distracting me from that.

She nodded, just slightly, her hair grazing my face with its sweet smell. "Okay. Okay. Thank you."

She should wait to thank me until I'd actually succeeded.

CHAPTER TWENTY-ONE

Rory

When I came out of my bedroom the second morning after the concert, most of my dormmates were hanging out in the common room, eating breakfast or just chatting. All of them got a little quieter at my entrance, which was normal these days even though I'd managed to get through the past night with no nightmares at all. They all also directed their attention away from the bedroom door farther down the room—the one that had been Shelby's.

Someone had conjured a burst of rainbow glitter around two words in twinkling silver script. *Goodbye feeb!*

The words set my jaw on edge. The message wasn't for Shelby. The glowing writing was clearly magical, and no one here would have dared to break one of the school's few but particularly firm rules: Never let the Nary students witness anything they'd realize was magic.

But no one in this room had to worry about a Nary student seeing that display. Shelby had been sent home yesterday. With her fractured wrist, she wouldn't be able to complete the last few weeks of the term or the special summer session. Unless it healed unusually fast, she probably wouldn't be able to keep up with the other student musicians for months after that either.

Chances were, she wasn't coming back. A fact she'd clearly known from the agony written on her face as she'd left.

As soon as I'd heard about the decision, I'd gone to Ms. Grimsworth in protest. This was a school for mages, for fuck's sake. If I could conjure dragons out of the earth and ice out of the air, surely someone here could meld a broken bone back together. Shelby didn't have to know it'd ever been broken.

"It's against school policy," the headmistress had said, so calmly I'd wanted to scream. "The safety of our students and their ability to continue operating within the Nary world undetected is our first priority. Several other Nary students witnessed Miss Hughes' fall. Miss Hughes saw and felt for herself how badly her wrist was injured. There's too much chance of someone noticing signs of the supernatural at work if we attempted to simply wipe the fracture away."

"It's not fair," I'd said. "She worked so hard to be here, and she only fell because of a stupid prank she had nothing to do with."

Ms. Grimsworth had been unmovable. "We provide the Naries with opportunities and training beyond any they're likely to find elsewhere in exchange for the benefits they provide to the other students' training. She was lucky to have gotten as much instruction as she did here, free of tuition. I'm sure she'll find plenty of options open to her in the Nary world once she's recovered—naturally, without magical intervention."

Shelby wouldn't see it that way. She'd kept trudging to classes half delirious with fever because it'd mattered so much to her to keep her spot. I hadn't been able to figure out anything else I could do for her, though. Even if I'd wanted to risk healing her myself with whatever fallout might come from that, I had zero medical training. I might have made her arm even worse.

And now someone—most likely the angelic-faced, viper-temperamented girl whose lips had curled into a smirk at the dining table—had decided to rub that failure and my friendship with Shelby in my face. I'd have liked to stuff a shovelful of glitter down Victory's throat.

"You look a little sick," Cressida sniped from her seat next to Victory. "Another bad night for Princess Bloodstone?"

The nickname Connar had used affectionately and then in taunting grated on my nerves. If I was acting weird right now, it was because of the crap they'd done with the full intention of upsetting me.

I held my anger in check and glanced over at the two of them, keeping my tone perfectly neutral. "I'm fine. Just thinking about how pathetic it is to slap someone in the face and then mock them for their cheek being red."

Victory's gaze snapped to me at that comment. She stood up, flicking her auburn hair over her shoulder. "I don't think 'pathetic' is the kind of word you should be tossing at other people. You want to throw down? Make it a real challenge. I'm right here."

Did I want to get into a magical battle with the queen bee of Villain Academy at this particular moment? Not really. I had enough on my plate without escalating the tensions between us into full-out war. Anyway, it would annoy her more if I acted like I didn't care.

"I don't want to fight with you," I said as evenly as before. "I never wanted to fight in the first place."

She made a derisive sound and dropped back into her seat. "Because you know you'd never win."

That might have been true at first, but she didn't really have a clue how far my skills had developed. We hadn't had a real stand-off. That would probably happen eventually, the way she kept pushing. I'd be happy to surprise her when push came to shove.

Today, I just walked out of the dorm. I'd already eaten one of the muffins I'd been keeping in my bedroom away from anyone's spoiling spells, so at least I didn't have to worry about breakfast. Someone, maybe Cressida, snickered as I stepped out.

Had my refusal to fight looked weak? I couldn't find it in me to care about my social status when people were getting kicked out of school or possibly dying here.

I made it down to the first floor before it occurred to me that I didn't really know where I was going. I didn't have any classes until late in the afternoon. The sight of the library's vast bookshelves just made me feel more hopeless. Nothing I'd found in there had let me help anyone I'd wanted to save.

I wavered in the hall as a few students wandered by, debating my options. Then a familiar lanky figure emerged from the stairwell.

A grin stretched across Jude's face when he saw me. It was hard to remember, seeing the genuine pleasure in his expression, that there'd been a while when every smile he'd aimed my way had been sharp, mocking, or both.

I wasn't sure which was stranger: that or the answering warmth that lit up in me as he walked over.

His appreciation wasn't enough to wipe away my sense of futility, though. His grin faded as he took in my face. He slipped his hand around mine as easily as if we'd been holding hands from the start rather than barely having touched until a short while ago. "What's wrong?"

"What isn't might be an easier question to answer." I let out a strained chuckle. "I'm just... tired." Tired of this place. Tired of having to keep a strong front while the weight of all the things I had to grieve or worry about piled higher. I missed my parents, missed my real home, with an ache that radiated through my chest.

Jude cocked his head. "Are you up for a drive? I had something special planned for our last outing—since obviously you hardly require my instruction anymore."

"Until we switch to piano," I said.

Jude's fingers tightened for a second, and I remembered how startled, almost nervous, he'd looked when I'd walked in on him that night. For whatever reason, he kept his hobby secret.

I made a gesture as if zipping my lips. "Sorry. I think I could drive. Where are we going?" Jude had proven himself good at coming up with excellent distractions so far.

His grin came back. "My secret. I promise it's good enough to take your mind off just about anything."

He swung our hands together casually as we walked out to the garage. A few of the students we went by watched us for a little longer than just a passing glance, but Jude didn't show any sign of caring. I guessed he'd already made a big enough statement about where he stood when it came to me.

When we reached my car, he stopped and tugged me a little closer. My head came up automatically to meet his kiss—our first kiss since the ones in the piano room.

The heat of his mouth lit me up like a torch, but what really gripped my heart was the gentleness of the gesture, as if he felt he had to leave plenty of room for me to pull away in case I'd changed my mind about the whole kissing thing.

Whatever was forming between us felt as fragile to him as it did to me. It mattered to him to be careful with it. Somehow that reassured me in a way nothing he said could.

He drew back with a satisfied hum. "I could do that all day, but I did promise you we'd take this car somewhere beyond the garage."

"I'm expecting big things from this secret surprise," I

said as I opened the driver's side door. "It'd better deliver after all this build-up."

He sprawled in the seat beside me. "What horrors should I expect if it doesn't?"

I arched an eyebrow at him. "I'm sure I could think of a few ways to express my disappointment."

He laughed. "Will I be frozen from head to toe this time, Ice Queen? I'm not worried. I keep my promises."

My pulse no longer sped up with anxiety when I eased the car out of its stall and drove out to the road into town. The motions were becoming automatic, the thrum of the engine more comforting than unnerving. The thought of driving somewhere completely on my own still made me a little uneasy, but maybe I'd start slow like I had with my drives with Jude. I could buy a lot more groceries at a time if I took the car into town.

The day was warm enough that we rolled down the windows. Jude leaned his arm partway out, the wind tussling his hair. "Do you want to tell me about any of the many things that are bothering you?"

He said it lightly but with enough gravity to make it clear he was asking honestly. I glanced over at him for a second as the shadows of the trees at the side of the road rippled over the car.

There was something different in his tone and in the general energy he gave off today. He'd pretty much always kept up a breezy, don't-give-a-shit demeanor when I was around, other than during the picnic when our conversation had turned briefly serious, but now... now he looked actually *relaxed*, in a way I hadn't realized that he wasn't before because I hadn't had the real thing to compare to. As if he didn't feel the need to keep up his usual frenetic pace and jokey attitude with me anymore.

My mind leapt back to that evening interlude in the piano room again—to the way he'd fallen so quickly into banter, the raw emotion I'd glimpsed vanishing beneath it as soon as he'd recovered from his surprise. If that wasn't how he acted when he was actually comfortable... how much of the joking and mockery was for his enjoyment and how much just a different sort of shield?

I didn't want to talk to him about Shelby. If I heard him call her a "feeb," I really might slam him with ice. His dismissive attitude about Naries was something we'd have to talk about eventually if this was going to become more than a little kissing here and there, but I wasn't in the mood to hash it out right now.

I could mention a different worry, though. "My mentor—Professor Banefield—has been really sick for a while now. No one seems to know exactly what's wrong, and I haven't been able to see him... He doesn't seem to be getting better."

Jude's forehead furrowed. "It's not often one of the professors is laid up for very long. Is there something you need to see him about?"

I also wasn't ready to tell him about my near-certainty that Banefield's sickness was part of some conspiracy against me. I shrugged. "I'm just worried about him. I was there when he first got sick. Maybe it's silly, but I feel like if I could talk with him, see how he's doing now, maybe I could help figure out what's going on."

"That sounds like the sort of thing you *would* think." Jude gave me a crooked smile. "But you're not thinking enough like a fearmancer. Someone told you you're not allowed to visit him? Who the fuck cares? If you can magic your way in without anyone realizing, that's your permission right there."

Oh. I... really *hadn't* thought about it that way, but he was completely right. That was how any other fearmancer would have looked at the situation. Rules didn't matter, only whether you could slip around them effectively.

"Those seem like extreme measures to take when I'm not sure what I'd be looking for... but we'll see," I said.

"Feel free to call on me if you need back-up," Jude said. "I do enjoy a good scheme."

We drove down the highway that we'd taken to our picnic spot until we'd gone about a half hour beyond that dirt track, and then took a turn to head farther south. Jude scanned the farms, forestland, and towns we passed rather than the street signs, as if watching for landmarks.

"Take a right here," he said after we passed a highway restaurant-slash-antiques shop. Five minutes later, he sent me left down a narrow but neatly bordered road through the thicker forest.

The road widened where it came to a wrought-iron gate in a high brick wall, the bars so close together I couldn't make out much other than a blur of green and brown on the other side. I eased us to a stop.

"Is this your family's place?" I said warily. The wall and

the gate gave me the same vibe as the main buildings at the university—fearmancer tastes in architecture. Did Jude figure he was going to impress me showing me around whatever grand home his family owned? I didn't think I was ready for the meet-the-parents step.

Jude chuckled. "No, this is *your* place."

CHAPTER TWENTY-TWO

Rory

I blinked at Jude, thinking I'd misheard him. "My place?"

"The Bloodstones own about twenty-five acres here," he said, getting out of the car. "All behind that damned wall. Your parents didn't usually take visitors here—no one I've talked to has ever been on the property. The guys and I have always been curious what's in there. I mean, you've got a big foreboding stone mansion that was the main residence too, but we all have one of those."

I stepped out after him. "Is this trip for my benefit or for yours, then?" I teased, but my heart had skipped a beat with excitement along with my nerves. My first glimpse of the properties I'd inherited. The whole reason I'd wanted to drive in the first place. I didn't know how much poking around I'd be comfortable doing with Jude around, but still… Whether I liked the heritage I'd stumbled into or not, whatever lay beyond that wall was *mine*.

"Oh, I'll freely admit I'm looking forward to this as much as I hope you are." Jude's eyes glinted with anticipation. "If you touch the panel at the right side of the gate there, it should be spelled to open for any Bloodstone."

I walked up to it and set my hand on the warm metal. It tingled beneath my palm, and a lock thudded over somewhere I couldn't see. The gate swung open ahead of us. I found myself holding my breath as I entered.

The paved road narrowed again on the other side of the gate, leading to a wooden garage building that stood next to what by fearmancer standards must have amounted to a cottage, even though it was three times as big as my parents' place back in California. The whole thing was dark fine-grained wood: two sprawling stories beneath a tented roof with a gleaming weathervane spire shaped like a rearing horse and a broad deck stretching around the two sides that I could see.

The yard sloped down toward a glittering pond with a beach of what looked like crushed quartz directly in front of the house. Closer to us stood a prickly looking hedge with an arched doorway that had been coaxed out of the brambles. The whole property looked perfectly maintained, as if the owners had only just stepped out for the day.

"Will there be anyone else around?" I said with sudden apprehension. "Ms. Grimsworth said there were people looking after the properties... and I guess there's my grandparents."

Jude shook his head. "I asked around. No one due today. And any grandparents of yours still around don't have any claim on this place. Bloodstones only."

"Not much respect for in-laws, I guess?"

"Not when it comes to baron holdings. And especially not when they make asses of themselves." He shot me a sideways glance. "I don't know how much you've heard about your dad's parents, but I've heard *my* dad and grandfather complain about them. Apparently from the moment your mom took up with your dad, they've been pushing in, grasping at every bit of prestige they could reach for."

Lovely. "I'm glad I told Ms. Grimsworth I wasn't interested in a family visit, then."

"A smart move, I'd say. Now let's check this place out." Jude started toward the hedge with a clap of his hands. "Is this what I think... Hell yes." He spun around by the arched entrance, grinning. "You've got yourself a puzzle garden."

"Am I supposed to know what that is?" I ventured closer and made out another hedge beyond the first forming some kind of passage. Like a maze?

"There aren't many of them built because it takes a lot of magic." Jude peered inside. "Apparently there's a huge one just outside London. It's the same idea as a puzzle box, except expanded into an entire garden... They're works of art, really. You make your way between the hedges, and you'll come to doors and gates you can only open if you figure out the trick to the magic. Usually they're made with funnel shapes and conducting pieces."

He'd had me at "work of art." I still couldn't totally picture what he meant, but that just meant I had to see it with my own eyes. "Let's take a look at it then."

Just inside the archway, twinkling gravel like the quartz down by the pond rasped under my shoes. The hedge passage branched in two directions. Several feet to our left, the way was blocked by a wall of brightly blooming flowers that gave off a pungent fruity scent. To our right, strands of silver and bronze appeared to be woven into a barrier of hedge brambles, forming an intricate latticework between the dark green leaves.

"Petals or metal?" Jude said.

The metalwork had stirred the artist in me. I wanted to get a closer look just to see how the pieces had been fit together. "Metal," I said, walking over.

Up close, the pattern became clearer. The strands of metal formed a sort of flower themselves, with expanding rings of interlocking petals around a circular center. Silver and bronze wove together to form that center, holding a shape like a closed keyhole in the very middle.

I touched the smooth surface like I had the lock on the front gate, but the barrier didn't budge.

"It's going to take more than that to get through." Jude leaned forward to consider the piece. "The idea of these gardens is to keep your skills honed—and take a measure of your friends, if you let them at it. There's a trick to each of the puzzles: something you have to nudge with one of your skills. If you choose the wrong one or aim it wrong, the funnels and conductors will throw it right back at you with a zap."

"Funnels and conductors?"

He motioned to the pieces that fit together to form the flower's center. "Certain physical forms can work with magic to direct it, focus it, amplify it, without having any magic imbued in them at all. Some you'll learn to recognize because they're used often enough, but even if you meet an unfamiliar one, you can usually get a sense by carefully feeling it out... This bit here is going to concentrate any energy you send along it toward the narrow end, for example."

The part he was pointing at had a ridged hollow in its curved silver body, wider at one end than the other. I bent down to study it. The narrow end led to a gold piece that was dotted with little craters.

The magic at the base of my throat tingled. I could picture how energy might flow through one part and then disperse in a dozen directions as it hit those marks.

But maybe the "funnel" could direct a spell toward just one crater, and it would bounce the magic somewhere useful? I touched the pock-marked piece, and it turned at the press of my fingers. A little gap formed between it and another gold piece above it, revealing a small channel carved there. The arc of that piece carried it around to the keyhole spot.

"How do I know what kind of spell to cast?" I asked.

"I think there should be clues in the design—or sometimes the puzzle will make it obvious. I've never actually been in one of these before, only heard about them." He cocked his head. "Flowers are usually a symbol of persuasion. Do you want me to give it a shot so I'll take the zap if I'm wrong?"

"No, I'll try it." A weird sense of possessiveness had come over me. It was my garden, my puzzle. I adjusted the first gold piece until I was satisfied with the angle, and then I murmured a spell into the silver funnel. "*Open.*"

The energy leapt from my tongue, and the metal pieces shone. The cratered bit shivered. Then the plate covering the keyhole snapped up, and all the metal strands pulled apart to form an opening we could walk through.

"Never mind. You've clearly got this all in hand." Delight lit Jude's face as he followed me into the hedge passage beyond.

He caught me by the waist from behind and pressed a kiss to the crook of my neck. My body lit up in turn. I lifted my head to catch his lips, and he spun me to face him so he could deepen the kiss.

Standing there with his arms around me, a prickle of guilt wound through my gut. Just last night I'd stood almost this close to Declan—I'd wanted to kiss him almost as badly as I wanted to keep kissing Jude right now. Nothing could happen between Declan and me, but still…

I drew back just a few inches. "Jude," I said, "what are we doing here?"

He gave my forehead a quick peck with a smile. "I think the idea was taking your mind off your troubles."

"No, I mean *everything* we're doing. What are you looking for out of this? I know—I know how the inheritances work. That if we were going to be together, really together, long-term, you'd be giving up the barony."

His mouth trailed down to brush my cheek. "What's the need to think about that just yet? I'm nineteen. You don't have to worry about me proposing after a couple of dates. Right now, this is just… getting to know each other."

I swallowed hard. It was difficult to think clearly with him so close, the smell of him filling my lungs with a spicy zing like pepper and coriander. "But, if it's never going to be possible, what's the point of heading down that road?"

"Who said it's impossible? There are options, if that's where we end up." He pulled back for a second, his expression puzzled. "Are you *asking* me to make that kind of commitment right now?"

My face flushed. "No. I'm nowhere near ready for that either. I just—I guess I'm trying to figure out how seriously we're taking this. If it's just having fun together knowing it won't go anywhere—whether we're making any commitment at all… *Are* we dating? Is that what you're looking for? You mentioned other girls…"

I wasn't sure I'd made a whole lot of sense trying to get my thoughts in order, but Jude's expression relaxed. "I thought we could figure it out as we go. I'm definitely not taking anything off the table for the future. But all my attention is yours right now, Rory. There's no other girl I want."

The words stuck in my throat for a second before I pushed them out. "What if I'm not sure I can say the same thing about other guys?"

Jude's eyebrows rose. "Are you seriously considering any of the jackasses who're being shoved at you to make a grab at the barony's coattails?"

No, but I couldn't admit what had passed between me and Declan without putting the other scion at risk. "I don't know. I haven't been making out with anyone else or anything." Only thinking about it. "My world got turned upside down just a couple months ago. I'm still working out who *I* am, how I feel about things—about people... If I decide I'd like to kiss someone else, does that mean we're done? Or is that an acceptable part of 'figuring things out' if I'd still like to be kissing you too?"

My cheeks heated more with that question. Jude let out a rough breath and brought his hands to my face, his thumbs tracing over my burning skin.

"I can't ask you to be all in yet," he said. "I know that. If some other jerk catches your eye, you do what you need to do to be sure. If you do go all in with me, I want it to be because you want me more than anyone else, not because you're afraid to find out what you really want. And if it turns out you really want someone else more, then that'll be my fault for not convincing you I'm your best bet." He winked at me. "I just promise I'll be very convincing."

I had to laugh, my embarrassment fading. "You've already proven that."

Jude kissed me again, just long enough to leave me with a pang of yearning when he stopped. He glanced down the passage. "Shall we see what other wonders await?"

The metal theme continued farther into the puzzle garden. Around a bend, we came to a wall like an immense shield made of overlapping plates. Jude rubbed his hands together as he studied it. "Let me have this one?"

He was so eager for the challenge that now that I'd handled one myself, I didn't mind stepping back. "Be my guest."

He ran his fingers over the plates, finding a few that lifted up. After a few minutes' inspection, he knelt down and whispered beneath one. I caught a glimpse of a lick of smoke vanishing into the shadow beneath. Something whirred within the shield. Then it spiraled open so we could step through.

"I guess you measure up," I said, tucking my hand around his elbow.

Jude beamed down at me. "Let's see what else we can find. I was under the impression these gardens usually had special chambers you could gain access to as well as the main path."

I studied the hedges on either side of us as we walked on, and my gaze caught on a metallic gleam deeper within the brambles. I tugged Jude to a stop. "There's something here."

An intricate metal sculpture like a multi-faceted star hung behind the dense foliage. We peered at it together. Something about the shape struck me as just slightly off. The top point—it didn't extend quite as far as the others.

I hesitated and then whispered, "Grow," pushing a thread of my magic toward it. Seeing how I wanted the silver surface already there to stretch and lengthen, until it touched—

The point brushed a bramble just above it, and the entire section of hedge unfurled, the leaves and twigs pulling back into themselves. My breath caught at the sight on the other side.

I stepped tentatively into the secret room I'd opened up. It was still bordered by hedges, but the colorless leaves on the walls gleamed as if they were made of crystal. The branches between them shone gold. More gold arced over our heads forming a lace-like roof. And by the far wall stood a high crystal seat—a throne wide enough for two or three to sit on.

Jude let out a low whistle. "Fit for a queen. Especially an icy one. Come here, Your Highness."

He swung me onto the crystal throne so swiftly I lost my breath. A pleasant warmth seeped through the slick surface beneath me. Then all I felt was heat as Jude brought his mouth to mine.

The seat put me at the perfect height for us to kiss without him bending at all. My legs splayed instinctively to give him more room. One of his hands settled on my thigh, staying there with a stroke of his thumb across my hip bone, the other tangling in my hair. His tongue teased between my lips, and I gave myself over to the pleasure racing through me.

We kissed, edging ever closer together until every nerve in my body was aware of the seam of his slacks grazing but not pressing against that particularly sensitive part of me. A giddy quiver traveled up through my core.

Jude traced a heated path across my jaw and over my neck. He stopped there with a swipe of his tongue and a nip of his teeth, and a gasp jolted out of me.

His hand slid up my body to cup my breast, and a different sort of jolt shot through me. The memory of my night with Connar on the cliff, the bliss of it wrenched through with the horror of his harsh words the next morning, flooded my head. My body tensed.

Jude stopped in an instant, his hand dropping to my waist, his eyes searching mine. A flicker of pain crossed his face before he schooled it calm again. "You're still scared of me."

I couldn't deny it. He wouldn't say that if he hadn't felt it, and my fear wouldn't have passed into him if he hadn't been partly responsible. I was afraid of giving myself over completely again, afraid of the harshness I'd already seen Jude was capable of.

"It's not just you," I said, to be fair. "The last time I was with someone else like this... things went badly."

Jude made an angry sound. "That asshole feeb? I can absolutely promise you I'll never treat you like you're *nothing*."

He knew from Insight class about my first boyfriend back home who'd ditched me and acted like I didn't exist after we'd slept together. Obviously word still hadn't gotten around about Connar and me. I didn't think I'd have wanted Jude to know about that anyway.

"I'm okay," I said. "But we don't need to rush anything, right?"

"Of course not." He tipped his head to nuzzle the side

of my neck, his lips brushing my skin as he spoke. "What if we made this not about me at all? I solemnly swear to keep my dick in my pants today, even if you end up begging for it."

When I snorted, he straightened up with a smile. "I'm serious. Would that take the fear out of it, if it was all about you? I can give and ask for nothing in return."

The promise in his voice made my skin tingle in anticipation. "That doesn't exactly seem fair."

"Sure it is. I was thinking too much about me when I was an asshole to you before. I know I'm not finished making that up to you."

Maybe it was fair then. My body leaned toward his of its own accord. "I suppose we could just... see how it goes."

His smile widened, and then he was kissing me again, tenderly but fervently. At the same time, he shifted backward so his hips no longer intruded on me quite so closely. Taking away that sense of impending expectations.

It was easier to let go when I knew he didn't expect me to open up to him completely. His fingers stroked over my breast again, but no panic sparked at their touch, only more heat. I gave a little growl and kissed him harder, and he rolled my nipple under his thumb with a pleased chuckle against my mouth.

He slipped his hand under my shirt to fondle me skin to skin, and my breath started to break apart between our kisses. Catching my lip between his teeth, he gave it a slight pinch that set off an even sharper flare of hunger, one that raced right down to my core.

Maybe I shouldn't have snorted at the idea of begging for him. An ache was building between my thighs with each skillful caress.

Jude returned his attentions to my neck, finding the sensitive spot that had made me gasp before. As my head tipped against the back of the throne, his hands dropped lower. One held my hip in place, and the other glided over my sex.

A whimper spilled from my lips. I couldn't stop myself from arching into his touch.

"I've got you," Jude murmured. "I can take you there."

My hips started to rock with abandon as he stroked me, first through my pants and then flicking open the clasp to cup me even more closely. His mouth came back to mine as his thumb swiveled over my clit, and I slung my arm around his neck as I kissed him back to try to counterbalance my growing shakiness. Pleasure spiked through me in waves as Jude's fingers delved deeper and curled right inside of me—one, then another.

"Good?" he asked breathlessly, and all I could manage was a stuttered gasp and a jerky nod. His fingers plunged deeper, all the way to a spot inside me that blazed with sudden bliss. Then I couldn't do more than cling to his shoulders and sway with him as he urged the flames higher and higher.

"Jude," I mumbled. "Oh!"

His voice came out ragged. "Rory, you're so fucking gorgeous. Fucking perfect."

He stroked that blissful spot inside even harder, and my orgasm burst through me like a firework. Jude captured my cry with his mouth. His hand kept rocking with me until the pleasure had burned through my body.

I sagged forward into his embrace, my head nestled against his chest, held by this boy I'd never have thought I could come to trust. This boy who'd offered me more in the last few weeks than anyone else at Villain Academy had been willing to.

———

"Was the outing sufficiently distracting?" Jude asked when we were on the road back to the university. The sun was still high overhead, only just starting to creep down with the waning of the June afternoon, but after exploring the puzzle garden and the rest of the grounds more thoroughly, we'd determined there was no food to be had in the Bloodstone country cottage. My stomach had already grumbled a couple of times in a demand for lunch.

"Absolutely." For a few hours, my mind had felt less like a hornets' nest and more like the placid pond beside the cottage. "I'd been wanting to check out my family's properties. Thank you for showing me the way out here."

"My pleasure." Jude sprawled back in the seat with a smirk that brought to mind all the pleasure he'd conjured in me this morning. "Any time you want to get out of town, I'm your man."

"I'll keep that in mind. It's gotten kind of crazy on campus with all the competing for credits."

"Everyone's got to support their league. I see Insight has been rising in the rankings. Apparently you've had a productive influence there. I expect Illusion can still rule the day, though. I don't plan on serving anyone a feast this term."

The members of the winning league of each term's competition got to eat a celebratory banquet prepared and served by the losers—who had to do a good job of it, or they'd get in trouble with the staff who were partaking too. There was a board up in Killbrook Hall regularly updated with the recent credit additions, but I hadn't checked it recently. I really didn't give a crap whether I ended up in the kitchen or at the feasting table.

"It's ridiculous," I said. "I guess I shouldn't be surprised by how far people are going, but I still think it's too much."

"It's just one more way to practice our skills. Why do you think the teachers encourage it?" Jude tipped his head to the sunlight with a satisfied expression. "You've got to admit that illusion during the concert was pretty spectacular, at least."

Something that was nothing like hunger twisted my stomach. "Illusion?"

"You know, rampaging bears and all. I thought it was a pretty spectacular way to top that last stunt nobody would stop going on about. It's no easy feat getting *three* bears that size moving independently and detailed enough that no one would suspect they're not the real thing."

My grip on the steering wheel wobbled. I'd assumed the bears had been shape-shifting students, but there was no reason they couldn't have been an illusion. I hadn't heard the credit called. But more importantly... "And you'd only know that if you were the one who cast it."

"Hey, I'm not looking for an ego stroke. We all have to do our part. It just so happens I could contribute a large part. The Illusion league is clearly the one to beat."

He was talking about it so breezily, as if it'd been nothing but a lark. My gut clenched tighter. "People got *hurt* because of that stunt."

Jude shrugged, glancing over at me with his brow knit. "A couple of Naries got bruised up a bit. No big deal. If they'd kept their cool, they've have been fine. I couldn't let the things really hurt them—any injuries they caused directly would have vanished with the rest of the illusion."

"There were plenty of injuries caused indirectly! They had no idea the bears weren't real. And my friend didn't just get bruised. She broke her wrist—she had to leave the school because she can't play her cello for who knows how long."

Jude paused, watching me. "Are you really this worked up about a feeb? They know the school is going to be tough. It comes with the territory. The profs make sure they get a good bang for their buck, especially considering they're not paying for anything. If she hadn't panicked, she'd still be here."

"If you hadn't made her think rampaging bears were charging at her, she'd still be here." I inhaled sharply, trying to keep my voice from shaking. I could stay calm. If I just put it the right way, he had to get it. "Do you really not see how that's a problem?"

"Are you really getting angry at me for doing an

amazing job at exactly what we're supposed to be learning how to do? That was the largest and most complex illusion I've pulled off in my life. I'd like to see anyone else top it in the next ten years."

"It's got nothing to do with that. What part of this person being my friend do you not understand? It doesn't matter whether she was a Nary or not."

Jude had bristled. His voice came out scoffing. "Of course it does. They're not at Blood U for us to make friends with them. They're there for target practice and forcing stealth. How can you be 'friends' with someone you can't tell the most basic thing about yourself to?"

My calm frayed. "By realizing there are a whole lot of other things that matter about people. How can *you* go around breaking people's bones and ruining their lives and not care?"

"I didn't hurt any of them on purpose! And that's the whole reason the staff bring them in—so we can use them. I'm sure she learned plenty from the experience."

He said the last bit so bitingly flippant that my stomach lurched right up toward my throat. I jerked the car over to the gravel shoulder and skidded to a halt just in time to throw open the door and vomit what was left of my breakfast onto the asphalt.

For a few seconds afterward, I just stared at the pale splatter on the dark pavement, my mouth sour and my head spinning. The guy saying these awful things was the guy I'd bantered and laughed with for the last few weeks. The guy I'd kissed, the guy I'd let touch me in the most intimate way just a couple hours ago…

He'd started being nice to me. That hadn't changed who he was to everyone else. I simply hadn't let myself think about it all that deeply.

He didn't give a shit that his stupid prank had cost Shelby her dream. He didn't even see her as a human being with a right to have those dreams. She and all the billions of Naries that made up the rest of the world had no rights at all to him.

"Rory?" Jude said, his tone abruptly uncertain.

I straightened up, wiping my mouth, and found I didn't even want to look at him. "Get out," I said as I yanked my own door closed again.

Jude stared at me at the edge of my vision. "What?"

I forced myself to turn toward him then. "*Get out of the fucking car.*"

I hadn't meant to hit him with a spell. I wouldn't have expected it to work even if I had meant to cast magic at him. But either his mental shields had faltered in his confusion or my anger had driven my persuasive magic right through them, because the second my voice crackled through the air, Jude groped for the door handle automatically. He swore as he stepped out onto the gravel, obviously compelled beyond his control. I leaned over to pull the door shut and locked it.

Jude grabbed the edge of the open window. Fear shuddered through me from him, but the whitening of his face looked as furious as it did horrified. "What the hell are you doing? *This* is ridiculous, Rory."

"No," I said. "What was really ridiculous was

forgetting that you'd already shown me exactly who you are. Let go of the car."

"You can't just leave me on the side of the road!"

"We're less than ten miles from campus. You were just telling me what a great mage you are—I'm sure you can figure out a way to make it back there. Let go of the car *now*, or you might end up with a few broken bones too. But I guess that's no big deal, right?" I tugged the gear shift from park into drive.

Jude jerked his hand back. "Rory," he started again, but I didn't wait to hear how he'd try to justify himself next. With my gut still roiling and my eyes burning, I hit the gas and tore down the road alone.

CHAPTER TWENTY-THREE

Rory

The voice echoed up from below as I climbed the stairs to the staff wing of Killbrook Hall. "It was awesome! He had this whole scheme planned out to transform a bunch of stuff, but it was all right there at the front of his mind, easy pickings. I pulled the rug out from under him in just a couple seconds."

"I think Insight really has a chance this term," someone said in answer.

The voices faded away when I headed down the hall, but they left me feeling nearly as queasy as when I'd kicked Jude out of my car two days ago.

It was still more than a week before the winner of the league competition would be announced, and all the students would just keep ramping up their efforts until then. And after that, the process would start all over again. Maybe my strategy of interrupting planned stunts was helping mitigate the damage a little, but at this point I just wished there was no such thing as credit in the first place.

Declan wasn't part of the competition, at least, having to stick to observing because of his teacher's aide position. I walked into the aide's office, and he got up from the table where he'd been paging through a book. But at the sight of his expression warming with a small smile of welcome I could tell he was restraining from getting any larger, I found it suddenly hard to smile back.

Jude had helped me, warmed me up with affection that might have been genuine… and I'd let that stop me from seeing or talking about how he was treating everyone around me.

How much did I really know about Declan Ashgrave and his views beyond the few subjects we'd talked about? He probably saw Naries as just as "feeble" as the other fearmancers. Who knew how many pranks he'd been part of before he'd taken this gig?

It wasn't just my heart I needed to be careful with here. It was the safety of everyone else I'd known and cared about or at least respected beyond the boundaries of this campus.

A couple of the other aides were standing off to one side of the room in conversation, so I couldn't say half of what I wanted to yet. "Should we pick up where we left off last time?" Declan asked, and I nodded, and for the first twenty minutes I tried to train all my attention on magical techniques and not on the motives and feelings of the guy leading me through them.

Declan was obviously wary of being overheard too. He

carried on as if everywhere were fine, even when I wavered a few times during the exercises, but his posture drew straighter when his coworkers headed out the door. The leash I'd kept on my tongue loosened at the same time.

"Is everything all right?" he said. "You're having more trouble focusing than usual."

"I've got a lot on my mind." I hesitated and then just spat it out. "Have you hurt people?"

His eyes widened. "What?"

I swiped my hand across the table top. "You were with the blacksuits when they killed my parents. Maybe you've gone on other missions with them where you didn't stand back. You were at this school for years before you had any rules about not picking sides—and that still doesn't apply to the Naries, right? Have people gotten hurt because of the things you've done, accidentally or on purpose, as far as you know? I don't think it's that hard a question."

Declan considered me in silence for a moment. My defenses stayed firmly in place, but he'd shown before he could put the pieces together without looking right inside my head. "This is about Jude and the thing with the bears, isn't it?" he said. "The Nary girl who had to be sent home —she was from your dorm."

"She was my friend," I said tightly, daring him to object. "The *only* friend I've made here who's never hurt me, I should mention." Which he should have already known if he'd heard about my falling out with Jude straight from the source. "Did you know it was Jude's spell? Did he tell you he was going to do that?"

Declan shook his head. "It was easy to guess after the

fact. I don't know any other student here who could have cast an illusion that complex."

"Fine. It was a brilliant spell, etc. etc. I've already told Jude exactly what I think about it. We're talking about *you* now."

"Okay." Declan inhaled slowly. "I've never done anything with the blacksuits other than that one mission. They only had me along because it was you—because of the similarities in our past. Beyond that... I can't tell you I've never caused anyone even a little pain, Rory. Can *you* say that, even in the short time you've been here? Striking fear in other people is how we operate. I can say that I've always tried to act in ways that won't do any lasting damage."

"What does that mean?"

"To the best of my knowledge, I've never outright traumatized someone, and I've definitely never intended to. I don't believe I've caused any physical injuries either. Scaring other fearmancers, within limits, is another way of teaching them how to handle themselves when they graduate and have to compete with mages who have far more experience."

My chin came up. "And the Nary students?"

"I don't target Naries," he said. "I think it's good that we have them here to prepare us for moving among them in the wider world, but tripping them up doesn't seem fair."

I studied him with a frown. Did he mean that, or was he just saying it because he knew it was what I'd want to hear? "Everyone else seems to think it's fair. What makes you so different?"

He paused, and a flicker of uneasiness passed from him to me. He was nervous about talking about this— about what I might do with the information? About what I'd make of it? I braced myself.

"I don't think I am so different," he said quietly. "I know my family isn't the only one that's started to feel this way. It's the way my father brought my brother and I up to believe, and from what he's said and the comments I've heard from the barons, my mother had similar feelings. There's always been jockeying for power and manipulation, but the kinds of aggressive harm a lot of the families are carrying out and encouraging… It's not necessary. It gives the joymancers an excuse to come down on us, and it puts us at risk by weakening our own bonds and getting us into precarious situations with the Nary population. We should be better, smarter, than being malicious just for the sake of it."

"So, you think we should be nicer to everyone for strategic reasons."

Declan held my gaze. "That's the best case I can make for it that anyone here is likely to listen to… which they're still not very likely to. If the other barons heard me say that, I could be accused of treason. I don't enjoy seeing people in pain. I don't want to ruin people's lives. That's my personal moral compass, where *I* draw the line, not an argument."

And yet it was the part that mattered most to me. "But you don't draw the line enough to stick up for me when I say anything like that to the other scions," I had to point out.

He gave me a crooked smile. "Did you miss the part about treason? I trust the guys more than I trust their parents, but they don't really know—they haven't seen— I can't be sure they wouldn't say something that would shatter everything I've worked for. And just because I don't enjoy pain, that doesn't mean I don't understand it can be necessary. This is how the world you were born into works, Rory. You were never going to be ready for it if you didn't have to face it."

I let out my breath in a huff. "I'm starting to get very tired of people deciding what's good for me. If all that is true, though, I'm really sorry for all of us that you lost your mom. If the joymancers had known she was pushing for peace…"

"That wouldn't have stopped them. They wouldn't have believed it. We're all villains in their eyes, believe me." He reached into his bag and pulled out a few folded papers I recognized as another report. I had three of them now stashed in the back of my wardrobe, so many words and images I didn't *want* to believe.

When I got out of here, when I could go back to the Conclave and prove I was better than they'd expected, maybe I could get a few answers from them too. Some of the fearmancer records *had* to be biased, but… the joymancers could have gone too far too.

Still, even the worst incidents the blacksuits pinned on the joymancers didn't compare to the attitudes my fellow students put on display every day here.

"Why are you giving me that?" I said abruptly. "What's the strategy there? Are you actually trying to help me by showing me all that stuff, or is this part of some plan Malcolm or your baron colleagues or whoever came up with? I'm *never* going to hate the parents who raised me, if that's the end goal."

A flicker of guilt crossed Declan's face. My hands clenched.

"You need to know the magical world isn't as simple as good guys and bad guys," he started, but I was already shoving my chair back to stand up.

"Why? Who says I have to know right now? Don't lie to me. *Everyone* here always has some other agenda—that much I'm figuring out."

"Rory." He got up to follow me.

I wasn't sure I could stand to hear more right now. I headed for the door, and Declan caught my hand partway across the room. When I glanced back at him, there was so much turmoil in his bright hazel eyes that my feet stalled.

"I'm doing my best," he said, his voice rough. "I'm trying to prepare you for everything that's going to be thrown at you. Sometimes that goal is going to line up with something someone else wants, and sometimes I have to make... concessions, but I'm not in this to hurt *you*. I don't want to see you broken. I want you strong enough to stand up with me in the pentacle of barons when there are hard decisions being made."

"I'm just a tool, then—a future ally you'll want to use."

"*No.*" He tugged me closer, and my heart stuttered

with the impression that he might try to kiss me again. Instead, he just tipped his head close to mine, dropping his voice even lower than before. "I've been as much of a shield for you from the people who *do* want to use you as I can without screwing us both over. Even telling you that could be a mistake. The barons are the most powerful mages alive, Rory. You don't fuck with them unless you want to end up with your head on a pike. But I am anyway, because the alternative is purposefully screwing you over, and I do have a goddamned line."

Strain radiated through every word he spoke. A tremor passed through his hand into me. My throat constricted as I squeezed his fingers. I'd thought I was carrying a lot of weight, but the pressures I'd felt were nothing compared to the tension in Declan's voice.

"I didn't know," I said. "You didn't *say* anything."

"The less I tell you about it, the less chance they'll pick up on it, one way or another. You're not the only one I have to look out for."

Not just himself, but his brother too. I swallowed hard. He was shielding both of us with all he had, even though those goals had to be in nearly direct opposition.

"Okay," I said quietly.

He pulled back, releasing my hand, and grabbed the report off the table. "Will you at least take this? Throw it in the garbage as soon as you get back to your room if that's what you want. At least then I can say I gave it to you."

I took the papers and shoved them into my purse. I didn't know what else to say in the face of the confession he'd just made. Maybe it was better to not say anything at all.

"Thank you… for the tutoring," I ventured.

The smile he gave me looked exhausted. "You're welcome. Keep those mental walls strong."

I didn't throw the report in the garbage. As soon as I was back in my room, I flopped on my bed and leafed through the papers. What other catastrophe had the joymancers supposedly caused?

This one wasn't as large scale as the others. It was personal. No one had died. No one had even been injured, at least not in a physical way. But there was a cruelty to the account that made me feel more sick than any of the others had.

Deborah scurried up to join me. *What now, sweetheart?*

"Another report on the joymancers. This one says they messed with a fearmancer they didn't like by forcing him and his wife apart. According to the blacksuits who investigated, anyway, someone cast a spell so that if either of them expressed affection for the other, they'd get violently ill. No one could figure out how to break the spell, so they just couldn't be together."

As I summarized it aloud, something sparked in my head. A spell that could trigger an illness only during certain actions…

That sounds more like a fearmancer spell than a joymancer one, Deborah said, but she'd hesitated first. I glanced down at her small body next to my arm.

"You've heard of something like this being done before."

Only for the good of the people involved, she protested. *And not so severe—no physical effects. There are times when we've implemented a repulsion in cases of unrequited love that was becoming harmful or other sorts of partners who always ended up in trouble if they associated with each other. Sometimes a bad relationship or friendship can be intoxicating, and those involved need a little help to break the habits. It doesn't come up very often.*

Often enough that she'd known about it. "You don't think... It sounds almost like what's happened to my mentor when he's tried to talk to me. Could a *joymancer* have done something to him?"

Deborah made a doubtful sound in my head. *How would a joymancer find him or know he had anything to do with you? Do you think he'd have gone to them of his own accord?*

No. I couldn't imagine any mage here risking the security of the school like that. And Banefield had seemed worked up about threats I was facing right now, while I was hidden away here where the joymancers couldn't reach me.

But that didn't mean a fearmancer couldn't have learned a trick or two from the joymancer technique in this report—if it hadn't been a fearmancer spell in the first place and the report a lie.

"How did those spells work?" I asked. "How did they get the magic to stay on the person so long? They wouldn't follow them around recasting it over and over."

No. There'd be a mark placed on the body somewhere, innocuous but designed to contain the spell.

A mark. That was something I could prove. I got up and shoved the report out of sight.

What are you going to do? Deborah asked.

"I'm going to see if I can finally figure out what's making my mentor sick."

I might object to Jude's attitude about a lot of things, but he'd given me one good piece of advice. A locked door and the headmistress's refusal didn't have to stop me. I waited until a couple students had left the teaching staff hallway in Killbrook Hall, and then I went to Professor Banefield's door and knocked, just in case.

No one answered. I waited a full minute, my ears perked for any sound on the other side of the door. Then I whispered a word to the doorknob, picturing the lock shifting to the side. Magic prickled up through my chest, and the door clicked open at the twist of my fingers.

The office on the other side was dark, only a faint glow seeping around the drawn curtain. I crossed the room to the door on the other side that led into Banefield's private quarters, disengaged that lock too, and slipped inside.

The apartment I found myself in looked equally gloomy. Shadows slanted across an old-fashioned living room set and an open-concept kitchen, the smell of stale bread lacing the air. I followed the rasps of breath to the bedroom.

It was brighter in there, the heavy curtain pulled back leaving only a gauzy one beneath in place. My mentor lay sprawled in his four-poster bed, the covers off other than where they were tangled around his midsection, fresh sweat beading on his flushed face. The air held the lingering tang of vomit.

His eyelids twitched but stayed closed. I hoped his dreams weren't too troubled.

He looked thinner than he had the last time I'd seen him, a couple weeks ago. His bent elbow stuck out with a knoblike shape that didn't seem right. How much had the health center staff been able to get him to eat?

I shifted on my feet. I was here now, but where did I start? The thought of peeling the sheets off him to examine his whole body for some sort of mark made me balk.

As I hesitated, his hand jerked lower to scratch at his knee. A memory sparked. Deborah had said he'd done that a few times while she'd observed him. Because something there was niggling at him, maybe.

I crept to the side of the bed and grasped the ankle of Banefield's pajama bottoms carefully. Inch by inch, I eased the fabric up over his calf. He was so deep in the fog of his illness, he didn't even stir at the movement. When I'd uncovered his knee, I stopped, studying the skin there.

Nothing looked obviously magical. Some reddish hairs, a nick of a scar, and a small brown mole protruding right in the middle of his inner knee.

When I focused on the mole, a quiver of energy passed through me. Was there magic in it right now, working on him, keeping him sick like this? If I could tell, why the hell hadn't the health center mages done anything about it?

But then, no one had been able to help the couple in

the report I'd read. A strong enough spell might be nearly impossible to break.

I had to try. Whatever the spell was, it had reacted to *me*—it was punishing him for talking to me. Maybe that would make the difference. If I could simply disperse the structure that held the spell...

I aimed all my attention on the mole. "Shrink," I said, picturing it shriveling up into nothing.

Magic tingled over my tongue, but the mole didn't budge. I tried again. "Disintegrate." And again. "Dissolve." And again. "Vanish."

I worked through a few dozen words and angles, leaning closer and stepping farther away, hovering my fingers over the spot as if that might help. The mole didn't so much as shiver.

I might not be trained in medical arts, but I should be able to have some physical effect, even if it was only superficial. The fact that the spot wouldn't change at all only reinforced my certainty that it was made of magic. A toxic magic that was draining the life out of my mentor.

A magic that no one who'd treated him had been able to cure. Did the doctors plan on just letting him waste away until he died?

I couldn't let that happen... but I'd just used up all the ideas I had. I didn't have the faintest clue how to save him.

CHAPTER TWENTY-FOUR

Malcolm

W hen I came down into the scion lounge, Jude was slouched on the sofa, a glass half-full of amber liquid in his hand. Even though he'd thrown my concern back in my face the last time we'd really talked and it'd been a couple years since I last saw him go overboard with the booze, I took a quick scan of the room for empty glasses or bottles that appeared significantly drained since I was last down here. There weren't any.

"Shut up," Jude said pre-emptively. He didn't look at me, but he didn't slur either, which suggested he was sober enough that I could lay into him instead of saving him from his stupid-ass self.

I ambled over to lean on the back of the couch at the opposite end from him. "Shut up about what, exactly? The fact that *she* hit and split on you?"

He glared at me then, with enough ire that I could tell I'd hit decently close to the mark. I didn't know exactly how far he'd gotten with our Bloodstone scion or what had led to him needing to call up Connar for a ride home a few days back, but from the little Connar had gathered and the way Jude had been skulking around since then it wasn't hard to figure out that something had gone sour between him and her.

"Self-righteous feeb-loving fucking bitch," he muttered, and downed the rest of his glass. He jabbed a finger at me with enough of a wobble to betray that he'd definitely had at least one other drink before that one. "Which doesn't change the fact that you're a fucking asshole."

"I don't remember claiming otherwise," I said. "Takes one to know one, doesn't it? What did you do that ticked her off?"

"It wasn't— I was only—" He smacked his glass down on the side table and got up. "I'm not discussing it with you."

He strode out of the room, brushing past Connar, who'd just come down, without a word. The Stormhurst scion glanced after him and then at me.

"He's still in a mood, huh?"

"As only Jude knows how to be." I went over to the bar cabinet to pour a drink of my own. "I don't know what he was thinking going after her in the first place. Anyone could have told him that wasn't going to end well."

And yet somehow without even being here, Rory's

presence had wormed into this room and drawn fault lines
through the bonds we'd spent over a decade forming. My
fingers tightened around my glass.

Jude would get over it. He'd have to get over it. All the
shit he'd said the other day—he couldn't really dismiss
everything we'd survived together like that. She'd gotten
into his head somehow, or he'd been peeved about
something else. We'd still be here when he finished
tending to his wounded ego. We'd all had plenty of
practice at forgetting the things he said when he let his
tongue right off its leash.

Connar's mouth had flattened into a pained line.

"He'll come around," I said to reassure him. "Faster if
we can finally knock her off that goddamned high horse."
Bring the Bloodstone scion to heel, solidify the pentacle of
scions, prove to my father that some prissy joymancer-
raised novice couldn't get the better of me—it shouldn't
have taken this long. She was cracking, but she still
wouldn't break.

My back prickled with the memory of the
disappointment that had loomed large in my father's voice
the last time we'd spoken on the phone—and with the
scars etched in my skin from his past judgments and
lessons. I was not going to let Rory make me look like a
fool. "You've still been throwing her off in class like we've
talked about, right?"

"When I can work it in without being noticed."
Connar folded his arms over his chest, his gaze dropping
to the floor. "It's harder to make sure she can't tell there's

outside interference as she gets better—and if the professor catches me, I'll get in shit too."

I knuckled his arm. "Live a little. Take a few risks. You can run circles around her. Maybe we can find another way for you to shake her up too. Sudden limb transformation. Shift the ground right under her. She can block off her mind, but she hasn't got full-body armor."

"That doesn't sound so subtle to me."

"Maybe we went too far in the opposite direction. Let's just get this thing done." I clapped my hands together, trying to shake off the jittery edge of the tension that had wound through me. This had gone on too long, this stupid feud, and not just for me. It had fractured the four of us too much. What was the point in being scions if we couldn't hold each other strong? "She has to be willing to stand up for us before we can stand up for her. That's the only way this can work."

Connar hesitated. "I'm not—" he started with a grim expression.

I waved off his worries before he had to say them. "Don't you think for one second you can't keep up with her. We'll all push together, and she'll topple. Let me think on it, and in the next couple days, we'll have a solid plan. In the meantime, just keep picking at her any opportunity you see. I know I can count on you for that."

"Of course," Connar said. "Whatever you need."

He left, which seemed a little odd considering he'd only just come down, but maybe he'd simply been looking for reassurance that we were on the right track. I wandered restlessly through the lounge as I finished my drink, but the emptiness of the space and everything I had left to accomplish ate at me.

It was just about time to let Shadow out of the kennel. I might as well head over there now.

Nothing looked particularly out of the ordinary on the way out to the little wooden building at the edge of the east field. I stepped inside, my mind already skipping ahead to watching my familiar bound joyfully into the woods, and froze at the sound of a human voice.

I was the only one with a large enough familiar to require the use of the kennel this year. No one else should have been in here.

"Oooh, you think you're fierce, do you?" the voice said in a teasing tone, with a scuffing of feet against the floor and a rasp that I knew was my wolf's claws. He let out a low growl, but not his threatening one—the eager one that egged you on.

That wasn't the problem. The problem was I knew the voice who'd spoken to him.

I marched over to the kennel stall and yanked the door open.

The heir of Bloodstone was standing in the middle of the large concrete space, her back to me, her hands clamped around a short length of knotted rope with which she was in the middle of a tug-of-war with Shadow. Her head jerked around at the squeak of the hinges with a tumble of her dark brown waves. Shadow dropped his end of the rope and bowed down with glinting eyes in a wolfish request that I join their play.

My gaze shot back to Rory. "What the fuck are you

doing with my familiar?" I snapped, every muscle in my body tensed.

Rory turned to face me, the rope toy—which I'd never seen before; she must have brought it with her—still dangling from her hand. Her stance had stiffened, but she raised one shoulder in a careless shrug. "What does it look like? He was bored. I figured I'd keep him a company when I had a moment."

The lift of her chin and the intentness of her deep blue eyes dared me to complain. I had outright *kidnapped* her familiar not that long ago, a fact I doubted she'd ever forget. If I freaked out over her entertaining mine, I'd only look like a hypocritical idiot. I reined in my emotions.

All of my emotions. Alongside the instinctive alarm, part of me couldn't help appreciating the fire and steel that radiated from her stance. Every ounce of my training, both formal and informal, had prepared me to welcome an associate like this: fierce but controlled, quick-tongued and quick-witted, strong down to the core. How could she be everything a scion was supposed to be and yet still hate the rest of our guts?

She should be with us, not against us. I felt it down to my bones.

She should be with *me*.

I shoved aside that thought as quickly as it rose up and snapped my fingers by my side. Shadow came trotting over with the same wolfish grin as if to say this was the best thing that had ever happened to him, and wasn't I just as pleased as he was?

I gave him a tight smile and scratched between his

ears. Didn't he remember pouncing on this girl a couple months ago?

"Shadow," I said, pointing at Rory, "we need to remind her who's in charge here. Take her down."

Rory's posture went even more rigid, but she held her ground. Shadow took a step toward her, but instead of lunging like he should have and knocking her over, he glanced back at me with an uncertain expression, asking if I was really sure about this.

For Christ's sake, how long had she been making friendly with him that he'd ignore a direct command?

Or maybe he could read my own mixed feelings about this girl. The familiar connection ran deep.

"It's all right, Shadow," Rory said in a gently cajoling tone that brought my hackles up even as it tingled over my skin. My wolf's ears swiveled right back to her, and his head came up as he watched her avidly. "You need to push me around to make him happy? Go ahead. I'll be fine." She held up her hands in offering.

Just when I'd thought this situation couldn't make me look any less effectual. Thank all that was holy we didn't have any witnesses.

"Never mind," I muttered. I could make my familiar follow the order, but it'd disturb him more than seemed worth it. I wanted to set her off balance, not torture him, and she wasn't the slightest bit afraid. Pushing the stall door wider, I stepped back to make room for Shadow to trot past. "Ready for freedom?"

My wolf didn't need any more encouragement than that to wheel around and lope out of the stall. The kennel door still stood ajar. He slipped out in a blur of dark fur.

"Why do you keep him shut up in here at all?" Rory tossed the rope toy to the side of the stall where his sleep blanket was. "It doesn't seem right for a wolf."

"I know it doesn't," I said tersely. "The staff are concerned about him roaming around during main school hours when the students are walking to and from classes. If you have a problem with that, you can take it up with Ms. Grimsworth, although even I couldn't persuade her, so good luck."

Rory had the decency to look a bit startled. "Oh. I didn't realize."

"I'd leave him at home where he can run free as much as he wants, but he'd be miserable that far apart from me," I added. I wouldn't feel that great about it either. The familiar bond started to gnaw at you if you were separated from your animal by a lot of distance for very long. "Whatever you've been doing here, you can stop it now." I motioned for her to get out too. "You made your point. I haven't even looked at your familiar in weeks. Leave mine alone."

She crossed her arms over her chest. "I think he'd rather I came back. What are you so worried will happen if I keep coming by?"

"I'm not *worried*. I just don't want you near him." Near the one living being in the world that had a direct line to my mind, although I wasn't going to emphasize that point for her. On the off-chance that she *hadn't* already considered that factor, I didn't want to put the idea in her head. "You know it's never fun for you when I have to make you do what I say."

She just gazed back at me with the calm defiance that rankled me all over again even as—damn it—it turned me on. "I don't think it's ended up being much fun for you either."

My jaw clenched. "If you really want me to show you I have what it takes to smash your defenses—"

She held up her hands again and walked past me, having to step close enough on her way into the outer hall that a whiff of a scent sweet as toffee reached my nose. The thought of Jude with his hands on her, with his mouth on her, and God knew what else sent a sudden flare of fury through me. Then Rory turned to meet my gaze, and there was something so unexpectedly vulnerable in her expression that my jealousy deflated.

"Do we really have to keep doing this?" she said. "The sniping at each other and the trying to get the upper hand? I don't like you, and you don't like me—so what? Can't we leave it alone and just ignore each other until we're done here?"

I don't like you, and you don't like me. The certainty with which she said that came with a jab to my gut. She had no fucking idea. As if I could ever ignore her.

"And then what?" I said. "You're stuck with me, Glinda. We're meant to work together until we retire decades and decades from now. Better we sort out our differences now."

"Is that what this is?" She shook her head in disbelief. "Let's just assume we'll tolerate each other's presences when we have to, then. It's probably going to be easier if we haven't been fighting the whole time before."

"You've got to know there's no chance of that. If I go easy on you now, then you win. I'm not going to look like a weakling so that you can have a little peace and quiet."

"But it's okay for me to look weak, if I finally give in and do what you want?"

I exhaled roughly. "What do you think? You have excuses. People hardly know you. You'll have tons of time to recover the respect you need. Hell, we'll *help* you get it back." But I—I had so much more to lose and so much farther to fall. Our peers here might never look at me the same way again. My father might never gain the confidence in me that I'd sweat and bled to gain.

She was smart—didn't she get how this worked?

For a few seconds, she just studied me. Was she really considering giving up just to put an end to the conflict between us?

I had the urge to offer her something to smooth the way, but what the hell did I have? Maybe there'd been a time when I could have turned the tension between us around the way Jude had, insomuch as he had before he'd fucked that up, but I knew without trying that I'd gone too far to have a chance now. The girl in front of me was *never* going to believe a friendly gesture from me until we'd beaten her down enough that she was begging for it.

The thought shouldn't have twisted my stomach the way it did. I couldn't even tell her I wished it was over too.

The moment dragged too long. I squared my

shoulders, drawing another biting comment onto my tongue—and Rory ended the moment.

"Then it's going to be how it's going to be," she said, and walked away without waiting to hear how I'd have responded.

CHAPTER TWENTY-FIVE

Rory

My nerves twitched as I walked out to the garage, even though there was nothing to worry about. The discomfort was partly because of all my memories of meeting Jude there, now clouded by all the reasons I had to regret allowing those moments to happen, but it was also because I wasn't sure whether the guy I'd invited today would turn up. I couldn't tell which made me more nervous: the possibility that he'd be there or the possibility that he wouldn't.

When I came around the aisle to my parking spot and saw Declan waiting in the dim light, my heart leapt with an exhilaration that was only partly anxiety. Plenty of relief was mixed in there as well, along with other feelings it was safer not to look at too closely.

He swept a few stray strands of his black hair back from his face, his stance wary as he watched me approach.

His gaze flicked from side to side to confirm no one else was around. It'd be hard to excuse this get-together as a tutoring session.

"What's this about, Rory?" he said when I reached him.

"I'll explain in a second. Hold on."

I scooted past him, more aware than I liked of the warmth of his slim body, and stood by the nearest window. "Hold the image," I murmured, willing some of my magic into the glass to fix the view of the empty passenger seat, ignoring the driver's seat where I'd be sitting. The spell came easily enough after the practice I'd had obscuring Deborah's hiding spots. I moved around the car, repeating the spell on all the windows, freezing for a second at the sound of an engine above.

Declan ducked down between my car and the neighboring one as a BMW cruised by. I finished my casting. When the other car had pulled out of the garage, he straightened up again, his mouth twisting.

Before he could argue, I motioned to the passenger door. "Get in. Let me make sure the illusion worked."

"Rory..."

"I promise I have a good reason. Go on."

He gave me a bemused look, but he climbed in. When he closed the door, he might as well have vanished from existence. I circled the car again, but the seat looked perfectly vacant from every angle. With a rush of relief, I got in on the driver's side.

"No one will see you're in here," I said. "If you want, on the way back I can drop you off in town and you can walk the rest of the way to campus, so there's even less chance of anyone realizing we went off together."

"On the way back from where? What's this all about?"

I looked at him, sitting where Jude so often had but with such a different presence—reserved and thoughtful and far more serious. His bright hazel eyes held mine with a glimmer of the longing I'd so often watched him squash. So many responsibilities and emotions he was juggling, and *my* presence in his life had made his so much more difficult.

"You've helped me so much, the last couple months," I said. "I didn't even realize how much until the other day… I didn't even think about the pressure you must be getting from the barons on top of everything else." My brief encounter with Malcolm's dad, Baron Nightwood, had made it clear that they didn't approve of my attitudes any more than the younger generation did.

"I want to take a trip out to one of my family properties that's near here," I went on. "I'd rather not drive alone. And I figured you might appreciate taking a break somewhere without having to worry about who might be watching or judging you. I've made sure the maintenance staff won't come by today. There won't be anyone else around. I'll do my thing, and you can just… chill out. Or you can say no and get out of the car. I'm not going to kidnap you."

Declan gave a laugh that sounded a little startled at that last remark. Maybe because the last time we'd taken a car trip of sorts together, the blacksuits he'd been with had technically kidnapped *me*. He ran his hand through his hair again, his gaze sliding to the windshield as he considered.

"It'll definitely be just us?" he said.

"The place is incredibly secluded. No neighbors around to see who goes in, and no one's going to get inside unless I let them."

He sank a little deeper into his seat. "All right. Maybe I *could* use a break. It doesn't sound like it'll hurt anything, anyway. And you're getting to practice your Illusion skills." He smiled wryly, but his expression softened when he looked at me again. "Thank you."

The flutter that look provoked in my chest was definitely not worth paying attention to. "Thank *you*," I said jokingly. "Today you can be my shield against having a panic attack in the middle of some country road."

I drove out of the garage and onto the road, pleased to find that whatever complaints I could make about Jude, his instruction in the car had left me reasonably confident. Declan watched without comment as I navigated the turns in town.

"You don't look like you need much help with this," he said.

"I've only ever driven about ten miles on my own," I said. "And that was fueled by being extremely pissed off at Jude. It's easier to feel secure knowing there's someone else here in case I run into some situation I haven't encountered yet."

"Not likely to be much trouble on these roads. Just don't go driving into New York City."

"Yeah." My thoughts leapt back to the story Imogen

had told me about Professor Banefield's wife. I couldn't do anything about that loss, but there was still a chance I could make sure my mentor didn't lose his own life. And maybe the answer would be somewhere in my parents' former home.

Jude had said they never had company over there. That'd make it an ideal place for hiding information they didn't want their enemies knowing about. Ms. Grimsworth had mentioned my grandfather Bloodstone packing things up for storage, which I'd determined meant it'd be off in Maine at the primary family home, but I had to at least check.

The shade of the scattered trees along the side of the road slipped over us. Another, smaller smile curved Declan's lips. "You know, this is how it should be. How it's supposed to be. The scions looking out for each other, supporting each other, as we need it... It's how the four of us have been since we were kids. I know you've had your problems with, well, all of us, but if we can get through this—and Malcolm can get over his vendetta—you have a family here."

A lump clogged my throat. "My family was murdered." *By your people.*

"I know," Declan said quickly. "I didn't mean— obviously it's not the same. But it's something. You don't have any other Bloodstones to rely on while you're figuring things out. I don't think you'd be in the same kind of danger if you did. We can fill that gap, is all I'm saying."

I had trouble imagining the other guys expressing the same sentiment, but I believed he meant it. "Is that why you've helped me even though it puts *you* in danger? Because you've decided I'm family?"

"In a way." He paused. "You remind me of all the things I'd like to do and say if I didn't feel my position was so precarious. Maybe it makes me a coward that it's easier for me to ensure you can keep doing and saying all that stuff rather than making a bigger stand myself, but… it's something."

"I wouldn't expect you to risk yourself or your brother for me," I said. It wasn't as if there weren't things I'd kept to myself rather than risk admitting them to the wrong person. My whole plan to bring Bloodstone University down, for example. "He's your real family."

"I don't think the bond of the scions is any less real. It's just different."

"I guess most families don't have to suppress the desire to kiss each other."

I'd spoken without really thinking that comment through, but Declan just laughed. "There is that. Not that it's been much of a problem until recently. You… have added an interesting dynamic showing up all of a sudden, let's just say. I'd suggest looking farther afield when it comes to the kissing thing, though. Plenty of eligible bachelors beyond the pentacle of scions."

Considering that I'd kissed three out of four in the last two months, that comment seemed fair. Heat crept up my neck. "I guess the thing is that with everyone else I have to worry about what they really want from me. So far the guys who've tried to chat me up—or worse—only seemed to care that I'm a scion and not about me as a person. At least with you or Jude or… whoever, I know I'm not just a step up the social ladder."

"But on the other hand, anything you have with us can't lead all that far."

"Maybe that's okay. We're in college. Isn't that supposed to be the time for experimenting and figuring out what you want without worrying about making big commitments?" I hesitated, and my voice dropped. "I don't really trust anyone at Blood U yet. But maybe the fact that I can't have a real future with any of you makes you safe in that one area. Just mutual attraction, no expectations."

Declan wet his lips. "You know, today, it can't be—"

"I know," I said. "I wasn't thinking—that wasn't the idea. I really did just want to do something nice for you, as foreign a concept as that might be in fearmancer circles."

"Sorry. I know I didn't need to say that." He looked over at me. "You might have shaken things up, and obviously the clash hasn't been easy on you, but I think we're lucky to have you the way you are."

I let myself glance away from the road for a second to meet his eyes. The honest appreciation there set off a whole lot more than a flutter inside me.

Maybe that was okay. He was the safest one of all, really, because he didn't *want* to want me. If anything ever happened between us, it'd be desire, pure and simple, not some other goal he thought he could use me for.

He reached for the radio, breaking the moment. "Do you mind?"

"No, go ahead."

He found a local station playing jangly pop music that I wouldn't have thought was his thing, but it reminded me of the songs I'd have listened to back home, three months and a lifetime ago. At least it was a pleasant memory of times past for once. The buoyant beats filled the car the rest of the way to the cottage.

There was no sign of anyone on or around the driveway, as expected. I'd gotten the contact information for the company that had been overseeing my family's properties from Ms. Grimsworth to ensure we had no interruptions today. As a secondary measure, just in case, I cast a little magic toward the gate's panel as I pressed my hand to it. "No one but me."

Energy shivered through the warm metal. As long as that spell lasted, it should reject any other attempts to open it.

On the other side, Declan exhaled slowly as he took in the grounds and the buildings, his shoulders relaxing with the clang of the closing gate in a way they hadn't quite while we were in the car. The sun beamed over us, glinting off the pond and turning the green of the yard and the hedges even richer. His family must have places just as nice, but I could tell he liked it.

I headed over to the house intending to begin my search, and he followed.

"What exactly are you up to here?" he asked. "This isn't just a break for you."

"No. Mostly I'm just trying to learn more about my family and what they did before my parents died. This seems like a good place to start." I didn't want to go into more detail about my hopes of helping Professor Banefield. I might trust Declan not to be involved with that plot, but he still had to report back to the other barons somehow or other, and who knew how they might be tangled up in this mess. "Feel free to take a walk around the grounds or find somewhere to just lounge around or whatever. Just enjoy having nothing to worry about for a little while."

Declan looked as if he wasn't really sure what to do with himself if he didn't have some pressing issue to deal with, but he nodded to me and meandered on toward the pond. I stepped into the house and started a much more intensive investigation than I'd felt comfortable getting into while Jude was around.

The great room on the main floor had a ceiling two stories high and a view from its picture windows down to the lake, but not a whole lot to look through. Somehow I didn't think my parents had hidden secret documents under the leather couch. Branching off from there, though, was a room that appeared to be a study, with bookcases filling two of the walls and a big oak desk by the window.

I'd only glanced in there with Jude. Today, I marched right in and got to work.

Every book on the shelves—some of them old novels, some volumes of magical theory, some more mundane business and legal reference texts—I slid out and flipped through in case anything had been secreted away inside. Then I started on the desk drawers.

The ones on the left side only held basic items like pens and paperclips, blank notepads not yet used, an old personal phone book that looked as if it hadn't been opened in decades. The yellowed pages crackled and started to tear as I flipped through it. Other than a few last names from the baron families, I didn't recognize anyone in there. I slipped it into my purse in case it'd come in handy later.

The drawers on the right side were locked. I fiddled with them for a while, testing my magic against each one, shivering with the deterring jab of the spells on them. Finally, my fingers managed to press the right spot with the right nudge of magic on the top drawer. It opened to reveal what first looked like just a bunch of scrap papers. I dug through them, and my fingers brushed a leather surface toward the back.

I pulled out a small leather-bound journal. The first page showed a list of notations—names, dates, jotted notes about the topics of meetings or phone calls.

I paged through, again checking for any familiar names. Whether it'd been my birth mother or father who'd kept this record, they'd been in touch with Ms. Grimsworth a few times in the year before their death. The name Crowford came up once, but I didn't know my Persuasion professor's first initial to be sure this was him and not some other member of his family. The information was all dry facts, no hint at how the writer had felt about any of the interactions noted.

After several unsuccessful attempts at the other drawers, I gave up for the time being. My stomach was starting to gurgle. I checked the fridge and found the fruit and premade sandwiches I'd asked the maintenance workers to drop off on their last visit. Digging into a peach, I went out to find Declan and see if he wanted anything to eat.

I almost didn't see him stretched out on the padded lounger on the deck. His arms lay loosely folded over his chest, his head tilted against the cushion as he dozed in the warmth of the sun. His lips had parted just enough to emphasize their soft cupid's bow shape.

My heart twinged. I guessed he really had needed a chance to properly relax. More strain than I'd realized was there had faded from his expression, leaving it completely at peace. An image popped into my head of waking up next to that striking face, of pressing my mouth to his, with a rush of heat I had to shake off.

In some ways, he really was as caught in his circumstances as I was. He didn't want the barony. He didn't agree with half the stuff he saw around him.

When I got out of here, when I could send the joymancers to topple the university and anything else it led them to, I'd tell them to make sure the Ashgraves stayed safe. Maybe the fearmancer world wouldn't be half so terrifying if all the barons had been like him.

The upstairs of the cottage held four bedrooms and a bathroom. Two of the bedrooms contained no personal items at all, so I figured they were guest rooms, presumably not used very often in my parents' day. The next one held a crib and a changing table.

Last time, I'd glanced in there briefly, Jude had made a

joke, and I'd walked on before the implications had really sunk in. Now, my fingers tightened where I'd grasped the doorframe.

This had been my bedroom. I didn't have the slightest memory of it, but it couldn't have belonged to anyone else.

For the first two years of my life, when we'd been here, I'd slept in that crib. My birth parents had changed me on that table. I'd watched that silver star mobile spin as I drifted off to sleep. I'd played with the stuffed animals sitting in their wicker basket next to the wardrobe.

I drifted over to the crib and looked into it. The sheet was neatly tucked, the furniture free of dust—the cleaner kept the place spic and span. Not a hair or a crease remained of my long-ago presence here. But just the sight of the room brought the idea of the family before the one I remembered crashing home.

I *had* had other parents, parents who'd set up this room for me, parents who'd cared for me. Parents who might very well have loved me, even if I found it hard to associate those tender emotions with fearmancers.

I shivered and backed away, leaving the haunted sensation behind as I moved to the last bedroom.

Just outside it, a framed photograph hung on the wall. My birth parents stood in a formal embrace in front of a marble wall. My mother in her deep blue gown looked like a slightly older version of me, with eyes a little closer set and dark chestnut waves that tumbled all the way to her waist. My father stood half a foot taller, broad-shouldered but narrow in his face, his hair a lighter brown both on his head and the neat beard on his pointy jaw.

They were posed the way you often saw in wedding photos, but their clothing didn't fit—unless fearmancers had different traditions. I tore my gaze away and went on into the room.

It was clearly the master. A king-sized bed with a mahogany sleigh frame dominated one half of the room, the other holding a dressing area with wardrobe, vanity, and a couple of armchairs. Like the rest of the house, the room was spotlessly clean, the air carrying a faintly citrusy scent.

I started with the wardrobe, hoping my search upstairs wouldn't be totally fruitless. The top shelf held a box that proved to be full of dry pressed leaves—who had collected those?

Groping as far as I could, my hand came to rest on a large clothbound book shoved right to the back. An old photo album, I realized as I tugged it out. The dates written on the cover showed a span of six years that ended a few years before my birth.

I sat down on the floor with the album and leaned against the wardrobe as I paged through it. My birth parents featured in most of the photographs, one or both of them. It started in their university days. There they were with a few other kids in their late teens standing on the green with Nightwood Tower in the background. There was my mother lounging on the dock with a friend, a big but elegant sunhat shading her eyes.

This wouldn't tell me who their enemies were, but it

might give me a better idea who my allies in the wider world should be.

I turned another page, and came face to face with a couple more familiar figures. The golden-haired guy with his hand on my mother's shoulder was the spitting image of Malcolm, if maybe a tiny bit wider in the jaw and a tad more smoldering with his gaze. His dad, no doubt. And next to him stood a willowy woman with Declan's smooth black hair and pensive eyes. She looked a little stiff, as if she hadn't wanted to be in the picture.

The creak of the floor brought my head up. Declan stood in the doorway, his face still a little languid from his sleep, his hair windblown.

"Sorry," he said. "I didn't mean to startle you. Have you found what you were hoping to?"

"I'm still figuring that out. I've found more than I had before, anyway. Have a good nap?"

He laughed with an embarrassed flush that only made him more attractive. "I didn't mean to drift off."

"It's fine. You must have needed it. I'm glad my mission succeeded." I grinned at him.

Something about his gaze felt more intense than usual, but maybe it was only the effect of that recent sleep. He took another step into the room—still several feet away, but my skin tingled with awareness of him anyway. "Is there any way I can help?"

I wagged a finger at him. "*You* are on strict orders not to do any work for what I'm starting to think is the first time in your entire life."

This time his laugh came easier. "That might not be a total exaggeration."

As I continued perusing the photo album, he wandered through the room. He drifted into the hall for a few minutes to consider the picture of my parents and then moved to the bedroom window to take in the view. Every now and then, I felt his gaze come to rest on me again, but he didn't say anything. He didn't seem to want to venture off on his own again either.

None of the photographs were labeled. Once they moved beyond the university years, I didn't recognize most of the places in them, let alone the people other than my birth parents. I set the album over by the door to take with me back to campus and hopefully do some cross-referencing—maybe I could get Declan to look through it on the drive home, come to think of it, when I released him from total relaxation.

One more glance through the wardrobe turned up nothing. I opened the vanity drawers and found them empty. With a huff of breath, I set my hands on my hips.

"Well, maybe I'm going to have to do some relaxing now too. I think I've run out of places to search."

Declan turned to face me. "You haven't exactly had the most peaceful time of it the last few months. You've got to deserve some down time as much as I do."

"There's just... so much I need to take care of, as soon as I can." I grimaced. "Okay, now I probably sound like you too."

He chuckled and ambled closer, and that impression

of intensity tickled through me again. "Yes, you do. Why do you think I like you so much?"

"I was hoping it was my brilliant wits and irrepressible spirit."

"Those too." He raised his hand to touch my cheek, and my pulse stuttered with desire. I expected him to pull back again, to let the moment pass, but instead he leaned in, so slowly my heart thumped faster and faster, until I felt like I'd die if he didn't kiss me.

And then he did.

CHAPTER TWENTY-SIX

Rory

This kiss wasn't at all like the one Declan had sprung on me in the library repair room, sudden and demanding. His lips brushed mine before catching my mouth more fully, the gentle motion setting off eager quivers all through my nerves. Even as I kissed him back, there was a tentativeness to the way he met my lips, as if he half anticipated the world to blow up with this transgression.

When it didn't, he tugged me closer, his fingers coming to rest by the crook of my jaw. He kissed me again, a real kiss, all determined longing, so heated I started to melt. His other arm looped around my back to hold me steady.

It was over way too soon. He drew back, leaving his arm around my waist, his hand at the side of my cheek. The tip of his nose grazed mine.

"Rory?"

I wasn't sure what he was asking me. He had to be able to tell from my response to the kiss that I had no objections. Well, maybe just a possible one.

"I thought you said we couldn't do this."

"I thought we couldn't do it." His breath had turned a bit shaky. It scorched my skin. "But being here, thinking about everything you'd said, finally having a chance to step back from all the stress hanging over me... Maybe I have a better chance of keeping it together and keeping us both out of trouble if I can let some of those feelings out while we're someplace safe. Maybe the fact that I want you won't eat at me so much if I can remember what it's like to have you."

I touched his chest and ran my hand down his slim but solid torso. "Are you sure?"

"No. Maybe I'm just kidding myself into giving in. I don't know. We still—we still can't be close after we leave here, as long as I'm an aide. And we still can't really *be* together in the long run. If that makes it too hard for you, we can stop right now. You just have to say it. I only want this if you do too."

No strings attached. No promises made. Nothing to figure out or wait and see about. After the messes of the last two guys I'd hooked up with, what Declan was offering felt perfectly simple. I'd been holding in the fire that kindled whenever he was around so long, it seemed to sear over my tongue as I answered.

"I do. I want you."

He didn't need any more answer than that. His mouth

collided with mine again, his dry cedary scent washing over me, and I gripped his shirt, tucking my other hand around the back of his neck. His silky hair tickled my fingers. His lips slid against mine, finding a deeper angle, and the fire inside me spread through every inch of my body.

We were really doing this—me and Declan Ashgrave. After all those weeks of restrained desires, he was giving himself over to me. Putting his livelihood, his security, and his family's future in my hands. So much trust, so much more than I could imagine having in anyone right now. My heart swelled with more emotion than I'd thought it could contain.

Declan walked me backwards one step, and then another, until my legs bumped the side of the bed. He reined in the urgency of his kisses, drawing the next one out long and slow, his tongue teasing over the seam of my lips. He pressed another kiss to the edge of my jaw and charted a path along the sensitive skin there all the way to my ear.

"This might be the only time we get to do this," he murmured. "So I'm going to take my time. I want to remember all of it."

"I'm not going to argue with that." I stroked my fingers up his neck into his hair. He let out a tight hungry sound and reclaimed my lips.

Between kisses, I started unbuttoning his shirt. When I'd made it halfway down, Declan drew back for just long enough to pull it up over his head, rumpling his hair even more. He looked younger like this, flushed and eager, more like he really was only a couple years older than me and less like the professional persona he put on so often. I liked it.

Compact muscles lined his slim body. I traced my fingers over them, and he tipped my head into another kiss. His tongue teased over mine and twined around it. I kissed him back harder.

When it felt as if he must have explored every inch of my mouth and my nerves were singing with need, he eased me onto the bed, following me as I scooted farther across the mattress to make room. His fingers slipped along my waist to grasp the hem of my blouse. I raised my arms in case he needed a definite invitation. With a crook of his lips, he tugged off the shirt and dropped his head to kiss my shoulder. My collarbone. The swell of my breast just above my bra.

My necklace with the glass dragon charm, its base broken from when Malcolm had forced me to smash the others, slid across my chest. Declan paused over it with a hint of a wince, maybe at the same memory. He kissed my skin just beneath it and eased it to the side to rest on the pillow.

His fingers traced heat over my shoulders as he eased down the straps of my bra. He tucked his hand beneath one of the loosened cups with careful attention, stroking the soft curve and then sliding over the peak. My nipple pebbled instantly. When he rolled his thumb over it again, pleasure rippled through me and jolted a gasp from my throat.

He unclasped my bra, and I pulled him down for

another kiss as he brought both hands to my breasts. My breath broke as he fondled them at the same time. I gripped his shoulders, massaging the taut muscles there.

Declan bowed his head over mine, watching my expression as he teased me, softly and then with a squeeze that provoked a shock of pleasure. I pressed my head back into the pillow with a whimper.

"Is that what you like best?" he said in a lightly teasing tone. He pinched my nipple carefully between his thumb and forefinger, and my back arched off the bed with the rush of sensation.

"Feel free to keep doing that," I replied raggedly.

He repeated the gesture a few more times until I was squirming with the tension building between my legs. Then he set to work with his mouth. His lips closed around one peak with a forceful flick of his tongue, and a sound that was half moan, half growl wrenched out of me.

I wanted to be the one taking. Calling the shots, leading the way. I was a fucking scion, wasn't I?

The pleasure we were stoking between us was mine as much as his. I would own it, and whatever happened after happened.

I would not regret *this*. I would make it exactly what I needed it to be.

For another minute, I trembled under Declan as he worked more bliss through my chest. When the need burning in me flared higher, I ran my hand down to his stomach and pushed. He eased away, checking my face with a flicker of concern, and I shoved him right over onto his back.

A smile curled his lips as I straddled him. I trailed my fingers up and down his torso, and he pulled me in for a kiss. My body rocked against him instinctively, flaming hotter at the solid length that met my core through our pants.

Declan groaned. He gripped my ass, encouraging the motion.

The friction between us left my head spinning. Fuck taking our time. I fumbled with the fly on his slacks, and he popped open the button on my jeans in turn. Before he tugged them down, he stroked his hand between my legs, earning him another gasp. We wriggled out of our pants between more hasty kisses.

I teased my fingers over the bulge in his boxers, and Declan tipped his head back with an inarticulate sound. I'd never really explored a guy's body this intimately before. The rush of my longing eased back as I caressed and then gripped his erection through the fabric. Declan stroked my breasts in turn, his eyes glazing each time I swiveled my thumb over the head of his cock.

"That feels so fucking good," he rasped. "God, Rory."

Something deep and distant twisted inside me, sharply enough that I couldn't ignore it. I leaned closer to him. "No regrets?"

His gaze cleared as he looked back into my eyes. "No regrets," he said firmly.

I yanked his boxers down, and he kicked them the rest of the way off. The smooth hardness of him felt even more thrilling skin to skin. I had the urge to kiss him there, to take him into my mouth, but I was getting too impatient for that. My panties were damp, my sex aching.

Declan pushed himself upright and helped me squirm out of my panties. He stayed there, sitting up to meet me, as I lowered myself over him. We kissed, his cock sliding against my clit, and my teeth grazed his lip with my whimper.

"Hold on," he murmured. "Let me..." He spoke a couple of casting words, his fingertips gliding between my thighs, and a similar protective tingling to the one Connar had provoked rippled up through me.

I drew him to me and sank down so his cock pushed inside me. Declan's breath caught, and I gripped his shoulder tightly as he filled me. A sudden swell of emotion nearly overwhelmed me.

Maybe there'd been no going back from the first moment I'd accepted his kiss, but in this moment, we couldn't have been any closer. He was offering up so much power to me that it left me breathless.

I cupped his face and kissed him with all the tenderness I had in me. With a shift of my hips and a rush of bliss inside me, our lips parted with a shared gasp. I flexed my thighs, pumping up and down over him, while Declan braced his hand against the mattress to hold himself with me. His other hand traveled over my side, stroked my breast, tangled in my hair as we kissed again, roughly now.

With each roll of his hips, each thrust to meet me, the pleasure building inside me soared higher. I bucked harder, faster, letting my body sway backward. Declan wrapped his arm around me and caught my nipple in his mouth, and that extra spark of ecstasy set off the final chain reaction.

I clenched around him with a cry I couldn't hold in, and my release blazed through me in a wave of fire. Declan let out a choked sound and plunged into me even more deeply. The sear of his cock sent me spiraling higher. He came with a groan against my shoulder, flooding me with fresh heat.

Declan tugged me to him, but not for a kiss, just to rest my cheek against his as my breath evened out again. I let myself relax into his embrace.

"I—" he started, and caught himself.

"What?"

He shook his head. "Never mind. Nothing important."

When I pulled back to look him in the eyes, he gave me a bittersweet smile. "I promise, it's not anything you have to worry about. It'd only make letting go of this when we leave here harder."

We snuggled together on the bed for a while, and then I dragged Declan downstairs for a late lunch he absolutely needed, sitting with my knee resting against his beneath the table. Drawing out the contact for as long as I could until I couldn't have it anymore.

When we finally headed out, I found myself taking his hand as we walked toward the gate. He twined his fingers with mine. I pressed my other hand to the panel to open the gate. It swung open—and my heart stopped at the sight of another car parked behind mine.

I dropped Declan's hand, but not fast enough that I was sure the two strangers standing by the second car hadn't noticed.

"Persephone!" the woman said in a gasp of a voice, and hustled over, her silver-white curls swaying around her broad face. The man, his short-cropped hair pure white, approached more cautiously, his broad shoulders and contrasting narrow face striking a chord of recognition in me.

I took a step back before the woman got all the way to me, tensing at the thought that she might try to hug me. She halted with a disappointed expression. "You don't know us at all, do you? How could you, you were so little? I told that headmistress at the university we should be allowed in to see you—"

"You're my grandparents," I broke in as the pieces clicked. My father's parents. "What are you doing here?"

"We keep in touch with the Bloodstone staff," my grandfather said in a more even tone. "They mentioned you were coming out here today. It seemed like an ideal time to introduce—or rather, re-introduce—ourselves."

"We knocked on the gate a few times, but I suppose the house is so far away, it's difficult to hear. You'll really need to get a new intercom system set up now that you're back." My grandmother peered at me, still looking like she was judging how she could finagle a hug out of me. "We have so much to talk about. You're all we have left."

That felt like an awful lot of pressure from two people that as far as I could remember I'd only just met. I was sharply aware of Declan standing tensed beside me, of the way they'd seen us coming out together. Of the fact that they'd seen us together here at all. And clearly Jude's account hadn't exaggerated their pushiness. The hairs on the back of my neck rose.

"I—I'm sorry," I said. "I really don't remember you. It's been a big adjustment, and I've been taking things one step at the time. Right now I need to get back to school. Maybe we could arrange a time for us to grab lunch together in town and talk, or something like that?"

My body balked at the idea, but I had to offer them something so we could get out of here. And they *were* family. I could give them a chance, even if their showing up here like this rubbed me completely the wrong way, just in case there was more to them than a regular fearmancer would recognize.

My grandmother's face fell. Her husband grasped her shoulder. "Of course you have your own plans. We'd only like to make the transition smoother in whatever ways we can. Let me give you my phone number so we can arrange that lunch."

As he jotted the number down on a slip of paper he retrieved from his pocket, my grandmother peered at Declan with sudden interest.

"Ah!" she said as if she'd solved a difficult puzzle. "You're the Ashgrave boy, aren't you? There's a lot of your mother in you."

"Thank you," Declan said, not quite able to smooth all the tension from his voice.

Her pale little eyes flitted between us. A knowing smile crossed her face. "The adventures of youth. I remember them well. You be good to her and don't promise anything you can't follow through on."

"We're not—It's not like that," Declan said.

Her eyes twinkled with even more curiosity. "Oh, is it not? This is a rather long way to come from the university for just a friendly romp. If you want to keep your adventuring quiet, you don't have to worry. We can keep it to ourselves." She winked at me.

Oh, fuck. I had no idea whether we could trust her, but every instinct told me no.

To my limited relief, when my grandfather handed over the phone number, my grandmother drew back beside him. "If you're sure we can't talk more now…"

"I have a tutoring session," I lied. "I'm almost late as it is. I've had a lot of catching up to do, of course."

"Of course," my grandfather said, but his face momentarily darkened, and for the first time I got the sense that he wasn't all that pleased with how their impromptu visit had turned out either. "It was a gamble, dropping in like this. It was good just to see you."

They got back into their car, turned it around, and headed back down the drive. I waited until they were out of sight before I slumped into the driver's seat of the Lexus. My hand shook when I pushed in the key. Declan said nothing.

If I'd just driven the car right up to the garage after I'd opened the gate—but that might have been worse. They might have spotted it through the bars and stuck around anyway, and I'd still have had to stop to talk, and they'd probably have noticed both Declan and the spell meant to hide him. Then it would have been even more obvious how secret we were trying to keep this excursion.

My thoughts tumbled around in my head as if they were caught in a clothes dryer as I aimed the car toward the university. I couldn't help searching for something different I could have said, something better. A growing horror filled the pit of my stomach with each passing minute that Declan didn't speak.

If they said something to the wrong person, my risky plan could completely screw him over. Why hadn't I left well enough alone? We'd been fine the way things were. No regrets—ha. He was going to regret ever speaking to me. Any lingering pleasure from our coming together had soured.

"I've taught you just about everything I can anyway," Declan said abruptly. "I'll talk to Professor Sinleigh tomorrow about starting up those advanced sessions she promised you."

Now that he was speaking, my stomach only squeezed tighter into a ball of misery. "Okay."

"It'll be better if we don't even talk for a while, just to offset anything your grandparents might say. That shouldn't be hard once we're done with the tutoring."

"It shouldn't," I agreed. My hands gripped the wheel harder. "I'm sorry. I know I shouldn't have—I dragged you out there. It's my fault. I—"

"No. Rory—" Declan motioned to the side of the road. "Pull over. We can't talk properly when you have to focus on driving."

I did as he asked, braced for the anger that had to be

coming. He'd snapped at me just for the fact that he'd lost control and kissed me that day in the library. This was a gazillion times worse. This time I really had fucked up.

As soon as I put the car into park, Declan set his hand over mine. When I met his eyes, his expression was solemn, nothing worse.

"I'm not saying these things because I'm upset at you," he said. "I'm not saying them because I don't *want* to see you. It's not your fault. You couldn't have known they'd come nosing around."

"I was still taking a chance, asking you to come out here. It was my idea."

"And I went along with it—I decided to take that chance. That's on me. Inviting me out here, giving me that space to really breathe and think, is the nicest thing anyone's done for me in ages. Okay?"

I sucked in a shaky breath. "Do you think they'll stay quiet about seeing us together? Would they even know that you're not supposed to—that you're an aide and all?"

"I don't know," Declan said. "But if word gets back to the university staff, it won't matter whether they knew how much shit I'd be in." He rubbed his hand over his face. "So that's why we have to make everything look totally professional and distant now. Maybe if someone hears what seems like just a rumor, they'll look at how we are with each other on campus and dismiss it. That's the best we can hope for."

"Yeah," I said quietly. I'd known we weren't going to keep anything like that brief intimacy after we left the cottage, but I'd thought I'd still have him in the ways I'd had him before.

Declan squeezed my hand. "I'll still do what I can to help you. It'll be harder, but—I'm not abandoning you."

"Okay." I couldn't seem to say more than that. I was afraid that if I did, the burn forming behind my eyes would spill over into tears. I couldn't cry over this. Over a relationship that had barely even existed in the first place. It was just the shock and the suddenness of the threat catching up with me.

"Hey." Declan let go of my hand to brush a few strands of my hair behind my ear. "I can't say I don't regret anything, but I've still got no regrets about what we did together."

"Are you sure?"

"Best day of my life, if we leave out the way it ended."

"That's kind of an important part."

"And I'll deal with it, because it's mine to deal with." He hesitated. His voice softened. "Come here? One last kiss, before we're all the way back to reality?"

My body shifted toward him automatically, my head tilting. He kissed me with a lingering desire that brought the flutter back into my chest and dulled the edges of my anguish.

I didn't know if everything would be okay, but with that, I at least believed that he didn't blame me. That we were okay.

I just couldn't believe that fact would be enough to shield *him* if the rest of the world came at him.

CHAPTER TWENTY-SEVEN

Rory

T he voice slid into my sleep, winding through the last fragments of a dream. "*Wake up.*"

My eyes popped open to my dim bedroom, morning sunlight seeping from around the curtain. My body had curled tight defensively beneath the covers while I slept. A sharp smoky smell filled my nose and seared down into my lungs.

I jerked upright, searching for the source of the scent, half-expecting to find my room on fire. But it wasn't flames that shifted along the walls. Before my eyes, the shadows of the furniture thickened against the fainter darkness.

They crawled along the walls and lunged toward the bed, maws forming in their wavering forms. One that looked like a snake sank its fangs into my foot through the sheet with a bolt of pain. I bit my lip trying to swallow a yelp as I scrambled back on the mattress, my pulse thudding so loud it seemed to echo through my head.

This wasn't real. It couldn't be real. I closed my eyes, shook my head, and looked again. The shadowy creatures loomed larger around me. And then the bed began to move.

It shuddered under me and hitched upward as if flying off the floor. The shadows clotted. The front of the wardrobe on the far wall sagged as if melting; the curtain billowed into the shape of a demonic face like the one that guy had conjured weeks ago in class.

Not real. Not real. I hugged my knees and buried my face against them, my breath coming ragged. But it wasn't enough not to look. The shadows nipped at my skin with icy mouths, alternately scraping me raw and pricking me with pain. An eerie groan filled the room, and then a hissing sound rose up, like bubbling acid eating away at something nearby. Through all that, the bed continued to sway beneath me.

I yanked my mental shields around my mind as tightly as I could, but that changed nothing. However much this was coming from inside my head, it was a seed already planted. And triggered. *Wake up*. It must have been Malcolm who'd done this. He'd sent his voice to me from wherever he was. How could I shut him out if he could hit me anytime he wanted without any warning?

I tried to dig inside my head for that malicious influence and rip it out, but my thoughts kept scattering with the horrible sensations around me. The nips and the noise and the sickening rocking carrying on and on. I clutched my knees tighter. A sound like a choked breath reached my ears, and every muscle in my body stiffened.

It was the gurgle of Mom's throat being severed. I'd heard it enough times in my dreams and in the desensitization sessions since to recognize it even without seeing anything. The thump of her body lolling, the fleshy tearing of the magic that had carved into Dad's chest…

I clapped my hands over my ears, but they couldn't shut out the sounds. I had the feeling if I let myself look, I'd see their bodies slumped right here in the room with me. A bloody metallic smell laced the air in place of the previous smoke.

Tears welled up behind my closed eyelids. I clenched my teeth against a scream.

Was it really worth it, keeping up this battle, having to endure this horror just on principle? Malcolm was never going to back down as long as I kept resisting. All I'd have to do was lie and pretend I'd seen the light, make a little show of surrender, and he'd end his campaign of torment. Maybe everyone who'd hassled me would leave me alone if he took me into his good graces, Victory and her crew included.

He *would* take me in. He'd meant what he'd said in the kennel the other day, just like Declan had meant what he'd said about the scions being their own sort of family. If I bent to Malcolm's will, they'd welcome me into their circle. It would be so fucking *easy*.

The thought filled my head for a moment with a twinge of temptation, and then a deeper nausea swelled to overwhelm it.

No. *No.* I was not going to give in to a sadistic asshole who believed provoking someone's worst nightmares out of them was a reasonable approach to getting his way. I was not going to let every other student at that school become even more convinced that torture was the path to victory. Fuck *no.*

The tears trickled down my cheeks. The chaos around me raged on for longer than I could keep track of. I pulled back as deep into my mind as I could go, focusing on my brightest memories: my first trip to the Museum of Contemporary Art in L.A. with my parents on my thirteenth birthday. Splashing through the waves with them at the local beach as a kid. The first moment I'd really felt and controlled my magic, known how much power I could wield. The way Declan had looked at me two days ago just before he'd kissed me.

Eventually I became aware of a small furry body against my hip and the quiet and stillness all around me.

Are you back? Deborah asked tentatively. *Are you okay, sweetheart?*

I swallowed thickly and swiped at my damp cheeks. "Yeah," I whispered. "I'm okay enough now that it's over."

My dormmates were moving around in the common room getting ready for the day. I stood up on shaky legs and peeked out just long enough to confirm that Malcolm wasn't hanging out there among them. Victory and her friends were sitting on one of the sofas, only the backs of their heads visible over the top, paying no attention to my room at all.

I ran all through the building when I saw the state you

were in, Deborah said, her voice reaching me more faintly because she wasn't touching me. *I didn't see anyone actively casting, just like before.*

Of course not. That would be too easy. I went to my window and yanked the curtain aside.

When I pushed it open, I could lean out into the warming air and get a good look at the grounds below. A few students were already heading to the Stormhurst building, and a couple were standing by the lake, but none of the scions were among them. The area near my side of Ashgrave Hall was vacant.

Frowning, I turned my attention to the building itself. Malcolm was reaching me *somehow.* He lived in the dorms here too—Deborah had determined on an earlier foray that his room was the one at the opposite end of the building on the same floor as mine. My gaze traveled over that side of the building.

The stone wall looked the same as it always had. When I'd studied it before, nothing had stuck out as concerning, but now my eyes halted on a small knob-like protrusion near the window closest to mine, belonging to one of the girls in my dorm.

The object was hard to make out from some twenty feet away—I must have seen it before and assumed it was just a normal part of the design. I would have again now if something about the shape of it hadn't triggered a prickle of recognition.

The curve of it, the impression of a hollow, gave the same impression as at least one of the pieces I'd had to work with in the puzzle garden the other day.

From watching the other girls come and go, I was pretty sure that room belonged to Cressida. It wasn't hard to imagine Malcolm managing to get in there for long enough to fix something to the wall outside. If he'd told her he was going to screw me over, she'd probably have given him an all-access pass.

She wasn't going to give *me* a pass to march into her room and get a closer look. I studied the ridges of limestone that formed the rest of the building. "Deborah?" I murmured.

My familiar darted across the floor to me, and I scooped her up to hold her by the window ledge where she could see outside. "Over there by the next window, there's something sticking out of the stone that I think might have magic in it—or be built for conducting magic somehow. Do you think you could handle the climb over there to check it out?"

Deborah considered. *With that groove there, it shouldn't be too much trouble. I'll go slowly.*

She hopped off my hand onto the sill and picked her way onto the thickest ridge of stone that ran along the side of the building. I watched, braced and starkly aware of the five story drop below, as she scurried along it toward the protrusion.

It only took her a minute to reach it. She climbed a little higher to sniff the shape, and a little shiver passed through her body. She darted back to me twice as fast as she'd gone.

It's had magic in it recently, she said as she scrambled inside. *It's built to store and amplify spells, as far as I can tell from the shape of it. We use pieces like that in our joymancy work too.*

Store and amplify spells. Amplify them enough that they could reach me in my bedroom without any more targeting than that? My queasiness returned, but a punch of resolve came with it.

"No one's going to be using that piece anymore," I said. "Come here?"

She let me scoop her into my hand, and I kept her tucked out of sight against my pajama shirt as I stepped into the common room. I didn't look at the other girls, didn't show any sign at all that I was about to infringe on anyone's privacy, just marched right over to Cressida's door as if I had every right to head straight in.

She hadn't bothered with a locking spell while she was right there in the common room. A small smile caught my lips as the doorknob turned in my grasp. "Hey!" a startled voice called out behind me, but I was already striding inside.

I dashed to her already-open window through a mist of lily-and-musk perfume and leaned out. The sculpted stone fixture was just within arm's reach. I grabbed it, yanked, twisted, and yanked again with a mutter of magical encouragement. It popped off the wall so abruptly I nearly tumbled right out the window.

I caught myself and yanked myself back into the room, shoving the fixture into the pajama pants pocket I'd never realized I'd be this relieved to have. Just in time, because a second later, Cressida burst into her bedroom.

"Get the fuck out of my room," she said in a taut voice. "What are you doing?"

"I'm so sorry," I said with an apologetic shrug as I headed over to the door, and held up my hand to reveal Deborah. "My familiar went roaming around farther than she should have. I was just getting her out of here before she disturbed you."

"Like I'd be scared of a stupid mouse," she sneered, but a little wariness had come into her eyes—in memory of the last time she'd been part of a plot involving my familiar, no doubt. "*I* didn't put her in here."

"Oh, I know! I think she just got turned around and lost her way. It's all good now. I'll make sure it doesn't happen again."

"You do that," Cressida said to my back as I crossed the common area to my bedroom, but she sounded more apprehensive than angry now.

If I was lucky, she didn't have anything to do with Malcolm's scheme other than letting him into her room. There was a decent chance she didn't know what he'd placed just outside her window or what spell-casting he'd done, considering he'd been secretive about it even with Jude. But I wasn't going to count on luck. As soon as my door had closed behind me, I set down Deborah and pulled out the stone fixture to examine it.

It did have similarities to pieces in the maze. I ran my thumb over the smooth surface, and a jolt of recognition shot through my head.

I'd had the feeling of holding this object in my hands before—no, of holding it in *Malcolm's* hands when I'd dipped inside his head that day in Persuasion class. This was one of the impressions I'd glimpsed. I just hadn't had any way of understanding it until now.

Maybe I couldn't prove it, but he'd definitely been the one who'd put this thing in place.

My jaw clenched as I considered how a spell would flow through the piece. Deborah had said it'd had magic in it *recently*, but I wasn't sure how accurate her magical senses were inside that mouse body. Were there more spells waiting to mess with me inside the thing right now?

If there were, how the hell did I get them out? In the puzzle maze, I'd needed to apply my own magic to the pieces' natural functions. This was a different problem altogether.

I hesitated for a moment before getting up. I had one person nearby who might be able to answer that.

This time, the two girls still in the common room looked my way the second I came out. I suspected Victory and Sinclair had joined Cressida in her room to check whether I'd done more in there than I'd claimed. Well, then they couldn't interfere with what I was doing now. I rapped my hand against Imogen's door.

She opened it with hair damp and mussed from a recent toweling. Her stance tensed. "Rory? I—"

"I need to talk to you," I said firmly. "Now. You owe me." I didn't care how uncertain she was about continuing our friendship—I wasn't looking for friendship. I was looking for a Physicality specialist.

Guilt flashed across her face, and she stepped back to let me in. Even if my weirdness over the last several weeks had made her cautious, she recognized she had a lot to make up for. Good.

"Congrats on the league win," she said as she closed the door.

My mind was so far elsewhere that it took me a second to process her words. They still didn't quite click. "What?"

"Insight won. It was announced last night. Didn't you hear?" Her mouth twisted wryly. "I'll be helping serve all of you people a big fancy dinner tomorrow."

Last night I'd been reeling from my encounter with my grandparents and the damage they might do to Declan. I wasn't surprised I missed the news. I couldn't summon much enthusiasm over the win. "I guess I was too caught up in studying. That's great. But that's not—" I held out the stone fixture. "Do you know what this is?"

Imogen took it from me and turned it over in her hands. "It's a conducting piece with a holding pocket." She glanced at me. "Do *you* know what that means?"

I nodded. "I've got the gist. Can you tell if it's 'holding' anything right now?"

She peered at it more intently, mouthing a few words under her breath. After a minute, she lowered the piece with a long exhale. The effort had left her face drawn. "There's a little something in there. Not much. I can't tell what the function is."

"You know how to stop this thing from working, though, don't you? That's got to be a Physicality thing— it's all about the physical structure."

"It is," Imogen agreed. "That's how pieces like this work.

I could tell you approximately how to *make* something like this. But the way they're constructed, the magical resonance contained in the design—these pieces resist any attempts to reshape or unshape them like crazy. *Maybe* one of the professors would be able to break the symmetry, but I'm not even sure about that. I definitely can't."

In that case, I didn't have much hope. I sucked my lower lip under my teeth in contemplation. "So there's nothing anyone can do to break one of these?"

"I didn't say that, although the other way is still pretty tricky." Imogen looked at the piece, her wry smile returning. "You can't brute force this thing into changing, so you've got to come at it from a different angle that it's not built for. With Insight aimed right, you could probably get a gist of any spells inside it. And I've heard of people 'persuading' the resonance to shift to throw the structure's natural capacity off. If you're strong enough. Those aren't my areas—I wouldn't have a chance. You, though…" She handed it back to me with a curious expression.

I had all four strengths. A quiver that was almost giddy ran through me. I focused my gaze on the holding side of the conducting piece and whispered my Insight casting word, too quiet for Imogen to hear.

It didn't feel like falling into someone's head. Only a piece of me seemed to tumble forward, with just a flicker of sensation meeting me in response from deep inside—a sensation that delved and burrowed with a prickling of hooked claws. I didn't like that at all. It definitely wasn't anything I wanted aimed at me, whatever exactly the spell was.

Could I persuade it out? Or persuade the form of the piece to alter so it couldn't hold the spell or conduct it anymore? I knit my brow as I inspected the structure again. The connection between the holding area and the amplifying part—that seemed like the key. If I could shift it even a little...

I pulled more magic onto my tongue and trained my attention on that area. "*Bend*," I ordered it, tasting the shape of the channel with the word.

I got no sense of it budging. Maybe I was focusing too much on the physical aspect still. Imogen had said to persuade the "resonance" of the thing. The way the shape mimicked the flow of cast magic.

"*Come out*," I tried again, thinking instead of that flow, the way the energy would bend with the structure. Nothing. I grimaced, my voice rising just a bit. "*Let* go."

A twitch passed from the stone into my hand. My heart lifted. I peered into the channel and spotted a tiny crack that had opened up in the middle of it.

Imogen let out a breathless laugh. "You did it. It won't work anymore like that—not unless someone else persuades it whole again, I guess."

Or Malcolm stuck another conducting piece in place. But the hitch of Imogen's breath had jerked my mind in a totally different direction with a rush of hope.

"Imogen," I said, "if I could persuade something like this to stop working... That strategy could apply to any physical form, right?"

"Any physical form created to conduct magic, anyway," she said. "The more intricate and condensed the form is, the harder it'd be to shift it, though. Why?"

I turned toward the door, my heart thumping faster. "I'll tell you later. Thanks for your help."

I had a life to save.

CHAPTER TWENTY-EIGHT

Connar

The last place I expected to see Jude going into was the junior cafeteria. I stopped in my tracks on my way through Killbrook Hall after my monthly check-in with my mentor, blinking a few times before I convinced myself that it really had been his lanky form slipping through the doorway few seniors ventured through under regular circumstances. There wasn't anyone else on campus with that dark red hair. It'd have been pretty hard for me to confuse someone else for him.

What was he up to? A tug of uneasy curiosity drew me to the doorway.

It was early afternoon, a little late for lunch. Only a few clusters of the younger students still sat around the wooden tables that filled the room. Tomorrow evening, those tables would be draped with fancy fabric and the sconces on the burgundy walls would be lit for the league competition banquet. Right now, the place looked unimpressive in the muted daylight that glowed through the windows. The meaty smell of whatever the staff had served for lunch hung in the air.

Jude had seated himself at the end of a table right next to one of the bunches of students. Not just any students either, I noted after a moment. Gold leaf pins glinted on all their shirt collars. They were Naries. What did he want with them?

Not much, as far as I could tell from simply observing. He pulled out a book and turned the pages absently, occasionally glancing up in the general direction of the Naries' table next to him. They chattered on without giving him much mind. Out of all the students here at Blood U, they had the least idea why he was anyone to be wary of.

After a few minutes just standing there in the doorway watching, I started to feel conspicuous. The puzzle in front of me still niggled at me, though. I pushed myself on into the room.

Jude's gaze shot to me with a startled twitch of his expression when I sat down across from him. He frowned. "What the hell are you doing here?" he said quietly, but there was no real venom in his voice, only mild irritation.

"Finding out what the hell *you're* doing here," I said. "What's going on? What's important about them?"

His shoulders came up as he slid farther down the bench so we were less likely to be overheard by the Naries. "Nothing. I just wondered."

I followed him, still confused. "Wondered *what*?"

Jude turned his frown toward his book rather than me. "What they even have to talk about. What *they* think is important. How someone could find their company appealing. I don't know."

Someone, huh? That last bit clued me in. "This is about—"

His gaze jerked back up. "Don't. We aren't talking about that." Then he looked toward the table of Naries, his brow knitting as if he found them as puzzling as I found his sudden interest in them.

What had Rory said to him when they'd had their fight anyway? He obviously wasn't going to tell me, but it was also obviously eating at him.

That question had niggled at me all the way down to my gut from the moment I'd picked him up on the side of the road, maybe because I had the most direct experience with having failed her. But he'd probably called me because he'd known I was less likely to keep prodding him about it than Malcolm or Declan. I wasn't going to hassle him when he was so clearly unsettled.

I wasn't sure I was any less conspicuous sitting here, and Jude hardly wanted my help with anything. "Well, good luck with it," I said, getting up. Malcolm had asked me to meet him in the lounge in a few minutes anyway.

Our private room below the library had always offered a bit of an escape—not as much as my cliff spot, but a place where I didn't have to be quite as aware of the fears and suspicions I provoked in everyone on campus. Normally, relief would have washed over me as I descended the stairs. Today, the tension in my gut clenched tighter.

I couldn't remember us ever arguing the way Malcolm and Jude had before. Declan had barely come down at all in the last few weeks, and I wasn't sure I could blame him. A deeper apprehension coursed through my body as I sat myself down to wait for Malcolm, to find out what he was planning now.

He came down a few minutes later with an energy about him that was eager but brittle. I didn't need any Insight spell to tell me something had frustrated him and he didn't intend to take it lying down.

"Good," he said, seeing me. "I've got it all figured out. We don't need anyone else—the two of us can build off each other's spells just fine."

I shifted forward on the couch, ignoring the jab of tension that comment gave me. "What have you figured out?"

He walked from one end of the room to the other, his eyes intent but distant as if picturing something a long ways away. "We're going to knock her down hard with the whole school as audience. The league banquet is the perfect opportunity. The girls in her dorm already think she's going bonkers. Victory and the others have been spreading that gossip, and probably some of the others too. Everyone's primed."

The jab turned into a dull ache that filled my entire abdomen. "Primed for us to do what?"

"To show just how out-of-control the star pupil has become in her insistence on going it alone. You can kick things off. Mess with her food or her drink, make her seat shift under her, whatever else you can think of that'll unnerve her but not be too noticeable to anyone else. While she's thrown off by that, I'll slide in there and take care of the rest. If she still isn't ready to bow to us, then I'll just make her do it."

The vehemence in his voice had taken on an almost frantic edge. My body tensed. Malcolm didn't let himself get overly caught up in anything—not usually. He observed and he made his moves with cool confidence. I didn't see that cool right now, and I wasn't so sure about the confidence either.

"Do you really think this is the best approach?" I ventured. "The banquet is sort of sacred. All the professors will be there too."

"That just makes it better. Let them watch too. We'll be ruling over all of them when the old guard retires— they should know what happens to anyone who challenges us." He spun on me. "Come on, Connar. I need you with me on this. We're so close."

If we were, I didn't think he'd have that wildness in his expression. I hesitated, and all the doubts that had been churning inside me since the moment I'd turned on Rory collided with a lurch of my pulse.

I trusted Malcolm. I'd have been willing to lay down my life for him if need be. But I didn't believe he was right about this, about her. And even though I'd called him my best friend and given him that trust, I was fucking *terrified* to tell him that.

That wasn't right, was it? We were all scions, no matter

how we'd come into that title. My opinion should at least matter enough for him to care without brushing off everything I said. He expected me to follow his lead and do whatever he asked simply because he said so as part of the loyalty between us, even though I'd never have pushed him the same way.

Rory had never pushed me. Even knowing how close I was with Malcolm, even when she'd been willing to open up to me, she'd never once asked me to so much as speak up on her behalf, let alone come right over to her side of the fight. When we'd talked the other day, despite all the anger I'd seen in her, she hadn't thrown my past in my face; she hadn't demanded anything other than that I leave her alone.

She'd only ever wanted me to be myself, to follow what mattered to me, whatever that happened to be. Wasn't *that* some kind of loyalty, one I could hardly say I'd earned? My hand closed around the memory of the dragon she'd made for me where it had once pressed against my palm.

I hope you don't forget that you're you *too*, she'd said when she'd given it to me. *At least some of the time, that's got to come first.*

If it didn't come first now, then it probably never would.

"Connar," Malcolm started again in his cajoling tone.

I stood up before he could go on. My entire chest had constricted into one big knot, but I propelled out the word. "No."

Malcolm blinked at me, momentarily speechless. "Excuse me?"

I crossed my arms. "No, I'm not going to mess with Rory during the banquet. I think we've done enough. She's still standing because she's strong enough to deserve to. *I'm* done with this."

His eyes flashed. "What the fuck is wrong with you? We've got her; we just have to—"

"*No.*" My voice came out louder than I'd expected, loud enough to cut him off completely. A strange exhilaration washed over me despite the ache inside.

I could make this choice. I wasn't even betraying him, no matter how he was going to see it. I was making this stand because it was better for *all* of us. "And if you try to hassle her tomorrow night, I'll step in. You want her in the circle? Find another way."

For a few seconds, we just stared at each other. Malcolm's jaw worked. "I have *always* had your back—"

"And I've always had yours. That's why I'm saying no, just this once. You're taking this whole thing too far. This isn't you."

"Don't you *dare* tell me who I am or what I'm capable of," he snapped. "You—She—" He shook his head, his entire posture rigid. "Fine. That's how you want things to be? Or maybe that's how *she* wants things to be. You think she's so above all this? When you get your head on straight, you'll see how she's breaking us apart. Until then, get the fuck out of here."

I wouldn't have wanted to stay anyway. As I headed up

the stairs, the clenching inside me started to release—and a new weight settled over me.

As far as I could see right now, it wasn't Rory breaking up the pentacle of scions. Malcolm was doing that all by himself.

CHAPTER TWENTY-NINE

Rory

I kept a careful distance from the cafeteria where the banquet would be held as I hurried to the staff wing of Killbrook Hall. Clinks and thumps carried through the doorway as the members of the other leagues set up the décor. The smells of roast pork and caramelized onions and all sorts of other deliciousness drifted from the kitchen. My mouth might have watered if it wasn't parched dry in anticipation of the spell I was about to attempt.

I'd waited until not long before the feast was supposed to begin so I could be sure any staff not teaching classes right now would be downstairs supervising the preparations. The hall of offices was empty and silent. I set my feet softly on the carpet on my way to Professor Banefield's door just in case someone had lingered after all.

The door opened with my whispered spell, even easier

now with practice. I slipped through his office and ventured into his apartment on the other side.

The smells of sickness had spread from his bedroom, even though I had to assume the health center staff who'd been coming to look after him must have been doing their best to keep things clean. Stale sweat, dried vomit, and something like rotting fruit mixed together in a sour cocktail that faintly laced the air. It got stronger as I reached Banefield's bedroom, enough that my stomach turned.

In the thin late afternoon light drifting through the window, his broad body looked even more diminished than it had when I'd been here only a week ago. The sheet had fallen off him and his undershirt had ridden up, showing the lines of ribs protruding from his side, shallower and then deeper with his erratic breathing. His hair no longer stood up in its usual tufts but clung damply to his scalp.

This was my fault. Whoever had attacked him had done it to hurt me, to stop him from helping me. So I'd better be able to make it right.

I sat down carefully on the edge of the bed by his sprawled legs. I'd spent all of my time between classes and meals for the last two days reading any information I could find in the library about using persuasion to influence physical objects. There wasn't a lot of it, and most of it related to the sculpted pieces like the one I'd found on the wall outside our dorm, expanding on what Imogen had told me. I knew a little more than I had yesterday morning, at least.

Had the health center doctors even considered this approach? Had they realized the mole was the likely source of my mentor's illness in the first place? It didn't seem right that I might have figured out a solution where they hadn't... but then, it was possible they hadn't looked all that hard once they'd realized it was almost certainly a magical attack.

It was possible they'd realized that whoever could conduct an attack like this could strike them down as well, and decided it was better to let Banefield's illness run its course.

I might face consequences from our enemies if I cured him, but at least I could face them with his help. If I could convince the mole to give up its magical resonance, he'd be able to tell me who our enemies were, maybe even how to protect ourselves from another attack. Or how to fight back.

As I tugged up his pajama pant leg like I had before, Banefield stirred. I froze, distinctly aware of how inappropriate it was for me to be sitting on a professor's bed while he slept, partly undressing him.

Banefield's head turned. His eyelids stuttered and opened just a crack. His voice was a weak croak. "Rory?"

"I'm going to try to make you better," I said quickly. "I know someone's placed a spell on you. I think I might be able to remove it. Will you let me try?"

He peered at me a moment longer before his gaze wandered off as if he hadn't heard me. His eyelids closed completely. A hacking cough sputtered out of him, and then he lay still.

Well, he hadn't made any attempt to stop me. I guessed that was as close to permission as I was going to get.

No sound but his breathing emitted from his chest as I uncovered his knee. Peering at the mole more closely than before, my pulse skipped a beat. I hadn't studied it that intently before, assuming it was meant to look like any mole. It... almost appeared to have a magically attuned shape to it, like a tiny version of one of those conducting pieces, only made out of flesh instead of metal or stone. The tiny dimple here, the barely visible ridge there.

Of course. That made perfect sense, didn't it? How else could the person who'd cast the spell have been sure the mole would hold its energy until it needed to activate? They'd built a conducting structure right on his body. Maybe it amplified the effects too, or some other awful function I hadn't encountered yet.

Imogen's words came back to me. *The more intricate and condensed the form is, the harder it'd be to shift it.* I'd better get started.

"I was going to have a daughter," Banefield mumbled, so low I wasn't sure I'd heard him right. His eyes stayed closed.

"What?" I said quietly, not wanting to disturb him if he was simply talking in his sleep.

"She was pregnant. Amara was. Twenty-two weeks, with our little girl. And they—they—" Another cough rattled out of him.

I rested my hand on his calf as if that might comfort

him, my heart wrenching. "It's okay. You don't have to talk about it."

He rambled on in the same mumbled, wavering voice. "They didn't call. They didn't do anything they should have. Stupid bloody feebs." His chest hitched. "They—she — But you. You would have forgiven them."

"I don't know. I don't know anything about it, really." I sure as hell wasn't going to blame him for being mad about his wife and their unborn child dying.

"You would," he said, with more firmness than before. "You would. Because you let yourself see." He trailed off for a long enough moment that I thought he was done. Then he added, "She would have been like you, I want to think. If my daughter had come. That's what— If I hadn't — She would have seen too."

For a second, I couldn't breathe, my throat was so constricted. I didn't totally understand what he was saying, but the gist was clear enough. "I'm sure she'd have tried to save you," I said. "So that's what I'm going to do too. Just rest for now, and I'll do my best."

I touched the mole lightly, fighting a cringe, letting my fingertip absorb the shape of it. A faint pulse of energy tickled my skin. I focused on the feel of it and the image of it in my mind, the toxic spell contained in a sort of chamber I could picture inside it, and rolled magic off my tongue with the command that had worked on Malcolm's stone. "*Let go.*"

I didn't sense any change from the form beneath my finger. Banefield's head twitched. "No. If you— They'll— I can't stop them."

"Maybe I can," I said in the most soothing voice I could summon. "It's okay." Please let it be okay.

It wasn't the structure but the energy its shape resonated with that I had to focus on. I couldn't forget that, even as the prickling pulse sent a queasy shiver through me. The tiny strands of a spell wound through the nub of constructed flesh—I could speak to them too.

"*Let go*," I murmured again. The energy didn't so much as tremble. Fuck. Okay, on to the untested strategies.

Think about the purpose the spell and its container. What was the right direction to untangle it from its target? Was the sickening spell leaching my mentor's health away from him or leaking poison into him?

No matter what I did, he couldn't get much worse off. I squared my shoulders and aimed my attention at the mole again. "*Release.*" Nothing. "*Pull back.*" Still nothing. "*Snap.*"

Sweat was beading on the back of my neck now. I was throwing all my effort into each casting, and they seemed to just bounce off the thing.

"No," Banefield muttered again into his pillow.

Could I take the spell into me? "*Come here*," I said to the fizz of energy. No luck.

Frustration gripped me. What if I just wasn't powerful enough? I only had three months of training. No matter how many strengths I had, they couldn't counterbalance all the time I'd missed when I should have been honing these skills.

Damn it. I was not going to let him die. I just was *not*.

The anger that came with that thought jolted through the magic coiled behind my collarbone. Without letting myself second-guess the impulse, I hurled it into my next command. "*Get out!*"

The pulse of energy jumped against my skin with a pinching pressure that faded in an instant. Beneath my fingertip, the mole deflated. As I jerked my hand back, it settled into a patch more like dark freckle. Banefield dragged in a heave of a breath.

My jaw went slack. I'd done it. I'd really managed to pull it off. Would he simply get better now on his own, or—

Banefield lunged upright so suddenly I startled in surprise, falling off the edge of the bed. His eyes popped open, ruddy with blood vessels crisscrossing the whites, and his hands snapped around the spot where I'd been sitting an instant before. A strained growl broke from his lips.

What the hell?

I scrambled backward and onto my feet. My mentor lurched out of the bed at the same time. Another angry, wordless sound escaped him. "Go!" he spat out, and threw himself at me.

I dashed out of the bedroom, my thoughts scattering in my bewilderment. Banefield charged after me with more speed than I'd have thought his wasted body could achieve. His hand shot out and clamped around my wrist. He wrenched me around with a heave so vicious that pain lanced through my shoulder cap.

"No!" he shouted, but I didn't think he was talking

to me. He propelled himself toward the kitchen, dragging me with him. His fingers dug in deeper, and his other arm whipped toward me. I ducked just a second before his fist would have clocked me in the head.

"*Stop*," I said, tossing a persuasive casting into my words instinctively. "*Let go of me.*"

The magic bounced off the solid surface of his mental shields.

"I can't," he rasped, and flung himself at the kitchen island. "A failsafe— They wanted to be sure— It's too deep in me. There's no way."

"If there's something *I* can do to stop this, tell me," I said, with a yelp as he twisted my wrist.

He was panting now. His free hand jerked toward me again, and he managed to slam it into the side of the island instead, hard enough that I thought I heard the crack of bone. Even in his agonizing grasp, I winced for him.

All at once, he hauled me past him, sending me hurtling to the end of the kitchen. My ribs smacked into the edge of the counter, but Banefield's grip snapped. He plunged his hand into the drawer he'd just opened.

"I'm supposed to crush the magic out of you," he said raggedly. "It won't let go of me until I do. They wanted you helpless. They want—they wanted to make sure you never trust anyone who'd help you again. Don't let it work. Don't let it *work*. There'll be people who'll mean it. There'll be people on your side."

"*Who* did this?" I spun around and ran for the living

room, but Banefield was faster. His punch rammed into my gut, knocking the air out of me.

"Fuck," he sputtered as I doubled over with a gasp. "The older barons, the other reapers with them. The cancer in the fearmancers." He fumbled across the island and snatched up a butcher's knife from the block there. As he swung it toward me, I wrenched away from him with a burst of panic.

His arm kept swinging, all the way back to his own body. He plunged the knife straight into his chest.

"Professor!" I cried.

He slumped, blood spilling from around the blade into his undershirt and streaking over his skin. I dropped down beside him. His breath came with a wet rasp.

"I'm sorry," I said, choking on the words. "I don't know what to do."

"Only way to stop them," he mumbled, his head rolling back to stare at the ceiling. Blood flecked his lips. "Only way. You need it. Stop the cancer. Maybe you can cure that too. If you go—"

The last word cut off with a seize of his body. His hand snatched after mine. He caught it as I yanked myself backward, clutching tight... and then going limp with the rest of his body as the light faded from his eyes.

"Professor Banefield?" My voice came out so hoarse I'm not sure he'd have recognized his name even if he'd been conscious to hear it.

He gazed blankly upward. Blood seeped into a puddle on the floor beneath him. I squeezed his hand as if that could jolt him back to life, and a solid shape pressed against my palm.

My fingers curled around it instinctively. I shoved myself to my feet and sprinted to the door. Maybe there was still a chance—maybe if a doctor got to him quickly enough—

But even as I burst into the hall with a cry of "Help!" bursting from my throat, an ache of loss was already spreading through me from head to toe.

I'd saved him, and then he'd saved me from himself. From the barons… From the "reapers"?

How many enemies did I have in this world—and just how much blood were they willing to spill to get to me?

I couldn't think through the blaring of grief and horror in my head. All I could do was shout, "Help!" again as I raced down the hall.

CHAPTER THIRTY

Rory

Not long after I'd dropped into the armchair in Ms. Grimsworth's office, I'd started shaking. When she came back into the room after doing whatever she'd needed to do to handle Professor Banefield's death, I hadn't stopped. My hands stayed clenched tight on my lap as I looked up at her.

The tensing of her expression told enough of the story before she even opened her mouth. "I'm afraid there was nothing any of us could do for him."

I swallowed the lump that had crawled up my throat and hugged myself. Tears seared in the back of my eyes, but somehow they hadn't spilled out yet. My head was whirling.

Ms. Grimsworth's gaze dropped to my right arm. To the purpling bruises in the shape of Banefield's fingers where my mentor's hand had clamped around my wrist.

The twinge at my side when I adjusted my position told me my ribs were probably bruised too, from when he'd thrown me against the counter.

He'd been trying to get me away from him right then, not trying to hurt me. I'd replayed the episode a hundred times in my head, and that was the conclusion I'd come to. There'd been another spell—a "failsafe," he'd said—that had activated when I'd destroyed the mole that held the one making him sick. Some kind of persuasion magic, I had to guess.

It had forced him to attack me against his will, but he'd fought against the spell as well as he could. I was pretty sure when he'd told me "no" while I was working at curing him, he'd been trying to warn me, knowing what would come. He'd done everything he could not to fulfill its purpose: to crush the magic out of me, however exactly that worked.

Should I have left him alone, not tried to cure him? It was hard to believe that. In another week or two, he'd have wasted away completely. The health center staff hadn't done anything useful for him. Either way, he'd have been dead.

This way was just more horrifying.

Ms. Grimsworth propped her thin frame against the edge of her desk rather than sitting behind it. "I can only imagine how distressing the experience you just had was, Miss Bloodstone. Can you tell me again, as thoroughly as possible, exactly what happened?"

I sucked in a breath. When I'd banged on her door and found her, mercifully, still inside, I'd babbled a fractured account of Banefield's death, and she'd ushered me in here before rushing off. Now I had to decide what it was safe to tell her.

She looked shaken by what she'd seen, but how much could I trust that impression? She wasn't a baron, but she could have been under their sway. She could be associated with whoever or whatever the "reapers" Banefield had mentioned were.

He'd given his life to save me. I had to make sure I didn't stupidly throw my own away before his body had even stopped bleeding.

"I've been reading up on healing spells in the library," I said, which was a version of the truth. "Maybe it sounds silly, but I wanted to see if I could do anything for Professor Banefield. He's looked out for me since I first got here... I used magic to get into his quarters, and I tried a couple of the spells, and nothing seemed to happen. Then all of a sudden he attacked me."

I rubbed my wrist. "I have no idea what was going on. He seemed delusional. He almost stabbed me with that knife, but when I dodged, he stabbed himself instead."

The headmistress's lips pursed. "I would say that sounds ridiculous, but our analysis confirms that he delivered the blow himself. Did he say anything to you during this attack? Any indication as to what provoked it?"

I shook my head. Better no one knew how much he'd managed to warn me. Better my enemies thought I was still totally ignorant. "He was mumbling and muttering, but I could hardly make out any of the words. I have no idea whether he understood who I was, even. He said something about a daughter... That's the only part I remember catching. It all happened so fast, and I was so shocked..."

"Of course," Ms. Grimsworth said, in a tone that I suspected was meant to be reassuring but that only came out as dour. "Of course you were. I hope you can see now why we restrict visitors in cases like this where we're uncertain of the illness—we can't predict how the patient will behave."

I hung my head. She sighed. "I expect that isn't a rule you'll ignore again. And your desire to contribute to Professor Banefield's healing was admirable if highly misguided. Clearly his illness was even more serious than we thought, affecting his mind as well as his body. Do you recall the specific spells you attempted?"

I tossed out a couple of the common ones I'd seen in my research, which seemed to satisfy her enough. "I can't imagine it was anything specific about you that provoked the attack," she said. "If you hadn't come, most likely it would have been the nurse who checked in on him in the morning. Don't make this any harder on yourself by feeling responsible."

"I know," I said quietly. I wasn't responsible for how the spell had made him act. I was only responsible for making him a target in the first place.

Ms. Grimsworth straightened up, brushing her hands together. "The health center may have more questions for you in the morning, but for now I think you've had enough. Let me see your arm."

She made a quick motion toward my bruised wrist. I

held it toward her awkwardly, and she murmured a word
under her breath with a swiping motion of her fingers.

Before my eyes, the bruise shimmered away, leaving
only unblemished skin. I touched it instinctively and
winced at the soreness that remained.

"It's still bruised," Ms. Grimsworth said. "The healing
arts aren't my area of expertise. I cast an illusion over it so
no one should notice anything's amiss tonight."

"Tonight?" I repeated.

"At the banquet. You'd better go on down there now."

Just the word "banquet" made my stomach lurch in
refusal. "*What?*" I said, wondering if I'd misheard.

The headmistress nodded, gesturing me to my feet.
"The food will be served in just a few minutes. Not having
their scion there will dull the celebration for the Insight
league. You'll be surrounded by friends and festivities
rather than left alone with your thoughts. Let the
festivities distract you, take comfort in the company, and
if it begins to wear on you, then make your excuses and
leave. We can't let this tragedy ripple even farther through
the school."

All I wanted to do was crawl into bed. My body
balked. "I—"

"I can escort you down to the dining room if that
would make it easier."

No, having Ms. Grimsworth march me down there
would be even worse. I could manage the walk. I could
stay five minutes, anyway, if that was my duty as scion
tonight.

Put on a brave face. If my enemies were watching, let

them think I hadn't been that fazed. When I thought of it that way, the idea sat a little more easily.

"That's all right," I said, forcing myself to stand. "I can manage."

My shaking had subsided as we'd talked, but the shock still clung to me like a layer of gauze that hazed my mind. The floor felt far away beneath my feet. Outside Ms. Grimsworth's office, the silence in the hall blared.

I tightened my jaw and kept walking, one foot at a time, out to the staircase and down and along the shorter hall to the front wing.

I'd just reached that space when a brawny figure moved into view at the far end. The light from the flames in the sconces wavered across Connar's chiseled face.

My legs locked. I couldn't deal with him, not now, not on top of everything else this awful evening had thrown at me.

He didn't come too close, just caught my gaze and held out his hand. A metal figurine gleamed in his grasp— a dragon, almost identical to the one I'd made for him. I stared at it.

"You said I had to make it myself," Connar said. "I'm going to be that guy."

He extended his arm a little farther. When I looked at him blankly, he brought his hand back to his side and slid the dragon into his pocket. It occurred to me only then that he'd been offering it to me as a sort of gift. Like I'd offered the one I'd made to him.

"It's just the beginning," he added with a pained smile. "I know it's hardly enough on its own."

He turned and left me even more shell-shocked than I'd been a minute ago, which I wouldn't have thought was possible. What had he expected me to say?

Warm lights and music trickled from the doorway beyond the hall. I stepped inside warily, and a girl from the Insight league grabbed my elbow, so abruptly I had to restrain a flinch. She beamed at me. "About time you made it. Come on—you've got the best seat in the house."

The tables throughout the room had been laid out with gleaming gold-embroidered tablecloths. Sconces glowed all around me. The crystal chandeliers overhead swayed and tinkled with the music.

One table at the front of the room was set perpendicular to the others. A few of the senior Insight league members were already sitting there, including the guy who'd led the meeting last month, and... Declan. The empty chair in the middle next to him was obviously meant for me.

I let the girl guide me over and sank into the chair, tucking my hands under the table. Declan gave me a quick glance and a quicker nod in greeting, the distant politeness of two people who'd never really talked, let alone fucked.

Chatter carried from around the tables ahead of us. Not a single person here had any idea that a man had just stabbed himself to death upstairs.

The door at the other end of the room opened, and our servers filed into the room, carrying the platters that held our feast. The other leagues had dressed in black pants and white shirts for the occasion. I might have found it mildly amusing if the circumstances had been different.

Three particularly familiar figures made their way to our head table. Apparently the rule was that scions served scions.

Jude reached us first. He set down a platter of carved pork near my plate with a mocking little bow. "For Your Highness," he said in his flippant tone. "May the food be tasty enough to wash away all memory of my sins."

The smell of the meat made my stomach churn. I couldn't find the wherewithal to come up with an answer to his remark. My gaze slid to Connar, who'd just set down a platter of asparagus and pine nuts near Declan. He was watching me, a flicker of concern crossing his face. Between how I must look now and how I'd responded to him in the hall—or rather, not responded—it couldn't be hard for him to pick up on the fact that something was wrong.

He hesitated, opening his mouth, and my hand clenched tighter on my lap as I rested the other on the table. I gave a curt shake of my head. There was nothing I wanted to talk about here, and nothing I wanted to talk about with him, whatever sins he intended to make up for. Not right now with the moments in Banefield's room still so fresh in my head.

As the two of them veered away, Malcolm set down the platter he'd been carrying—skewers of garlic grilled shrimp—between Declan and me. He met my eyes with a glower, his posture radiating displeasure. I looked right back at him, refusing to cower despite the implicit threat in his gaze.

We weren't done? Fine. I might be shaken, but I had so much fight left in me.

He swiveled on his heel and stalked away. Beneath the table, I uncurled my fingers just slightly. Just enough to run my thumb over the warmed metal of the object Banefield had pressed into my hand as he'd died. A little silver key.

He must have grabbed it from the drawer—it must have been why he'd wrenched himself over to the kitchen despite the spell's compulsion. He'd given every last bit of will he had to placing it in my grasp. I'd thought he might be the key to navigating the treacheries of the fearmancer world, and he'd turned out to have a completely literal one for me.

The spell had taken him over before he could tell me where to use it, but that was all right. I'd mourn tonight, and tomorrow I'd start searching for the lock that matched it. Whatever this key opened up, he'd believed I needed it. To heal the cancer he saw among the fearmancers? Maybe.

Or maybe I'd just burn this whole place to the ground.

ABOUT THE AUTHOR

Eva Chase lives in Canada with her family. She loves stories both swoony and supernatural, and strong women and the men who appreciate them. Along with the Moriarty's Men series, she is the author of the Moriarty's Men series, the Looking Glass Curse trilogy, the Their Dark Valkyrie series, the Witch's Consorts series, the Dragon Shifter's Mates series, the Demons of Fame Romance series, the Legends Reborn trilogy, and the Alpha Project Psychic Romance series.

Connect with Eva online:
www.evachase.com
eva@evachase.com